Praise for

Babyface

"*Babyface* is enthralling. Gibson's original voice,
which is at once comic and accurate,
exactly captures the lofty and
lowly moments of being a new mum."
—Adele Parks, author of *Larger Than Life*

"A bittersweet take on bringing up baby
in modern times and a great first book."
—*Heat*

"A winsome debut about first-time motherhood."
—*Observer*

"Gibson provides a running commentary
of observations on the curve-balls life throws you
when you're dealing with a fresh first-born."
—*Sunday Herald*

Babyface

Fiona Gibson

RED
DRESS
INK
™

First North American edition July 2004

BABYFACE

A Red Dress Ink novel

ISBN 0-373-25064-9

www.RedDressInk.com

Printed in U.S.A.

ACKNOWLEDGMENTS

For support and tireless egging on, huge thanks
to Jenny Tucker, Kath Brown, Sue Wheeler,
Marie O'Riordan, Michelle Dickson, Jane Parbury,
Fliss Terrill, Nick and Helen Fisher, Cathy Gilligan,
Ellie Stott, Gavin Convery, Wendy Rigg.
The brilliant Dolphinton writers—Pam Taylor,
Vicki Feaver, Amanda McLean, Elizabeth Dobie and
Tania Cheston—for suggestions and enduring rants.
Jane Wright at the *Sunday Herald* for morale
boosting. Cheryl and Stephen for long-ago Burgundy
frolics. My brilliant agents, Annette Green, for
putting the book thing in my head in the first place,
and Laura Langlie. All at Red Dress Ink, especially
Farrin Jacobs. Margery Taylor and Keith Gibson for
unfailing encouragement. Sam, Dex and Erin for
sweet inspiration. Jimmy for keeping sanity mostly
intact. My writing lifesaver, Wendy Varley, for
constant support, ideas and hawk-eyed glitch
spotting, beamed from the Isle of Wight to my Inbox
from the start to the finish of this book.

For Jimmy

1

Birth

Something has broken into our bedroom. It zaps past my ear and lands on Jonathan's cheek.

Pain sneaks in, swelling, clenching my middle. "It's started," I tell him.

He twitches, and the bluebottle buzzes away. "Are you sure?"

"Think so. It goes away and then—" I grope for something to cling on to and find his hand.

"I'll phone the hospital. Keep breathing."

Jonathan has assembled the flat-pack crib at the foot of our bed. A Winnie the Pooh mobile arches over the space where a baby will sleep. Soft toys—a penguin, a bear and an otter—nestle at the head end. My hospital bag contains Bach Rescue Remedy to aid relaxation, plus button-front nighties for easy access to breasts.

It's not a big thing, having a baby. People do it all the time. In the moment it takes you to squeeze out a tea bag so it doesn't drip on your way to the pedal bin, five miniature people will have emerged into the world.

Jonathan reappears in the bedroom. He extracts balled-up socks from the top drawer and his favorite baby blue sweater—the one he handwashes himself in case I make it go felty—from the one beneath it. "Put on something warm," he instructs, easing me into a fleece that has been so stretched by my stomach it appears to be forty-one weeks pregnant, even when no one is wearing it.

He guides me out of the front door, a hand resting gently against my back. His cheeks are flecked with red blotches. He has that kind of skin; the sort that mottles easily, especially when he's stressed. The postman hovers on the path. "She's having a baby," says Jonathan, as if he needs to explain things. The postman has a round potato face and a waterproof jacket which rustles. In an attempt to remove himself from our property, he teeters backward, bouncing gently against the hedge. Perhaps he fears that the head will emerge and he'll be obliged to assist, seeing as delivering stuff is his job.

Jonathan lowers me onto the car's back seat. I have looked forward to this journey, imagined it over and over: swerving past slow-moving vehicles and juddering to a halt beside a rectangle of battered grass where, with some vigorous panting, I will plop out the infant onto

Jonathan's tartan travel rug. Men will run out of the barbers, haircuts half finished, clapping and cheering like there's a fight going on, and I'll think: "All this attention. It's not so bad, being a mother." Jonathan will wrap the three of us in the rug and a photographer will arrive from the *Hackney Gazette*. "I didn't do anything much," Jonathan will say. "Nina managed it all by herself. A natural mother."

Jonathan will, of course, know what to do. One lunchtime he bought *Babycare: Your Essential Guide to the First 12 Months* by the softly permed Dr. Hilary Dent. I read a chapter each night while marinating in sweet almond oil in the bath. "We need to bone up," Jonathan said, pleased to see me taking the whole business seriously. I studied pastel drawings of baby at breast, baby having its hair washed ("important to remove city dust and dried food, though unlikely to be your infant's favorite activity"). But still I know nothing. I have never held anyone younger than myself. One time, when my magazine's Art Editor came into the office to show off her new baby, I made sure I was busy with phone calls and an urgent feature shimmering on my screen. Wendy appeared at my desk with knackered eyelids and a hopeful smile. "Would you like a hold?" she asked.

I forced myself round to face her, feigning surprise. "I'd love to," I said, "but I'm bunged up with a cold. Don't want to breathe my germs all over him." I even shut down the back of my throat so I'd sound really ill.

"It's a her," she said. Wendy's smile congealed and she backed away to find people who were good at admiring babies. She knew I was lying. That wobbly newborn neck: I didn't want any part of it. Not when the child appeared so fragile that holding it wrongly might cause its head to snap off.

And now, as we park in a space meant for hospital staff only, I can't get over the neck bit: a person, independent of me, with a wobbling head of its own. The cot is assembled but I'm not ready, not really. Another month—extra time, like in football—and maybe I'll get there. At least, when the baby takes a breather from booting my innards, I can pretend it's not really happening at all.

"Good girl, good girl," he says, passing me a clear plastic mask for a breath of gas-and-air. Do-the-right-thing Jonathan. Apologize-when-the-condom-splits Jonathan. His fine sandy hair clings to a wet forehead. The lambswool sweater is discarded. His gray T-shirt has dark splodges under each arm and a mysterious brown splatter on the front. And I am no longer bracing myself for contractions but sensing an enormous shifting downward that no one can stop, no matter how hard I scream that I have changed my mind and want to go home to my flat where I live alone, fry all my food and wake up in tepid bathwater.

Finally I feel it, wedged for a second, then out and squealing. "It's here," says Jonathan, "the baby's here. It's a boy."

Jonathan's upper body is over mine, heavy and damp. He is replaced by the infant, who is deposited on my stomach, skinny-limbed, wrinkled as bacon.

"Look at him, Nina," Jonathan says. I can only stare upward at beige ceiling tiles with black speckles, like ants. When I do look, the child is regarding me with moist, swimmy eyes. A woman with coarse yellow hair delves between my legs.

And the voice comes, sharp and metallic above hospital clatter: "So, Nina, see what you've got yourself into this time?"

2

Early Days

I didn't intend to have a baby. I didn't even intend to live with someone. All I wanted was: fun-loving man for companionship.

I started again: female, thirty, likes classical music.

It wasn't true, that last bit. I owned one classical CD— *Duets from Famous Operas*—purchased with a notion of throwing open my living-room window and filling the street with big men shouting. I planned to play it so loudly you'd hear it over the buses that revved and belched exhaust outside my flat. The man from the Asian grocers would run out of his shop and stare up, wondering what kind of dramatic and passionate creature might live on the second floor. Then I remembered I couldn't stand opera and never bothered to remove the cellophane wrapper. I certainly did not wish to date a man who would force me to endure three hours of whining violins and discuss them afterward over dinner.

I wrote, "Attractive, lively female"—aware that I was marketing myself as an appealing spaniel puppy—"seeks loving, adventurous man for meals and maybe more." I copied it neatly onto the form, reminding myself that I didn't need to do this. A bit of fun, that's all it was. I phoned Eliza to report that I had sent the ad and hadn't been able to get the damn thing out of the postbox, no matter how hard I'd tried to jam in my arm.

"Don't be embarrassed," she said. "The junior in my department advertised herself, and she was really attractive." Eliza was chomping her lunch. She was the wrong person to call. Our friendship resembles one of those cocktails incorporating five different spirits plus peach juice: you love it and want loads, even though it makes you feel bad. Sick, sometimes.

"So I'm not attractive?" I said.

"No, loads of men fancy you. I bet." She swallowed loudly.

"Then why am I doing this?"

"It's getting harder," she struggled, "to meet men in normal ways."

I wondered where I might hire heavy-duty metal-cutting equipment to slice through the postbox.

I expected a heap of replies to skid onto the cracked brown lino of my hall, from wise and dazzlingly attractive men who would find my savage nose interesting. It was the prospect of receiving letters to sort into three piles (yes, no, maybe) that had made small ads more appealing than the Internet. If notepaper was involved it wouldn't feel sleazy, more like an avalanche of male penpals.

The letters came together in one flimsy brown envelope. There were four:

Laszlo, musician, with many body piercings.

Leo, whose startled, side-parted face peeped meekly into the bottom half of the photo booth.

Jerry, white-blond hair sprouting vertically from his head, naked on a brown velour sofa.

And Jonathan. A nondescript man, smiling hopefully as if waiting for you to open his present. Unthreatening eyes (possibly blue, more likely milky-gray). Someone who would hold a door open rather than let it bang in your face. He wrote: "You are probably looking for someone more outgoing and adventurous. But let me tell you a little about myself." In careful, forward-sloping writing, he detailed his interests: cooking, gardening, interior décor. I examined the handwriting, scanning for hints of a murky secret life: a penchant for highly flammable camiknickers or at least a criminal record. No one was this ordinary once you'd peeled off a layer or two. But no matter how hard I stared, he smiled reassuringly like the presenter of a gardening program where they burst onto your property, dig up your flower beds and wear soft, ambivalent expressions to convince you that they're doing the right thing.

"He works with computers," I told Eliza, in a coffee

shop done out to resemble a shabby living room. She pulled off her sandals and tucked her feet under her bottom on the cracked leather sofa. One knee was grazed, and looked sticky. Eliza is always damaging herself, probably because she forgets how long she is. Her size nine feet are perfectly formed for clanging into inanimate objects.

Smooth-faced waifs lolled on battered armchairs. A boy and a girl barely out of primary school leaned across a low Formica table, kissing wetly over a mound of shattered biscuits. Eliza held Jonathan between her thumb and forefinger. "I'm nervous," I said, "about meeting a stranger. He could be *anyone.*"

She dabbed her graze with a paper serviette. "He's just a regular bloke. Mr. Normal."

"It might be a cover-up, the looking normal thing. Ordinary people do horrible stuff. Weirdos always look normal."

She laughed, and crunched a brown sugar cube. "Meet him in a public place. A pub stuffed with millions of people, so there's witnesses." She jabbed his photo, leaving a sticky fingerprint. "He's reliable," she added, "I'd give him a go," as if he were a Ford Fiesta.

There was scarier stuff I hadn't told her. "He reads those poncy interiors magazines where no one has any CDs or a telly. Just a plain white vase on a mantelpiece."

"Meet him. You've got nothing to lose."

"You don't think he's too ordinary?"

She squinted, trying to bring him into focus. "No," she said. "Ordinary is good."

* * *

I rehearse the call:

Hello, Jonathan? I'm the woman you wrote to. The one who can't find a man in any normal kind of way. I don't do this sort of thing, not usually. It's not a habit of mine. But I travel a lot and don't have time to meet new people. You know those dog-eared magazines you find scattered on doctors' waiting room tables, full of shocking real-life experiences? Well, I write those. I interview people with trusting eyes who feed me tongue sandwiches and stories. This involves jetting off all over the place: to Sheffield, Woking, Walton on the Naze. So you see, I'm busy and successful and very, very happy. Perhaps you'd like to meet?

He answered by saying his number as if at a desk with a work hat on.

"Hello, Jonathan? It's Nina." *Nina the lonely heart. Nina the desperate.* "From the ad," I explained, my tongue flapping extravagantly. There was too much saliva. It was seeping into my mouth like my body was wringing itself out.

"How nice to hear from you," he said calmly. "Imagine you got lots of replies. Didn't think you'd—"

"I've never done this before," I blurted out.

"Neither have I. So what made you…"

I told him that I was away a lot and worked mostly with women. That was true(ish). I added that I wanted to expand my social circle, which wasn't.

He said, "Your ad sounded friendly."

There: I knew I'd come out like a puppy. I toyed with boasting that I was house-trained and rarely sniffed strangers' crotches but reminded myself that I didn't know him, that it wasn't the time for jokes. Instead I said, "It's difficult, selling yourself in less than twenty words.

You wonder if you should stick in the physical stuff—height, hair color, whether you're all right looking." I regretted saying this. Now he would ask what I looked like (key phrases formed instantly: five foot one, probably due to my mother chuffing filterless cigarettes throughout her pregnancy; puddly eyes with vaguely interesting rogue flecks of amber; would that be enough? Or were measurements—bust, waist, hips—required at this early stage?).

He laughed kindly. "I wouldn't think of it as selling yourself. It's brave, I'd say. I'd like to meet you, Nina. Perhaps you'd come over for dinner."

I saw myself gagged with shiny gaffer tape, bundled into the cupboard under the sink among the Brillo pads and Toilet Duck. "I'd rather meet in a public place, if that's okay."

"You choose. I don't go out much."

I pictured a too-normal man who stayed in with the curtains shut. "Do you know Gino's in Old Compton Street?" I asked. Gino's was the latest reincarnation of a bland Italian café that had changed hands several times in a year, yet retained its wipeable moon-and-star-printed tablecloths and concrete fountain, dribbling water. No one went there. At least no one who mattered.

He said he knew it, but I could tell he was bluffing.

"How will we recognize each other?" I asked.

"Well, you know what I look like."

"So I'll spot you, and you'll know it's me, when I come over."

"I'll look forward to that," he said.

★ ★ ★

He was easy to find. Apart from a waiter feeding salmon-colored carnations into a crystal vase, Jonathan was the only life form in the restaurant. I had planned my entrance: confident strides, non-desperate smile (no kiss; too much potential for the awkward bobbing of heads and the cracking of skulls).

When he saw me, he stood up and smiled mildly like a man greeting a cousin. The smile from the photo: *It's okay. There is nothing remotely peculiar or unnerving about me. I have no unexplained wounds and won't feel you up under the plastic tablecloth.*

Unasked for grilled vegetables arrived on skewers before I'd taken off my jacket. The waiter mooched away to busy himself with unnecessary tasks: repositioning salt and pepperpots on vacant tables and flicking the backs of red metal chairs with a wet cloth. He seemed nervous, as if expecting bailiffs to burst in at any moment and carry out the greasy cappuccino machine. Occasionally he looked up hopefully when passersby stopped to read the laminated menu in the window. They would peer through the glass, between the spindly green letters that read "Gino's Trattoria," and see just one couple—no, not a couple. Cousins who were close as children, and still liked each other enough to meet up occasionally at this soon-to-be-boarded-up restaurant (but only on a Monday; never a valuable weekend night).

I ordered trout because it sounded light and unobtrusive. There wasn't a hungry cell in my body. Jonathan dithered over the trout but politely ordered a chicken breast lolling in a muddy sauce so we wouldn't be too matching.

My trout came with an unwieldy salad, incorporating too many ingredients. Slices of plum and blood orange slumped uneasily against a heap of spring onions. An uncut beetroot seeped into a slagheap of Russian salad from a tin. We talked about the areas of London we liked and didn't like. I felt as bland as my trout, but with heavier bones. When I told him where I lived, Jonathan gnawed gamely at his chicken and said, "That's an interesting area."

"It's up-and-coming," I lied.

Jonathan had wisely bought in the chunk of East London bordering mine, which boasted two organic pubs, a comedy club and fabulous Thai take-away. Where I lived there was only a grocers, a minicab office and a mysterious store crammed with dead sewing machines.

Jonathan used phrases like "foot on the ladder" and "long-term investment." I didn't confess that my own flat was rented and that a strange man from Dundee lived upstairs with a boisterous Alsatian that lollopped unattended among the junk mail in the hall. Jonathan's cheesecake sagged stickily beneath its yellow skin. I couldn't eat dessert. My stomach had shrunk to the size of a broad bean. I was running out of steam.

An inquisitive face peered in through the "O" in Trattoria. On spying the cheesecake, it hurried away to the new, instantly popular restaurant two doors down, which offered white bowls of noodles to models and fashion students at rowdy communal tables. As we left, a mouse darted between the red chair legs, diving for cover behind a chipped gold radiator. The waiter presented me with a slimy-stemmed carnation plucked from the vase. "Enjoy the rest of your evening," he said, as if the meal had been just the start of it.

We stopped at the tube platform, wondering what to do with our hands and mouths. Our train rumbled its approach. "Sorry about the restaurant," I said, looking up at him. He smiled expectantly. I liked that smile. "Maybe next time we could—" There: I'd said it.

He looked surprised. "Next time I could cook for you. If you feel okay about coming round."

A man tumbled out of the train and beamed soppily into Jonathan's face. "Hey, mate!" he said. His tie was askew, cheeks scribbled with veins. "Who's your friend?" the man asked.

"This is Billy," Jonathan said to me through his teeth. "An old school friend. Billy, I'm just—"

"Who are you?" Billy blasted in my face.

"We just ran into each other," said Jonathan.

"Why don't we all have a beer? It's too early to go home. Come on, my shout."

Billy rummaged in his pocket, rattling coins. Jonathan bit his lip. "I'll call you, Billy."

"He always says that," Billy laughed, and ricocheted along the platform, lobbing a fistful of coppers in the vague direction of a busker's open guitar case.

"Sorry," said Jonathan.

"Why? He was only—"

The kiss came from nowhere. He started it, taking my

face in his hands. Then there were lips. I dropped my carnation onto the platform. His mouth was still on my mouth, hot hands tightly holding my hands, as our train clattered out of the station, without us.

Jonathan took to cooking for me. He said I didn't eat right. Too much cholesterol, furring up my insides. He seemed happy to rattle around in his sleek, grown-up kitchen, stirring things. Better than going out, he said. He knew where he was. Everything at hand.

I had never dated a man who knew what to do with capers. At least I assumed we were dating, which sounded creakily old-fashioned, but I couldn't say I was going out with him as I only saw him at his flat. The one time I coaxed him to my place, we lay on my grazed sofa where he gave me a back massage and the Dundee man's Alsatian barked above our heads.

Jonathan was happier on home turf where everything was shiny and smelt lemony. I would watch him at work with yellow rectangular sponges and dimpled blue cloths. He would tell me about the inner workings of computers, which I found comforting. His job sounded terribly precise. Software developers were either right or wrong. There were no gray areas.

As he prepared supper, I would hover on the sidelines, observing ingredients in plain glass bowls: roughly-chopped herbs. A lime, halved, ready for squeezing. I had only ever seen TV chefs prepare everything beforehand. When I cooked, shifting a solitary object around in a frying pan, I would pretend to be such a chef. I'd say, "Now we're cracking the egg, sliding it into the pan…a little black pepper please…" My left hand—the assistant—would pass the grinder and I'd ask, "Doesn't this look tasty? Shall we let the studio audience have a try?" I would flip the egg into a torn-apart roll and bite into it, bursting the yolk. "Mmm," I'd say. "Delicious."

Perhaps Jonathan had come along in the nick of time.

"You can't be pregnant," he said, "after one little accident." He had turned up at my office off Leicester Square, clutching his briefcase nervously. We crossed the road to the nearest pub, one I never drank in. They still did meals in baskets. On the bar was a plastic tub of whiteners, for coffee. "I did a test," I said.

He ordered a glass of white wine which came in an oily glass. I asked for water. "You're serious," he said.

"It's not the kind of thing I joke about."

We sat in a corner, bordered on two sides by smeared windows. He placed two abandoned chips, coiled like slugs, in the ashtray. "So what do you think?" I said, helplessly.

"What do you think I think? I'm pleased." He squeezed my hand bravely across the table.

"It's too early. We're not at that stage, not nearly."

"Could it be wrong, the stick thing?"

"I don't think these things lie." I fished it out of my pocket and showed him. I'd wrapped it in paper from the office loo, which fluttered toward the maroon carpet like a miniature sail.

"What do you want to do?"

"Have it, what else?" This wasn't strictly true. I couldn't think of any reason not to have it.

"How do you feel?" he asked.

"Sick. I was doing an interview yesterday, this woman whose husband made her move out of their bed so his dog could sleep with him. Massive Afghan hound thing, stinking of wet fur. Even when the woman put it out of the kitchen, I could still smell it, stuck to my coat."

Hair clung to my forehead in a miserable droop. Jonathan pushed it away. "Poor Nina," he said. "It'll be okay, I promise."

Anyone would have thought we were a proper couple.

3

Taking Your Baby Out

Martha's cleavage looms dangerously close to my eyeball. A wooden beaded necklace bounces lightly between her freckled breasts. "Everyone finds it painful at first," announces my breast-feeding counselor. "But the nipple toughens up into a hard little *nub.* In no time you'll be popping it out in cafés, on trains, even in the theatre, darling, without a second thought."

It is Martha's purpose to convince me that a four-day-old infant can be nourished solely via one gnarled nipple. The other nipple (for I have two) has withered to a mean-looking raisin and is therefore temporarily out of service. As a result, the breast to which it is attached has grown so bulbous that I fear it might burst, splattering

Jonathan's seventy-eight-year-old mother, Constance, with sweet fluid.

"I want to put him on formula," I tell Martha. She shakes her head quickly, as if I'm a child demanding to tightrope walk on live electrical wires. Secretly I have bought some factory-made milk. I crept into the chemist's, pulling up the collar of my jacket. It's tucked behind the organic rolled oats with a tea towel folded over it.

"But you're managing fantastically," insists Martha. "And think of all the good you're doing your baby. Less risk of gastroenteritis, higher intelligence. You know, breast-fed babies have a far higher chance of getting into university."

This suggests that my son might leave home at eighteen rather than lying on the rug and demanding bags of crisps and his pants to be ironed at the age of thirty-seven, which can only be a good thing. Martha rests a stubby hand on my knee. "A woman I know made a rubber ball from elastic bands. Built it up for weeks before the baby was born. When it came to feeding, she had this rubbery globe to bite on."

"Biscuit?" asks Constance, hovering with a sugar-speckled plate. Constance is my pretend mother-in-law and has brought her own biscuits. Jonathan and I are not married. As the baby was conceived before we had learned each other's surnames, we haven't had time to get married.

"Jonathan was bottle-fed," blares Constance into the anxious air. "I'd put in a rusk to thicken it up and fill his belly so he'd sleep the full twelve hours." She arranges finger Nice biscuits to form a perfect fan shape. She's a small, busy woman with a fallen-out perm that looks rained on. "He was a guzzler," she adds. "But I routined him. We did that in those days. Weren't you on the potty at fourteen months?"

"I don't remember," splutters Jonathan.

"Oh, he was. Not completely trained but only one serious accident, in Boots, and they were ever so good, let us use the staff facilities."

Jonathan smiles sadly at his feet.

"On his second birthday," she rattles on, "I took off his plastic nighttime pants and said, 'We don't need these anymore, do we?'"

Jonathan tweaks the heel of his sock.

"And that was that," announces Constance. "Dry as a bone. A late developer in other ways, though."

My redundant breast oozes milk. The baby cottons onto what is required and gulps thirstily, then plops off again, leaving the in-service nipple spurting milk. I stop the flow with a clamped-on hand. Jonathan lurches forward with a tissue, dabbing the air around my breast. "Perhaps you're not relaxed enough," suggests Martha.

"I think I'll make dinner," says Constance. In the kitchen, drawers are opened and banged shut. "Don't you have any mince?" she shouts.

The baby coughs, spraying milky saliva. I tip him over my shoulder and pat his back, forcing out a curdled jet.

"Believe me, it gets easier," says Martha, now looking hopeless around the eyebrows. She crunches the last Nice biscuit and wipes her hands on tenty brown trousers. She locates her bag beneath Constance's bundle of knitting. "Jonathan can help," she adds. "I know he can't feed *per se*—doesn't have the equipment—but it's good for bonding, to involve Dad in winding and settling. You know the key to successful breast-feeding, Nina?" Her tongue shoots out, desugaring lips. "Looking after yourself. *Loving* yourself. Saying: I may be a mother but I too have needs."

"Yes!" I say, too eagerly.

"And you're lucky to have a supportive partner." She smiles richly at Jonathan and strides past the glossy black door to her next appointment where New Mother is managing marvelously, intending to breast-feed until the child is able to position itself on the bosom while watching an R-rated movie on TV.

Jonathan peels the sleeping baby off me.

"You must have a heavy-bottomed frying pan," mutters Constance.

I flop backwards onto the sofa, aware that one breast, an orb of veiny Stilton, is fully exposed. "I'm putting him on a bottle," I croak.

Constance emerges from the kitchen clutching an open packet of Bisto. We don't use it; she must have brought her own. She holds it in one hand and a teaspoon, loaded with ashy powder, in the other. Her eyes rest on the baby. He lies on the sofa, drunk on my milk, ready to be decanted into his cot. Pink legs and arms are splayed, as if he has tumbled from an airplane.

"Funny," she says. "He looks nothing like you."

★ ★ ★

We live in the ground floor flat of a converted three-story Victorian terrace. The hallway is never littered with junk mail or neglected Alsatians. Jonathan owns the square front garden that juts from the flat like a table leaf. He had it paved with reclaimed slabs (for low maintenance) and edged with galvanized pots of lavender (for fragrance). There's a backyard, too, where Jonathan plans to introduce more plants, perhaps bamboo and some elegant climbers.

He has lived here for several years. He gutted the place immediately after moving in, chucked other people's appalling taste into a skip. Before renovations started he had the forethought to take Polaroids of old-person's swirling rusts and olives. His mother thought he had ideas above his station, flinging out perfectly usable fixtures and fittings. He ignored her, he told me, and marched past with faded velvet curtains and a bathroom carpet stinking of ammonia. The Polaroids were stuck into an album alongside shots of each room as it is now, with shades of creamy vanilla and blue everywhere.

"I know what you've done," I said, when he showed me the album on my second visit to his flat. "You've made it look awful in the before pictures like they do in makeovers. So the woman looks even better afterward."

"What are makeovers?" he asked.

"You know. Before and afters. In the before picture they slap Vaseline on her face to make it look greasy."

"Isn't that cheating?"

I laughed and flicked the album's pages. Polaroids were

captioned: *Hall—before. Bathroom—after. Back door—sanded but not painted.* There was even a photo of the skip with a shower curtain lolling over the edge. "You're so particular," I said, "for a man."

"What do you mean, for a man?"

"I mean it's unusual. I've never met anyone like you."

"Is that a compliment?" he asked, shutting the album firmly.

"Just an observation," I said.

I moved in with Jonathan six months ago. This changed me in small ways. I noticed that my toothbrush splayed untidily and bought a new one (turquoise to tone with Jonathan's white-and-blue-tiled bathroom). Instead of bundling underwear into a drawer, I took to folding my pants.

We were a real couple now and proved it by inviting friends to dinner. Jonathan's friends were mostly from work, and talked about their roof terraces and how great it would be to have a shed. They always left by 11:00 p.m. I preferred Billy who would roll in several hours late with a hot, pubby face and his dinner dried up in the oven. The tube was a challenge for Billy. Each visit, he'd blame his lateness on falling asleep on the train and completing a circuit of the Circle Line. Occasionally he ventured farther afield, and found himself in Barnet or Ongar where he'd dawdled to study tiny frogs on the platform. He felt in his pocket where a frog should have been, but found only tobacco fallen out of its pouch.

In the old days, when I was normal, I might have

stayed up with someone like Billy, talking nonsense. But Jonathan would become agitated and start jigging his knee. He'd throw Billy a blanket and me a look that said: *time for bed*. In the morning I'd find Billy sweating on the sofa, fouling the minimalist décor with his breath.

Mostly, though, we saw the work people. After cheese and dainty slivers of celery, Jonathan would pass round the album of Polaroids. Everyone would agree that we had made dramatic improvements, forgetting that I was a recent addition, quickly moved in with my expanding belly. One night, when the friends had gone home, I asked, "Have you lived with anyone before?"

Jonathan continued polishing wineglasses and said that he had. Billy had lived on the sofa for a couple of weeks, following a disastrous affair with a flight attendant. When Billy had lit a roll-up from the gas ring—setting his fringe alight and filling the kitchen with vile fumes—Jonathan had suggested he might go home and try to repair the relationship. "Can you imagine," he said, "how awful burning hair smells?"

"I meant have you lived with girlfriends."

He edged a wineglass into its rightful position with a middle finger. "There's been no one," he said.

"What? No one serious? No one you wanted to have a child with?"

"No one special," he said.

I watched him wiping surfaces he had cleaned already, wishing I could jam my stupid questions back into my mouth.

★ ★ ★

Leaving the house with your newborn according to *Babycare:*

1. Start with a short, local trip. If anything happens, at least you can get home quickly.
2. Head for open spaces, not busy streets.
3. Take nappies, wipes, barrier cream, breast pads, dummy, a bottle if necessary, a book or magazine, extra blankets if it's chilly, a sun hat if it's hot and a spare outfit in case your baby's nappy leaks.
4. Stay calm.

Jonathan returns to work. He smiles encouragingly as he steps into the car, leaving me with sandpaper eyes and a baby with no instructions attached. Back inside I turn to find the chapter in *Babycare* entitled: What to Do with Your Newborn During the Day.

There isn't such a chapter. A two-week-old human doesn't appear to be capable of anything much, other than feeding and sleeping. He can't hold a rattle or make biscuits with a heart-shaped cutter. He hasn't even been named. Jonathan's suggestions (David, Anthony, Martin) feel enormous for a person fifteen inches long. Eliza contributed a fashionable list: Milo, Dylan, Spike. Couples from the antenatal group favor dowdy (but ironic) names suggesting persons old enough to remember the Second World War and bang on about it endlessly: Fred, Walter, Stanley. My mother called, shouting, "You haven't thought of Colin?"

I'm warming to Benjamin. It's a flexible name, hanging comfortably regardless of a person's size. He sleeps now, the blanket rising and falling gently. Confident that he won't catapult himself from the sofa onto the polished floorboards, I tread lightly to the bathroom.

I have piles, and waxy white pellets to put up my bottom to make them go away. After poking one in I inspect the kitchen, in search of tasks. The coriander is out of alignment with the other herbs. Something else is wrong: a sour whiff. The kitchen never smells bad when Jonathan is here. He has been at work for less than an hour and already the flat is decaying. By the time he comes home, it may be derelict.

Jonathan has tidied the fridge, transferring eggs from their box into dimples in the door. Nothing bad there. It can't be a nappy; soiled offerings are swiftly bagged in peach-scented sacks and dumped in the outside bin. Jonathan bought a nappy disposal unit but I can't figure it out. More switches and buttons. Equipment overload. The smell intensifies when I twist to the right; sicky and acidic. Perhaps it's on me. But there's no stain, no evidence of anything spewed up. Stay-at-home mother fills her people-free days with lining up herb jars and obsessing over odors.

I call Jonathan to announce that we're going out. "Good idea," he says. In the background phones ring, colleagues babble. Clearly they're having a wonderful time.

"I don't think it'll rain," I tell him.

"No, but take the rain hood in case."

"And the mobile."

"Make sure it's charged. Sorry, Nina"—a pert female

voice has interrupted him, possibly to call him to a meeting but, more likely, to announce an impromptu office party—"someone wants me. Go easy now."

I ram the buggy, which doubles as a carrycot and incorporates far too many knobs and levers and a padded pouch called a Snugglebabe, into the street, gouging a sliver of black paint off the door. A cluster of mothers is ambling towards the park, dangling toddlers on reins. If Eliza were here, she would point at the most dollied-up one and whisper, "Not a good look." A MILT, she'd call her: Mother in Leather Trousers. I've read the term on the "fun" page Eliza writes for her fashion magazine: snippy comments about celebrities' outfits. I used to help her think them up. We'd balance drinks and Eliza's lilac suede notebook on the wall outside the Dog and Trumpet, back in the sixteenth century when I frequented licensed premises.

"Do you know a baby's face can burn in *seconds?*" An elderly woman with a soft puff of double chin has squashed next to me on the park bench. "Babies' skin is ever so sensitive," she scolds. "Don't you have a canopy for that?"

The sun shines weakly. Yet the woman's concern—plus the fact that she appears to be wearing several tweed coats on top of each other—makes me doubt my heat-sensing abilities. The sick smell is still noticeable, too. That means I've brought it out with me.

The woman peers into the pram. Satisfied that Ben's epidermis has not formed a blistered sheet, she squeezes his cheek. This wakes him instantly. His lower lip puckers, and his cries—though not as alarming as when heard in the flat—are enthusiastic enough to suggest that snack time is upon us.

Stupidly I am wearing a dress with a zip at the back. In order to extract a breast I have two options: hoist it over the neckline which, given that each is fully inflated, will alert the attention of teenagers dogging off school and possibly even the police. Or I could raise my entire dress and sit naked apart from my knickers and a ring of bunched-up fabric around my neck.

I delve into the baby essentials bag and extract a bottle. "Mine were breast-fed," says the woman. "All nine. One died." She stares at me with small, sticky eyes.

"This is the first bottle he's had," I explain. "It's just a backup."

"You'll get your figure back quicker if you breast-feed. It drains the fat out of you."

Babycare warns of the tricky progression from breast to bottle but Ben's eyes bulge with delight at the sight of clear plastic, his vigorous sucks flattening the teat. Along the path, a copper-haired woman marches toward us, her necklace bouncing in time with each stride. "I thought it was you," announces Martha, my breast-feeding counselor. "You look fantastic. Aren't you coping amazingly well?"

"Thanks," I say. "I *feel* fantastic."

"And look at you—out and about already. That's an achievement in itself."

I am rather proud of having made the arduous journey from flat to park, past potential dangers such as the organic pub and the paper shop. "So how's…" she begins.

"Benjamin. Ben. He's doing fine."

But Martha has stopped listening. Her eyes swoop on the bottle plugged between Ben's lips. As he gulps, emitting appreciative *um-ums* after each swallow, I realize there is little hope of passing off a factory-made bottle as a genuine human breast.

Perhaps I'm not cut out for this job.

4

Sleep Deprivation

Eliza has a beautiful neck. It is long, like a candle, and waxy smooth. She rubs cream into it; special cream containing minerals from the Dead Sea. She buys two fat pots at a time: one for home, one for the drawer of her desk.

She is a fashion stylist on a magazine. There appear to be two strands to the job: urging her readers to spend several hundred quid on a plain gray cardigan, and traveling to exotic locations "for the light." The majority of Eliza's fashion shoots require trips to sunnier climes. Occasionally she'll go somewhere freezing and force models to trudge through the snow in dangerous sandals. Apparently the light in the parks around her office isn't good enough.

On these trips abroad, Eliza's main role is to sympathize when the models complain about the heat or the cold, and to bribe indigenous peoples to stand next to them, adding local color. While Ben naps and I wonder whether to shine up the stainless steel hob that Jonathan has already polished, I amuse myself by imagining Eliza in Lapland, bellowing, "Bring on the Hopi tribe!" at which time a cluster of pissed-off locals troop into shot, wondering why a thin, scowling girl is wearing a cream beaded gown on a mountain.

Before Ben, I worked on *Promise* magazine. Its flimsy pages featured "real" people (i.e., not thin people) telling dreadful true-life stories: like coming home from bingo to a burnt-down house. Chase, my editor, liked a twist (ideally the woman whose house had burnt down should unearth a winning lottery ticket in her handbag which, fortunately, she had taken with her to bingo). He called such stories "triumph over tragedy." They gave hope, he said; that no matter how cruddy your morning had been so far, something wonderful might happen to you, too.

Chase was lying. *Promise* was successful because it made you think, "Maybe my life's not that bad. At least we haven't been persecuted for our love and forced to live in a henhouse." And you'd pour yourself a cup of tea and reflect that, while your husband had left you for the nineteen-year-old baby-sitter and something sinister was bubbling up in the toilet, things could be worse. You could be in *Promise*.

Ben and I have spent five days shuttling from flat to park and back again when a cab pulls up outside the flat.

Eliza's neat bottom bobs as she bends to pay the driver. "Could I have a receipt?" she asks. "Put fifteen quid, would you?"

Eliza has brought a present for Ben: a black velvet teddy devoid of facial features or any child-stimulating embellishment apart from a Louis Vuitton ribbon lashed tightly round its neck. It smells of floral-scented soap. I suspect it's an unwanted present from a PR flack that has lain in Eliza's desk drawer for several centuries. "Thanks," I say. "He'll love it."

Ben lies on his back beneath a vivid plastic contraption called an activity arch. Jonathan winced when he saw it, complaining that its primary hues and bashy noises were out of keeping with our vanilla-toned living room. But the activity arch has turned out to be a fine acquisition. Ben will gaze happily at the dangling plastic balls for anything up to a minute and a half. I place the Louis Vuitton teddy beside him. Drool slides down his chin.

"Are you feeling all right?" asks Eliza.

"I'm fine."

She narrows her eyes at me. Her lashes are dusty with old mascara. "Are you really all right?" she says in a softer voice. "You seem…"

"It just takes some getting used to."

She sinks into the sofa, propping turquoise heels on the tan suede cube. Her shoes look badly treated. "I'm supposed to be on appointments," she sighs, "but I've sneaked off to see you. You sounded so hollow."

I know what appointments mean: gliding around the offices of fashion publicists to select a belt or maybe a necklace. On an extremely busy day she might have her hair blow-dried straight or select a bias-cut skirt to use on a shoot. "I was probably tired," I say, trying to sound unhollow. "I just feel a bit flat, that's all."

"You're spending too much time at home. Daytime's weird, isn't it? There are people about, but they're aimless. It's creepy."

I wish the phone would ring or that someone would burst in with a belated congratulatory bouquet.

"When you're busy at work," continues Eliza, "you don't think about daytime people, popping out to the shops, trimming hedges…"

"I don't trim the hedge," I snap. "Jonathan does it."

"So what do you do all day?"

"See people. Make new friends."

"You mean coffee mornings, stuff like that?"

In fact, I have attended one prelunch gathering where hot beverages were offered. Being at home so much, I worried that I had lost the ability to converse with adults. Ben was six weeks old but I felt like I'd not spoken to anyone big—apart from Jonathan—for several decades. My mouth had started to work stiffly, and when Jonathan came home I'd burble minutiae until he escaped to the bathroom. Even Eliza kept our phone calls short, and often yawned.

I'd surprised myself by enjoying the coffee morning. I ranted non-stop—which required a tricky kind of circular breathing—until the lifeless woman I was talking to said she had to see to her baby, even though he was propped up on cushions, happily licking his chin.

"It's good for me," I tell Eliza firmly. "I need to meet people with babies."

She picks up Jonathan's interiors magazine and flips its shiny pages. It's called *InHouse*. She studies a concrete sweep of building clinging precariously to a cliff. "You need to get back into the real world," she says.

"It *is* real."

"I know. This is what mothers do. But I thought you might fancy something different."

"What kind of different?"

"We need a baby for a shoot," she says, glancing quickly at Ben. "Week after next. Not doing anything, are you?"

"I'll have to check," I say, staring at her feet. The heels have formed little square indents on the suede cube.

"Don't look so worried. He wouldn't have to do anything. He'd just be a prop."

"Don't you have people who supply babies for that kind of thing? Baby model agencies?"

She nods dismissively. "Too cutesy. Rosebud lips, big eyes. Cliché, isn't it? I'm looking for character."

Ben has stopped gazing at the dangling spheres and glowers at Eliza. I notice, perhaps for the first time, that his eyelashes are particularly dark and luscious. "You're saying he's ugly."

"No, just unusual. Cute, in a weird way. Doesn't look like either of you."

Ben's deep pink lips part, hinting at a smile. I wonder if it's a real smile, or just wind. Or perhaps he's about to fill his nappy, and this is his concentration face.

But the mouth rises at its corners. A wobbly half smile

hovers uncertainly, as if it might pop in an instant. I want to tell Eliza that this, his first smile, is some amazing thing that even *Babycare* doesn't mention.

"Three hundred pound fee," she announces. "I'll send a cab so you won't have to cart all that baby equipment you lug about. And you'll get lunch."

"What kind of lunch?" I have taken to punctuating long, adult-free days with around fifteen small snacks: the odd slice of ham, a fistful of gherkins. No plates or cutlery.

"Organic buffet. Roasted peppers, seared salmon. Dinky goat cheese pastries you won't believe."

Ben's smile wilts. He turns back to the activity arch, regarding himself in a swinging mirror like you'd find in a budgie cage.

Sold, for a goat cheese pastry.

Before Jonathan, my boyfriend selection methods were more haphazard. I met Ranald in the Dog and Trumpet's downstairs room. Wendy, our pregnant art editor, was having a party to celebrate her departure from buff-colored office life. She danced, grazing the embarrassed post boy with her pregnant dome. You could see her belly button jutting through her flimsy white tunic.

No one had proper parties in houses anymore. Gatherings were held in pub basements that were used three times a year and reeked of damp and disinfectant. The manager would attempt to create a celebratory atmosphere by plugging in a fan heater. You never found anyone promising in these downstairs rooms.

Ranald had wandered in after taking a wrong turn during his hunt for the toilet. He emitted outdoorsy freshness, even while picking at a dish of aging Bombay Mix. The music was so loud I couldn't make out his words. I stared, mesmerized by his mobile lips. His teeth were white as Tipp-ex.

The music stopped. "I'm going camping next weekend," he shouted. "Want to come?"

"What? In a tent?" I roared back.

He laughed. "You've never done it, have you? You media lot. Fond of your poncy hotels." He scanned the room with flinty eyes. Wendy took one puff of the junior writer's cigarette. There was grit in the bottom of my glass.

As Ranald was so attractive—of a high enough standard, in fact, to model casual separates for mail-order catalogs—I said I'd rather sleep in a tent than one of your poncy hotels any day of the week. We set off for North Devon at 8:00 a.m. the following Saturday and arrived at his uncle's farm before lunch. I had limited myself to one item of skincare: tinted moisturizer with sunblocking properties. I explored his sucked-in body under drab green nylon and he told me off for being too enthusiastic. We woke to rain, battering the tent. Ranald made me wash in a feeble stream with orange industrial soap. He glared as I dabbed on moisturizer afterward. From that moment his mood soured and he accused me of not helping enough. When we dismantled the tent, he shouted at me for losing the tiny drawstring bag into which an enormous heap of rustling nylon was to be stuffed.

"I didn't lose it," I said. "I put my jumper in it and used it as a pillow."

He whirled around and—in something of an overreaction—flung a tent peg at me. It whipped past my cheek and lopped into the long grass. It took us twenty-five minutes' hunting to retrieve it.

We drove home without speaking. He kept the engine running outside my flat. "Thanks for a great weekend," I said.

I called him later that night to break it to him that I wasn't in the right frame of mind for a relationship.

"Okay," he said. I waited for him to add something else, like, "It's been fun, though, hasn't it?" or, "You're a lovely person, Nina."

"Are you still there?" I asked.

Ranald yawned. I remembered then that he hadn't chosen me or even found me attractive. He had simply been hunting for the toilet and gone down too many stairs.

I can't sleep for the looming horror of Eliza's shoot. I'll call and say I've changed my mind, wasn't thinking straight. Sleep deprivation: it makes you say yes accidentally. Before having Ben, I considered sleep a tedious but necessary procedure for promoting cell renewal. I didn't look forward to going to bed. Nor did I wake in the morning and immediately calculate how long I would have to remain upright before sliding back under the duvet.

Now, however, I think about sleep constantly. In my

fantasies, rather than being pleasured by an assortment of unfamiliar men, I am simply lying down with my eyes shut. Sleep-related garments creep into the picture: cotton nighties, flannel pajamas. Even bedsocks. In these fantasies I lie on my back, diagonally across the mattress with arms splayed to occupy maximum space. No room for an adult male or even a baby.

Ben operates on an upside-down schedule: drowsy in daylight, alert after dark. "Human beings are not designed to sleep at nighttime," warns *Babycare*. "It's the safest time for hunting. We should be out, foraging for food." This appears to be accurate as, approximately every two hours between 10:00 p.m. and dawn, Ben's eyes spring open and he assumes the eager expression of one who would rather be thrashing through undergrowth than snuggling beneath a blue blanket appliquéd with rabbits.

Some nights, it hardly seems worth going to bed at all. I research the consequences of chronic sleep deprivation: lethargy, mood swings, clumsiness, dizziness, skin irritations, an inability to cope, a tendency to lose perspective, temporary memory loss and other things I've forgotten. Sleep occupies so much of my brain space, there is little room for anything else. I can barely dress myself without mislaying my bra and discovering it, hours later, dangling from the chrome hook where the oven glove should be. During a march around the park, I somehow part company with my front door key and have to summon Jonathan home from the office.

I loiter at our gate, trying not to attract the attention of the surly couple across the road with their threatening *This Is A Neighborhood Watch Area* sticker. To appear friendly, I hum a lullaby, even though Ben is asleep. Finally a vehicle lumbers into our road and Jonathan springs out, my rescuer, key poised to jab in the door.

As my intellectual capabilities appeared to be crumbling, so Jonathan becomes Patron Saint of Getting Things Done. I watch as he measures formula for Ben's bottles; capable Dad-hands, simultaneously stirring basil-scented sauce to accompany the fresh linguine he picked up at lunchtime.

"I can't do the things you do," I tell him.

"You're fine," he says. "I'm proud of you."

Eliza told me to relax about Ben's shoot, not to deck him out in a sailor ensemble like some revved-up showbiz mother would. "Don't go to any special lengths," she instructed. "Put him in one of those button-up things with the legs in them."

"A babygro."

"And don't bother about his hair. We'll deal with that on the shoot."

As I peel off Ben's damp night nappy I consider simply not showing up. Something terrible's happened: a baby emergency. He has a rash. She wouldn't want him, would she, with festering spots? Or some domestic disaster. I've been attacked by the nappy disposal unit. The blades flew off the food processor, lacerating my arm. I must think of something. I only agreed from a self-centered desire to be out of the house with someone fetching me snacks. Enticing, yes, but at what price? If anyone comes near him with their hairspray or fierce eyebrow tweezers, we'll be out of there. Ben's well-being is my priority. I am his *mother.*

While he kicks on the bed, delighted with his naked-ness, I lay out miniature clothing. Obviously I can't put him in anything knitted by Constance. The range includes frilly-collared sweaters from which Ben's head pops out as if emerging from a cake, and knitted coats called mati-nee jackets, even though it will be years before he goes to the cinema. I might have considered one of Constance's plainer creations, but all have puckered seams and gaping buttonholes. They appear to have been knitted on forks.

I ease his pliable body into a plain white all-in-one. He gazes at me, clearly of the opinion that I am some remarkable human being. Sometimes I wondered why he likes me so much.

The buzzer sounds. My cab has arrived early deliber-ately to catch me in a state of undress. To save time, I consider pulling on outer clothing over my dressing gown. But what if I arrive at the studio with the cord dangling at the back, like a tail? Eliza would worry that I have deteriorated from merely sounding hollow to being unable to dress myself. It's a short step from wear-ing your bra on top of your coat.

The buzzer sounds again, repeatedly, as if being pressed by a child. A singsong voice calls: "Neee-na. It's us. We're back."

I open the door. A tricycle hovers at eye level, its rust-ing frame flecked red and blue. Frayed washing line lashes a wicker basket to the handlebars.

"She forgot we were coming," says Dad.

"Of course I didn't forget."

"Let's see him then," says Mum, tottering past me. "What is he now, three weeks?"

"Two months."

"Gosh," says Dad, "how did that happen?" He places the tricycle on the floor, pointing it towards Ben.

"Thanks, it's lovely."

"We didn't know what to give you, did we, Jack?" says Mum. "Thought you'd have everything already."

To ensure a respectable distance between herself and Ben—presumably to minimize any risk of being asked to hold him—Mum rests her bottom on the suede cube. She is wearing a snagged lemon skirt which she tweaks with insecty fingers. "He's like you," she says, peering down at him. "Like you when you were that age."

Occasionally something happens to remind me that I am the result of an unspeakable act involving the coupling of my parents. Mostly, though, our family tree twigs seem wrongly connected; a line might link me to Mum but it was surely a slip of the pen. I can see where I'm coming from with Dad; we share weighty noses, an all-over doughiness and slump into chairs, knees thrust apart. Mum's narrow brown legs are pressed tightly together. She has pinned up her peppery hair with a smattering of plain brown kirby grips, the kind you buy at the chemists, 15p for several hundred.

"How was France?" I ask.

"Nothing done to the house, of course," says Dad. "Damp seeping into the back bedroom. Terrible smell."

Mum splutters, stops a laugh with yellowing fingers. "We bought Camembert and you know, with the damp and stuffiness, I went to take a piece off it and the whole thing—" her dainty shoulders quiver "—was a mass of teeny white weevils."

"I thought you weren't supposed to eat cheese?" I remind her. Mum sees Ashley, an alternative practitioner of dubious pedigree. He has advised her to banish gluten, dairy products and citrus fruits from her diet and sends her home after each visit with huge, flecked tablets, possibly intended for horses. She sticks the horse pills to her forehead with tape. It's for her brain blockage, Ashley says. He's worried about her brain.

"If I can't have a nibble of Camembert in France—" she says, tetchily.

"Don't you think you should sell the place?" I suggest. "It's a liability."

"Oh, no," says Dad. "It'll all come together eventually."

Several years ago, on a driving holiday in Western France, my parents noticed a crumbling structure slumped at the end of an overgrown lane. Any sensible adult would have driven swiftly onwards to Dijon and booked into a snug hotel. My mother made Dad perform a reckless U-turn and check that the house was as awful close up.

The English owners invited them in. They had intended to transform the rotting heap into a lucrative holiday let until their drunken stupors wore off and they wisely decided to hurry home to a centrally heated town house in Holland Park. It was meant to be, my mother said. She failed to notice that, as the house hugged a grassy bank, it will forever be a stinking pile unless someone removes the hill.

This does not appear to concern my parents. The decaying property provides a handy excuse to amble to and from Burgundy, checking that the heap of slates has still not been arranged to form a new roof but is simply becoming a little more moss-covered with each visit. "The garden's looking wonderful, though," adds Dad. "We brought you back some rosemary. Did we leave it in the car, Kate?"

"Mmm," murmurs Mum, inhaling deeply. I suspect she wants a cigarette. Ashley doesn't know she smokes. He can't understand why the blockages aren't clearing or what makes his pendulum rotate in an alarming anti-clockwise manner when he dangles it over her lungs.

"I'm just popping out to the garden," she says.

"Mum, I'm sorry, I should have remembered and let you know, but this isn't a very good time to—"

Ben gives a little squeak.

"Gosh, hello!" says Dad.

"Would you like to hold him?"

"Oh, I don't know."

"Would you like a cuddle, Mum?"

She makes for the door, scrabbling in her tasseled shoulder bag for a lighter.

Ben cries shrilly. "Does he do that a lot?" asks Dad. He sinks into the chair, trying to melt through the soft leather to a place where there are only springs and stuffing and no spluttering infant.

Smoke meanders in through the open front door. "There's a man here," says Mum. "He keeps saying Lavender Hill. He looks awfully cross."

Remembering that I am still wearing a dressing gown, I dump Ben on Dad's lap and hurry to the bedroom.

"Will you be long?" he calls pleasantly.

"Pop him over your shoulder and walk up and down."

"The man says he was told to pick you up at ten-thirty," shouts Mum. "What does he want?"

I tumble out of the bedroom, flinging items essential for Ben's survival into the baby-changing bag. "Sorry, Dad, but we're due on this shoot thing with Eliza."

"This what?" asks Mum, grinding her cigarette into the doorstep with the toe of her shoe. Ben arches stiffly, writhing in Dad's arms.

"Here, let me take him." I scoop up Ben, allowing him a couple of seconds' false hope that he is about to be cuddled, then slam him into the car seat. "It's for Eliza's magazine," I say over my shoulder. "They want a baby as a, as a…"

I belt Ben's seat into the minicab. Dad eases himself in beside it.

"A sort of prop?" suggests Mum, exhaling fag breath as she shimmies into the front seat.

5

Your Sociable Baby

The cab rattles to a halt in a cobbled alley scented with a pedal-bin stench from the canal. My parents bound out of the car. "So," says Dad, "this is where these photographers do their pictures. You'd never think it."

I have met plenty of photographers but not the kind who work for glossy magazines. When a "real" person was having their photograph taken for *Promise,* we called upon someone from a local paper—your man at the *Cherrow and Spalding Advertiser*—who, while not obviously grubby, appeared as if certain nooks and crannies would benefit from closer inspection. I encountered one of these photographers while interviewing a woman from Hull who had given birth while still wearing her leggings. She hadn't known she was pregnant.

The photographer winced as she plugged the roaring baby on to its bottle. "It's all pretty tragic, isn't it?" he whispered. He had a glossy, oval face, like an olive.

Our hostess peeled cling wrap from a plate of grated cheese sandwiches and set them on the smallest table from a nest of three. "So," she said, "are you stopping the night in Hull?"

"God, no," said the photographer. "I'm on the next train back to Leeds. Got tickets for a-ha's comeback tour."

Which struck me as more tragic than carrying a baby to full term and being blissfully unaware of it.

Smoke shoots from Mum's nostrils as she crams in a fag before being forced indoors again. The reception-ist glances up from a chaotic desk. Her inky hair is se-cured in sticky-out bunches with cheap plastic hair bobbles. An owl pencil case rests by the sticker-cov-ered phone.

"Model?" she rasps, jet eyebrows scooting upward.

"Not me, I'm here to—"

"The *baby*. It's for the shoot, yeah?"

I nod, hoping she realizes we've been forced into this. Her eyes shoot to the left, indicating that I should pro-ceed through a battered swing door. I nudge it with my backside and swing Ben's car seat into a vast, chilly stu-dio, the heavy-breathing specter of my parents behind me.

The state of Eliza's hair suggests that the shoot is not running smoothly. It slumps around her face, weighed down by anxiety. "Greg's having a tizz," she whispers. "Stay out of his way until he's ready for you."

"It's not what I wanted," snaps the photographer. "Not the color we talked about."

"I thought you wanted blue," says a hollow-faced boy holding a paint roller.

"I said turquoise. A diluted, wishy-washy, rained-on turquoise."

The assistant's roller drips onto the studio floor.

"He's painted the cove the wrong color," hisses Eliza. "Greg's not pleased. He's very particular—that's why he's so good." She holds an iron and a flimsy dress of pale lobster hue. Things are not looking good on the color front.

"What's a cove?" I ask.

"Infinity cove. That curvy wall. It's supposed to be blue."

"It *is* blue," protests the assistant. He has knobbly elbows. His green eyes look disappointed with life. A small, snuffly dog pads through a spillage of paint and cranes upward to sniff his crotch. The assistant teeters back, clearly not having the authority to bat the quivering animal away from his toileting region.

Greg tries a gentler tone. "I said pale, Dale. Almost pastelly. Like last time."

"It *is* pale."

"It is pale, yeah, but I wanted really fucking intense."

A balding man carrying a tray of oozing pastries pauses to glance at the cove, imagining, perhaps, his own particular shade of blue, but is interrupted midthought by Greg, bellowing, "I wanted fucking *larkspur,* Dale." This outburst prompts Ben's eyes to ping open and his face to crumple and deepen to a subtle, yet really fucking *intense* shade of fuchsia.

I hadn't realized how many bodies are required to create a photograph of a girl in a limp, sleeveless dress. "And they wanted, like, glossy lips," the makeup artist tells a dressing room jammed with assorted persons, all busily patting knitwear. "I told them *no*. I don't do glossy. If you want glossy you have totally the wrong makeup artist."

"Nightmare," agrees the hairdresser. He has triangular sideburns and is combing something snotlike—possibly serum—through the model's marmalade hair. "You're only trying to be creative and say something."

Several weightless women tut sympathetically and tear into the pressing task of arranging necklaces in perfect oval shapes on the cluttered dressing table. Perhaps these are Eliza's assistants: Collator of Shoes, Editor in Chief of Accessories.

Ben mews timidly from his car seat.

"Is that yours?" asks the hairdresser. "It must be sweet, having a baby."

"Oh, it is."

"Ahh. Anyway, I was thinking of messing this up and leaving it rough-looking for texture, what do you think?"

"I think my baby's too young for that," I cackle.

No one laughs. The model blinks slowly on to the mascara wand, regarding me with uncertain eyes.

My parents have settled themselves on an L-shaped sofa. Mum coils herself on the black leather, snuggling into its creases as if it were a nest. She fiddles with an untidy heap of model cards, each depicting a headshot of a girl on the front, and a variety of poses on the back. She can smoke as much as she likes and blows out quick puffs, as if learning to whistle. Dale brings my parents coffee in trembling plastic cups.

"Mum," I say. "Ben needs feeding."

"Oh. I might have some barley sugars in my bag."

"He doesn't have barley sugars. He has milk. I'll need to heat it up." I consider asking her to locate the kitchen while I comfort Ben, then decide against it. She might blunder outside and drop his bottle into the canal or, if she located a source of hot water, heat it to such a temperature that it would strip his throat lining. Sometimes I wondered how I scrambled through babyhood without being singed or horribly damaged. I carry Ben to reception to ask where I might warm a bottle. "A what?" says the girl, fixing her bunches.

"Baby's milk."

She scowls as if I'd asked her to express fluid manually from her own, upwardly-mobile breasts. "Prrr, I don't know. Maybe hold it under the hand dryer?"

"It won't—" I begin, but she has returned to the urgent matter of grooming her owl pencil case.

I carry Ben, now rigid with misery, into the dressing room. Four lit cigarettes teeter on an ashtray. There must be a kitchen; what about the tempting snacklets Eliza talked about? Trays bearing edibles appear briefly and are carried swiftly by the balding man to another studio.

"Poor baby," says the model. "What's wrong with it?"

"Maybe it's got a pain," suggests the makeup artist. "An

ear infection, don't babies get that? Is anything pussy coming out?"

I ease Ben over my shoulder and bounce gently.

"Urr, he's puked," says the model. The Managing Director of Earrings swipes at my cardi with a cotton wool ball, leaving a streak of white fluff. At each inhalation, Ben's abdomen pulls sharply in on itself. I wondered if it is possible for an infant to implode through sheer grief.

"Isn't there a kettle?" I say desperately.

The model sucks black coffee through a straw so as not to dislodge her lipstick and points to a corner of the dressing table. High Priestess of Hosiery tries—unsuccessfully—to stab its plug into the socket. "Now how do you work this thing?"

The small dog yelps, scratching the concrete floor. Greg turns up the music. It's dance music, which you need a birthdate in the eighties to understand. Although the kettle has been switched on, little appears to be happening. To stopper Ben's mouth—and expecting him to reject it immediately—I jam the bottle between his lips. He sucks experimentally, pulls off in disgust, then decides that fridge-cold milk is preferable to fruitless howling.

"Let's party," says Greg. He dances, arms bouncing like inner tubes. "Where's my model? Fern, are you ready?"

Fern steps out of the dressing room, smiling weakly. "I thought there was a guy in the shot. Weren't we waiting for a guy?"

"There he is," says Greg, indicating Ben.

"I mean a man."

"The male model hasn't shown up," explains Eliza.

"He's in a band, doesn't really want to model at all. We were lucky to book him actually."

It strikes me as a weird kind of lucky when he hasn't even bothered to show up. But at least he'd agreed to the job in principle. Eliza seems grateful for this. "We should wait another half hour," she says. "It's the whole point of the shot—girl, guy, baby. Kind of slutty looking."

"Slutty?" I say. This term hadn't featured when Eliza first mentioned the shoot.

"The idea is, they're dressed up and spaced out but pissed off because they're stuck at home with a baby."

"They could have booked a baby-sitter," I suggest.

"It's not literal. Just a feel."

"And what do you want Ben to wear for this slutty thing?"

"His suit's a bit naff. Just a nappy, I reckon. We don't want him widdling all over that dress. So if you could strip him off while we wait for our guy—"

"Let's get on with it," says Greg. "I'm not hanging around for that arsehole."

Dale lumbers up beside me, jaws pounding a pastry. "The guy's not really a model," he explains, "but that's what they all say, you know? That's a nice baby you've got."

"Why do they say that?" I ask.

Dale shrugs. Perhaps there is something unsettling about making a living solely from one's appearance. It's not as though you've had much to do with it. Your genetic makeup is down to your parents; by rights, your earnings should be dispatched directly to Mum and Dad.

Maybe that's why models are quick to point out that they're only doing it for a bit. You can't do that with motherhood: pretend it's not what you do *really*. The baby certainly knows who his mother is. You can't pass yourself off as a casual baby-sitter who'll be off, clutching a couple of tenners, when the real mum and dad teeter back from the pub.

Fern hovers before the blue background, her arms cradled, awaiting a baby to fill them.

"Mum," says Greg with a finger snap. "We're ready."

I have become Universal Mum, devoid of name or, come to think of it, the promised goat cheese pastries.

"He's asleep."

"For how long?"

"An hour, maybe more. He tends to go off late morning after a bottle, though sometimes he needs a jiggle in his pram and then—"

"Mum, we're doing a shoot. We are *ready*."

While it is acceptable for an adult male not to show up for work, an eight-week-old baby is not allowed to sleep at naptime. I pass Ben to Fern. He opens his eyes momentarily, apparently content with this substitute mother.

"It's not working," says Eliza. "We need a man. Let's have someone stand in, any old guy, so Greg gets into his head what the shot's about."

"What *is* it about?" murmurs Mum, scattering ash onto a model card.

Eliza's eyes roam the studio.

"What about him?" suggests Dale. "The old fat guy?"

"Would you mind," asks Eliza, "just for a minute?"

Eliza has never met my parents before. Dad smiles uneasily. She steers him across the studio as if he's a supermarket trolley with a busted wheel and positions him next to Fern. He squints into the lights. He's wearing clapped-out cords with the knees worn smooth. Next to Fern, he looks 103.

"That works," Eliza says.

Dad smiles uneasily.

"Nice," agrees Greg. "A bit closer to her, Papa."

"It's great that he looks so uncomfortable," whispers Eliza.

Bile simmers in my throat. Ben flops in Fern's arms, eyelids drooping. "Mum," commands Greg. "Keep. Baby. Awake."

I clap my hands. Ben's eyelids tremble, then shut firmly.

"Sing," demands Greg.

Which song? "Twinkle Twinkle" isn't rousing enough. "Old Macdonald" has a habit of chundering on for weeks if you're not careful but I clear my throat and begin:

> *"Old Macdonald had a farm*
> *Ee-eye ee-eye oh*
> *And on that farm he had a…"*

A farmyard flashes into my brain: cockerels and piglets and ponies, crowing and snorting and whinnying together. Which to choose? I can't decide, not on four hours' sleep. I'll have to speak to Jonathan about spending a night on my own in a hotel.

"Mum?" says Greg. "Are you with us?"

The small dog yaps. From a distant corner of the studio Dale's tremulous voice rings out:

> *"And on that farm he had a dog*
> *Ee-eye ee-eye oh.*
> *With a woof woof here and a yap yap there*
> *Here a howl. There a growl, everywhere a yip-yip.*
> *Old Macdonald had a farm*
> *Ee-eye ee-eye oh."*

Ben flinches. A glimpse of eyeball, an awakening smile. "Closer now, Pops," urges Greg. "Lean on her. Arm round her waist. Look at her. Look at me." Dad's eyes swivel as if operated by joystick. Ben leers at the lens like it's a bulging, milk-filled breast. Dad stares at Mum, pleading for help.

"Relax, Dad," Greg urges. "Feel like you're a puppet and your string's gone loose." Dad's knees tremble. Next to Fern, he has aged, collapsed in on himself. The studio door swings open. A male model saunters in, just in time to do the shoot with Ben. I know he's a male model because he's carrying a black portfolio, and a guitar.

Dad's so tired I have to ease him into the cab. His knees click irritably. Mum clutches a stash of goat cheese pastries, wrapped in an oil-stained serviette.

Dale buckles Ben's seat into the back seat. "I loved

your song," I tell him. "All those different barks. Do you like dogs?"

"No," he says. "I fucking hate them."

I intend to tell Jonathan about the shoot as soon as he comes home but it doesn't feel like the right moment. "Minimalism is dead," he reads flatly from *InHouse*. "Go crazy for eccentric florals after too many years of good taste. It's time to chuck *in* the chintz."

"I'm sure it won't happen," I reassure him. "It's just someone making stuff up."

He places the magazine on the polished floor. "What do you mean, it's made up?"

"They're paid to spurt waffle. I did it myself for ten years."

Jonathan sips from a wineglass. In the year and a bit we've been together, his hairline has snuck back. I only notice the change when I stare at that lonely hearts photo. He looked amiable then, and unruffled. "Why would they make things up," he says, "when there's real stuff to write about?"

"Real isn't grabby enough." Where did I hear that? From Chase, my old editor. I had submitted a piece about a woman who survived solely on rum and raisin ice cream. I'd been especially proud of the story—it had that crucial "thank God that's not me" factor—and had taken along a carton, plus wafer biscuits, to get on the woman's good side.

"It's not enough," complained Chase when I handed in the story.

"Well, I think it's pretty extreme. Think of what it's doing to her intestines. It's hardly normal."

"No one in *Promise* is normal, Nina. We need an edge. I know…"—and now I was about to discover why he was editor of Britain's bestselling weekly while I was a lowly features writer—"…say she wakes up in the night, feels that familiar urge—the desire for something creamy and sweet…her husband's asleep. She knows it's wrong but can't stop herself. She pulls on a housecoat over her nightie and sneaks out to, to…"

"The freezer," I suggest.

"A twenty-four-hour Tesco. That's the photo—her in a flowery housecoat creeping out of the supermarket with a family-size tub under her arm."

Jonathan drains his glass in one gulp. "I can't believe he'd manipulate people in that way."

"He didn't do it. I did. I even took along a nylon housecoat with a gathered yoke and ribbon at the neck and told her it was *Promise* policy to supply the clothes."

Jonathan stares gloomily at *InHouse*. "Your magazine might do that. This sort doesn't."

"Of course they do. They can't show flats like yours every month. They pretend it all changes, like fashion."

"Ours," corrects Jonathan. "Flats like ours."

His eyelids are heavy. He places the wineglass on the floor and edges over to make room for me on the sofa. "Come here," he says, patting the space.

He curls around me, breath warm on my neck. A hand edges up my T-shirt, loitering inside my bra. Immediately—although Ben has not ventured near this region for several weeks—baby lips form in my brain. Jonathan and I have yet to resume our sex life. We should have done it by now. *Babycare,* which generously allots one and a half pages to the well-being of the parents and 377 to the nurturing of the child, states, "You may resume intercourse after your six-week postnatal checkup."

There is no reason not to do it, or at least to have a go and see what happens. Dr. Strickland assured me that my stitches were healing marvelously, yet I fear that, at the sight of a naked adult male, everything will ping open again. I read that new parents should "seize the moment even if it's in the middle of the night. No matter how sleepy you are, sex can rebond you as lovers, not just new mum and dad," but can't imagine Jonathan being delighted by such clumsy treatment, even if I felt like it.

"You're tense," he says. I wonder how long it will take for his fingers to stimulate milky seepage. *Babycare* acknowledges New Mother's reticence, suggesting, "Subconsciously you may fear becoming pregnant again. Make sure you are confident with your method of contraception." Condoms: fat lot of use they were a year ago. Jonathan's other hand shuffles tentatively up my skirt. "Massage each other sensuously," *Babycare* advises, "with aromatic oils such as ylang ylang and tuberose. You may find it helpful to explore the vaginal area with your fingers or even examine it with the aid of a mirror." These days, looking at my face is terrifying enough.

"Are you all right?" asks Jonathan.

"I feel funny."

"What about?"

I want to say: where do I start? I can hardly remember how all this came about. What was sex like, before sperm skidded through a tear in the helpless beige rubber, my breasts ballooned and a squiggled line appeared on my belly? I don't recall that we did it that much. We didn't need to. Once was all it took.

"It's not right," I say, "being in the same room as Ben. He might see something."

"He can't. He's asleep."

"He might wake up."

Jonathan sits upright and silently flicks through *In-House*. He stops at a page offering decluttering tips: *Don't view the process as insurmountable. You'll feel overwhelmed and never get started. Take it one step at a time.*

Later that night I turn to the sex bit of *Babycare:* "No need to rush back into penetrative sex. However excited you may feel, the perineum may still be bruised and tender."

The fact that the perineum is mentioned at all confirms that New Mother might have a more pleasurable time extracting her own teeth.

6

Introducing Solids

Jonathan brings coffee and two croissants on a plate. It had been a pleasant surprise to wake up with the bed to myself. For a moment, I thought my nightmare about losing Ben in the park, along with my front door key, had segued neatly into the flannel pajamas fantasy.

"Eliza called," he says. "Something about the pictures being great, just what she wanted. What pictures?"

I bite into a croissant, sucking its butteriness. "Probably Cuba. She was in Havana last week. Complained that she couldn't find a building that looked run-down and Cuba-ish enough."

He laughs. "Funny she's your friend, being so different."

"You know what's even stranger? You're her type, exactly. You'd never think it."

"And what type is that?"

I don't know how to put this. Eliza favors conventional men. Nothing excites her more than polished black shoes, a brass-buckled briefcase, an evening paper tucked under the arm. She cites banking as the ideal profession but is also partial to lawyers, librarians, computer programmers (as long as they don't talk about work) or, in fact, any job requiring a hushed environment and serious, grown-up clothing. When we're out, her neck swivels at each glimpse of charcoal suit. Perhaps they offer respite after the difficult colors she has to deal with at work.

Unfortunately such men rarely respond well to Eliza. She has a fondness for short, slithery dresses that look like underwear, as if she'd started to put her clothes on but lost interest halfway through. It's something you might expect a new mother to do: the fashion equivalent of starting a sentence and forgetting what you're going to say.

"You mean conventional men," Jonathan says.

I think of the suits she says hello to, who make excuses to go to the bathroom and reappear armored with girlfriends in pastel blouses. Morning aromas drift into the bedroom. Jonathan has clearly been busy. The absence of clattering from the activity arch suggests that Ben has been fed and lulled to sleep.

"You're not conventional," I say.

"But I wear a suit."

"You have to."

"I like wearing it. I'd wear it even if I didn't have to."

I know that. Dress Down Fridays cause Jonathan a degree of anxiety. I vacate the bedroom while he sifts through insipid polo shirts, flapping fabrics before the full-length mirror. He was born to inhabit a suit. Constance showed me a photo of him as a child, possibly attempting to fill me in on his history. Jonathan aged seven or eight, wearing a paper crown like you'd find in a Christmas cracker, squeezed between two robust adults. Constance smiling at a fiercely attractive man in suit and tie—presumably Jonathan's father, although his identity was unconfirmed and I didn't like to ask. Jonathan wore a suit and tie, too, its knot tight against his throat.

"Was it Christmas?" I asked unnecessarily, as a glistening turkey and torn crackers littered the foreground of the shot.

I rest the plate on my lap, transferring croissant crumbs to my mouth with a wet finger. "Just because you wear a suit, it doesn't mean you're—" My head empties itself of all logical thought.

"What am I?" Jonathan asks.

"You're a great dad."

"What makes you say that?"

"The way you comfort him and have patience—much more than me. The way he loves you."

Jonathan takes my empty plate and brushes croissant crumbs from the duvet.

"I know he does," is all he says.

★ ★ ★

Beth and Matthew chose the restaurant. I wonder why—out of the seven couples in the antenatal class— we've stayed in touch with this one. Between them, they radiate so much smugness you can smell the pinkish haze around their heads. Beth took to calling me after Ben's birth, enquiring whether I was "coping" before moving on to detail how easy everything was. She had a head start on me. Her daughter, Maud, was born four days before Ben. "It's all in the attitude," she'd remind me. "Relaxed mother, relaxed baby."

Beth had been big on relaxation during our classes, breathing like bellows as if poised to give birth on the teacher's sea grass matting. I preferred the look of a fat girl who smelled of mushy peas, wore a gravy-stained sweatshirt and announced, on day one, that her boyfriend couldn't be arsed to come. She slouched with thighs thrust apart on a batik-printed cushion and declared that she intended to take full advantage of the pethidine, di-amorphine and any other goodies on offer. I hadn't seen her after that first class, so presumably she couldn't be arsed to come again either.

"Lucky us," smirks Beth, bobbing onto a chair facing the waterfront. She wears a pale denim dress with short puffed sleeves and white flowers embroidered on the collar. A rabbit knapsack clings to her back. Beth has tumbled from a Beatrix Potter book.

The restaurant hums with grown-up Sunday lunchers. Beth unbuttons her dress and pops Maud's head into a white broderie anglaise bra. Of all the names available, why Maud? Already, they are mulling over which school to send Maud to should she—as already suspected—turn out to be gifted. Beth thinks she might be musical as the kid slaps the keys of Grandma's piano when they visit her in Oxfordshire.

"Such a happy feeder," announces Beth to no one in particular.

"So is Ben," I say. "We've started giving him solids."

"At three months? Isn't that early?"

"Our health visitor suggested it. Said the odd little taste won't do any harm." I like our health visitor. She has a crisp Northern Ireland accent and bit Ben's fingernails when I couldn't find the baby scissors.

Beth frowns, running a palm over her child's colossal forehead. "Maud has only had breast," she says. "Incredible isn't it? Every little bit has been made with mummy's milk, hasn't it, sweetheart?"

"Ben's food is all homemade," I blurt out. "Pureed carrot and broccoli and all sorts."

"Gosh," says Beth. "How do you find the time?"

Jonathan fills everyone's glasses from the water jug. He has the good grace not to point out that I have yet to locate the blender's on button. He has taken on the matter of Ben's nutrition, appearing perfectly happy to spend one evening a week finely chopping and steaming organic produce to be whizzed in the blender, frozen in ice cube trays and popped into plastic bags, labeled and dated and stored in the freezer. I assist by writing with an artistic flourish, Pear and Apple Medley.

Beth props Maud on her denim lap and expertly rubs her back, easing out a polite belch. She places the snoozy child in the car seat at her feet. "You know, we're thinking of having another," she says. "Not trying exactly, but not *not* trying, either. Aren't we, Matthew?"

Matthew and Jonathan have been muttering together, discussing the function of each building across the river. "We'll see," chuckles Matthew. "Now, have we all decided?"

Unused to the concept of eating out, I stare at a menu that consists of too many choices with baffling terms such as tagine and coulis.

"What about you, Nina?" chirps Beth.

"I can't decide. I might have monkfish but dill chicken sounds tasty."

"I mean, do you want another baby?"

I gulp air. My mouth feels formless. "We don't know, do we, Jonathan? We haven't got to grips with this one yet. Have we, Jonathan?"

"No," he says, dipping his nose into the menu.

"What's annoying is there's only ever two or three things for vegetarians," grumbles Matthew. "They palm you off with a vegetable bake and never stipulate what a bake actually is."

"We could have gone to a vegetarian restaurant," I suggest.

"I'm having salmon but not with the roast pepper chutney," says Beth.

"Aren't you vegetarian, too?"

"I am. But I eat fish."

"And chicken," adds Matthew.

Beth smiles tersely and folds Maud's blanket to form a neat oblong. "Funny how your baby's made from the best bits of each of you," she says. I glance from Beth to Matthew. Oily complexions that haven't got their acts together postadolescence. Beth's skinny plaits peter out at her shoulders. Matthew has slippery lips. "Everyone says Maud should be a model," she adds. "But I hate that, don't you? Little girls with ringlets. Pushy mothers wanting a share of it all."

"It is rather naff isn't it?" Matthew is whirling the wine in his glass and sniffing it.

I bite into a rosemary-infused olive.

"Aren't they the best thing?" says Beth. "They marinate their own. We come here all the time, don't we, Matthew? Maud's very good in restaurants."

I wonder if now might be an appropriate moment to announce that Ben was dragged by his fame-grabbing mother to a studio dense with cigarette smoke. I could add that he was stripped to his nappy in a cavernous, unheated space, force-fed cold milk and manhandled by strangers barely able to operate a kettle. I wonder how that might go down in present company.

"Does Ben have much personality?" asks Beth, staring down at him.

I am tempted to brag that when he wakes up he will astound her with a repertoire of juggling tricks but mutter only, "He likes his activity arch."

"One of those gaudy plastic things? Maud only has wooden toys. Did I tell you she can already hold a crayon?

Boys lag behind, of course. You're talking years before he'll sit quietly with a dot-to-dot book."

I toy with the possibility of kicking over the table and its glinting array of glasses and porcelain dishes filled with black pepper and sea salt. But they'd assume it was my hormones.

Ben's eyes open. I reach down to lift him from his seat. He howls and spews a bellyful of vomit onto his striped cotton top and the white tablecloth.

"Oh dear," says Beth, leaning backward.

The initial retch is followed by a screech of such volume that the entire restaurant appears to swivel one gigantic, chomping face, praying for the offending infant and his liquid emissions to be removed immediately.

I grip Ben to my chest, not caring that splodges of partially digested peach puree are sopping straight through my T-shirt. "We've got to go," I cry.

"Yes, of course," says Jonathan. He springs out of his chair, upending the black pepper dish and slapping several ten-pound notes on the table, even though we've had only four olives each.

Ben's simmering cheek meets my face. I feel the back of his neck like proper mothers do. He arches backward, not wanting to be held and not wanting to be put down. As we gather up his possessions and turn to hurry along the riverfront, I hear Beth telling Matthew, "It's all that solid food they're stuffing into him."

Ben times his next vomit for when he's being carried into the flat, and splatters the floor with soupy fluid.

"How hot is he?" asks Jonathan.

"Bloody hot."

"No, I mean *how* hot? With a thermometer."

Even if we possess such an item, I wouldn't know where to locate it.

"Bathroom cabinet," growls Jonathan. "Little white thing in a see-through packet."

"I can't bear to do this," I babble, when I return with it. Ben gulps timidly into Jonathan's neck.

"Can't bear to do what?"

"Put it up his bottom."

"God, Nina, he's not a farmyard animal. You stick it on his forehead."

Ben huddles into Jonathan's chest. The cries rev up again, peaking to a nerve-shattering screech that refuses to subside, even when Jonathan paces the living room and points out two dogs embarking on a lewd act on the pavement.

"Get the Calpol," he shouts.

"Have we…?"

"Right-hand kitchen cupboard, above the spices, next to coffee filters."

I spring to the kitchen and notice with admiration that Jonathan has arranged first-aid items—plasters, Savlon, bandage—neatly in a Tupperware container marked "Medical Supplies." I return with a wobbling spoonful and hold it before Ben, expecting him to gulp it greedily. He flings back his head, apparently disgusted. I lurch forward to try again. Ben thrashes wildly, causing the spoon to collide with his cheek and fire sticky pink liquid onto my wrist. "Hold him down," I instruct, pouring another spoonful. Ben yowls like a cat, kicking the spoon.

"Let's take him for a drive," suggests Jonathan. "That'll calm him down."

"He's going to hospital."

"Why? It's not—"

"He's got an infection." That was it: an infection caused by filth and bacteria. From inhaling fag smoke in Greg's studio. Or being close to a rank canal where rats live with their stinking diseases. I spotted something bobbing in the water and assumed it was a partially deflated football. Perhaps it was a rodent, long dead and bloated.

Or what about the studio floor that the dog had scratched and licked and done its business on? I can virtually *see* germs, swarming around in Ben's belly. What terrible things will they do to him? I've heard about conditions caused by dog mess: blindness. Madness. Beth is always scribbling petitions to ban dogs from pavements, parks and possibly even the planet, and no wonder.

Or maybe he swallowed something. One of Mum's kirby grips. He plucked it from her hair and ate it. She wouldn't have noticed.

Jonathan loads Ben into the car. "It's okay," he soothes. "Easy, now. Easy."

"Would he scream like this," I gabble, "if he's eaten something bad?"

"He hasn't eaten anything bad."

"Maybe he's too little for all that mushed–up food. His intestines can't cope."

I feel mean for trying this tactic, attempting to deflect suspicion that our son has ingested an eyeshadow applicator or lipstick lid, now embedded in his stomach wall. What was I thinking of, bringing a baby into contact with adults whose sole function is to decide whether a side parting is very now, or very not now?

"There's something inside him," I announce, crying now as the car lollops over speed bumps. "They'll have to X-ray him. How will they get it out?"

"Get *what* out?" shouts Jonathan.

"Whatever it is. The sharp thing. Will it come out of his bottom or will they open up his stomach?"

The lights turn red. "There's nothing inside him, Nina. Nothing that shouldn't be inside him."

I picture Ben's innards: miniature stomach, spleen and intestines quivering with the effort of expelling something hard and shiny. "I'll go through his nappies," I rant. "I'll pick through them and see if it's there, like they do with owls' dung to find the little skulls of animals they've eaten."

"Nina," says Jonathan. "Please stop. It's probably a virus." Perhaps he's right. More than four weeks have passed since the shoot. Yet that makes it potentially fatal: the object, festering slowly, already smothered in barnacles. Ben growls like an electrical appliance on the brink of going horribly wrong. When that happens you try to ignore the rumbling sounds and behave normally but you know it's a sign that all is not well; that you're heading for inexplicable jolts and shakes, culminating in a mini-explosion and terrible stench of burning. Then you're calling in experts who exhale heavily and rummage in filthy canvas tool bags, saying there's a small chance of recovery—a grain of rice-size chance—but it would have been more hopeful if only you'd called an hour earlier.

I smear tears onto my T-shirt with the back of my hand. My nose is streaming. How can Jonathan remain so grown-up and capable throughout all this? It's only when sunlight glints on his sweaty upper lip—and we're nudging fifty in a thirty-miles-an-hour zone—that I remember he is just an ordinary man.

7

Running a Fever

A young man with a bleeding cheek is involved in an angry exchange with the hot drinks vending machine. "Call it a cappuccino?" he shouts, clutching a brown plastic beaker which quivers dangerously.

I perch on a molded orange seat. Jonathan clutches Ben, who's awash with snot and tears but mercifully silent.

"I said cappuccino," says the man, slamming a flattened hand against the machine. Toffee-colored liquid slops onto his coat sleeve, which looks like it's been run over by a tractor. "Cappuccino," he bellows into the air before him, "allegedly involving the passing of steam through milk to create a bubbling action and make proper froth instead of this piss which is *not* cappuccino." He boots the machine.

"Careful," warns Jonathan, "you might scald yourself."

The man stumbles round to face him. "Who are you?" he growls.

Jonathan glances at his watch.

"I said, who are you?" the man demands.

"Jonathan," says Jonathan, fixing his gaze on a pro-breast-feeding poster. *Lunchtime and not a breast in sight.* A woman with a swingy bob is laughing with colleagues in a café. Her baby is tucked neatly into her top. No vast, veiny breast, no bitter nipple.

"Nice baby," says Cappuccino Man. "Nice woman. Are you married? Have you made her *decent?*"

"Will we be long?" Jonathan asks the receptionist.

She is busy with a middle-aged man in a football top who's shouting about his hamstring.

Cappuccino Man whirls coffee under my nostrils. "Have some," he offers.

"No, thanks."

"Not good enough for you, Miss lah-di-dah, with your boring bloody husband."

Jonathan's hand lands on mine. I study a poster depicting contraceptive methods: the Pill, IUD, cap, implants and injectables. Below it, a handwritten notice reads: Do Not Allow Children To Play With Vending Machine. Very Hot Liquid.

"Good job the baby looks like its mother," grumbles Cappuccino Man, "because you know what your face is? It's sick, mister, you in your crappy weekend clothes."

Jonathan rubs the sleeve of his fawn-colored shirt.

"Excuse me," I shout. "We have a young baby. This is an emergency."

"Is it really?" says the receptionist, tapping primly on a keyboard.

"Yes. I think he swallowed a kirby grip."

"Did he?" says Jonathan. "Why didn't you say that before?"

A young doctor appears, milk-faced and clearly no more than eleven years old. This child is to be trusted with the removal of an unidentified object from my son's innards? He can't have studied at medical school. Becoming a proper doctor takes five years at least. I wouldn't trust him to stick on a plaster.

In the curtained cubicle Jonathan details Ben's symptoms. Ben eyes the doctor fearfully, aware that his stomach's about to be opened. "I'd say gastroenteritis," says the doctor. "His temperature's coming down now. Keep offering him cooled, boiled water."

His voice has barely broken. He is probably a virgin. There comes a point when you start noticing that you're in the company of a young person, which means you no longer are one. You use words like "cool" and try to befriend them by saying, "I love your..." and tail off into silence because you don't know the name of that particular type of trouser.

"It's the in thing," says the doctor.

"What?" I bark.

"Gastroenteritis. We've had a wave of it."

"Aren't you going to X-ray him?" I snap.

"No need," says the doctor. "But you were right to bring him in."

"I want him X-rayed," I protest.

"She's just upset," says Jonathan. "Let's go."

As we drive home I think: maybe it's not so bad being ancient. You don't have to hang out in damp-smelling basements, plucking at dusty snacks that too many strangers have dipped their fingers into on their way back from the urinals. This baby stuff, it's what we're designed for. It keeps us out of mischief. Forces us to grow up, to cook meals requiring ingredients.

Jonathan lowers Ben into the cot. It's 8:20 p.m.

"I feel stupid," I say.

"Don't. You were scared. That's natural."

Jonathan heads for the kitchen and a vegetable mountain to be mushed with the addition of finely chopped herbs from his new windowbox. I hadn't seen the point of filling a silvery trough with compost and scrawny plants. What was wrong with the dried stuff in jars? But within weeks leaves had bushed out and Jonathan appeared with a fistful of parsley, instructing me to sniff it.

I creep into the bedroom. Ben snores throatily. Cappuccino Man was wrong; he's not like me. He's not like either of us. Perhaps he really did drop out of an airplane.

Warbly voices come from the answerphone. Eliza, sounding like she's smoked several packets of filterless cigarettes and slept with her head in a drain. "Where are you?" she rasps. "You never go out at night. Listen, there's a pile of makeup at work that no one wants. The colors are a bit manky but I thought it might perk you up."

Beth enquires: "Is everything okay? Shame about lunch today, but don't worry, the manager was very good about it."

The third message plays: "Hello, Nina? You don't know me. I'm Lovely. Model agent. We've heard about your little boy from Greg Moore, the photographer. Sounds like he'd be perfect for us. Do call me." She rattles off an assortment of numbers so I can reach her any time.

"Who's Greg? Who's Lovely?" Jonathan stands in the bedroom doorway, holding a bundle of leaves.

"Maybe someone to do with Eliza."

"She wants Ben to be a model?"

I nudge his blanket into position and check his forehead: normal service restored. "No idea," I murmur.

"You will tell her we're not interested?"

"Of course." My eyes grow accustomed to the dark. A cheek forms in the cot; a perfectly rounded, utterly photogenic cheek.

"It's exploitation," comes Jonathan's voice. "Babies can't agree to this kind of nonsense and give permission."

"I know."

"They can grow up disturbed and in therapy."

"Yes."

I watch Ben, overwhelmed by the beauty of him sleeping there. Unable to stop myself, I superimpose a logo above his head: Pampers, perhaps, or Cow & Gate.

"Maybe she called a wrong number," he says.

"Yes, that's probably it."

I follow him into the living room where he's staring

at the phone as if expecting it to perform a somersault. "But she knew your name," he says.

Sunday was just the start of it. Ben thrashes irritably, punctuating nights with vomit explosions and helpless crying. He kicks the bars like a bear kept in inhumane conditions and forced to perform for grown-ups. His cheeks radiate anger and hotness. The rear end assumes an equally unhappy hue. It seems a terrible design fault that babies are not born with the ability to explain, in reasonable terms, that they don't hate you, they're just feeling lousy.

I develop diagonal gray lines under my eyes. My pores gape like tea bag holes. Ben has taken to swiping my face with a fist as if the wretched illness is my fault. Each morning, when Jonathan heads for the office, I clamp my mouth shut so I can't beg him to stay. One day, with Ben's cries piercing my brain, I can think of no other way to appease his displeasure than summoning Jonathan home from work. "There's a systems failure," he says. "I can't leave."

I inform him that something similar is taking place in his own home. In less than an hour he appears with a paper bag containing more Calpol because the last lot got kicked over, plus his bleeper, which goes off several times to remind me that he should be at work, salvaging systems.

Next morning I pack the changing bag with supplies for a day in the park. The playground smells of wet metal. A dog wees against the seesaw. At least the irritable swans and bigger kids twisting the swings' rusting chains will keep Ben occupied. But even the squeaking roundabout fails to enthrall Ben for long. His wailings attract swarms of unsolicited advice—teething powders, cold flannel on the forehead, keeping him wrapped up indoors *and not out in the park, poor mite*— that buzz around my ears as I hurry back to the flat, batting them off.

An elderly lady appears at my shoulder, her permed head jutting from a buttoned-up coat. "You're the one who's not breast-feeding," she says.

I hurtle into the flat.

"He's hot, that's why he's crying," continues her far-away voice. "You don't want him in woollens, not when he's running a fever."

I bare my teeth at her, willing her to go. She stands at the gate, glowering. "You'll get your figure back if you breast-feed," she adds, then continues her search for other new mothers to advise, gripping her handbag like a weapon.

I've stopped worrying about my body, even the apron stomach, as Beth calls it, correctable only with an operation called an apronectomy. It's not so bad, the collapsed flap of belly. I can fold it in on itself and tuck it into my knickers. With Ben temporarily appeased after a bottle, the phone rings. I know it's someone in an office because I can hear the happy background babble of adult voices. "Nina?" he says. "Chase here. Thought I'd check you were still in the land of the living."

I jam the phone under my jaw. Ben starts bleating. His

nappy has leaked orangy-brown onto his babygro. "How's it going?" I ask, trying to radiate alertness.

"Great," says Chase. "We've just had new figures. Just over six hundred thousand." So he's calling to brag about his booming circulation. The phone digs into my ear as I place Ben on the sofa and strip off the putrid nappy. "Noticed the new regular columns?" Chase asks. "Seen the last few issues?"

"Briefly," I lie. I have encountered little in the way of reading matter since Ben's birth. Magazines have become distant blurs of gaudy color spied briefly through the newsagent's window. Beth lent me a novel with a pastel drawing of a beach hut on the cover. I had to reread the first chapter three times to remind myself who George was.

"I thought you'd like it," Chase chunters on. "This new thing—My Operation—with the pictures?"

"Very brave," I bluff.

"Everyone says that. I never imagined readers would get the pictures, let alone send them in—but they do. With all that going on—their bodies being delved into and God knows what—they're making sure Auntie Myra's there with the disposable camera."

"Amazing," I say, gripping Ben's ankles with one hand while wiping vigorously with the other. His bottom glowers at me.

"The new girl, Jess, set it up," Chase explains. "She's in Features till you come back. Keen, but doesn't squeeze the juice out of people like you do. When *are* you coming back?"

"I'm not sure," I say. "It depends on arrangements."

"What kind of arrangements? Aren't there nannies and nurseries for that sort of thing?"

"I haven't looked into it yet."

"I've heard," he continues, "about these twenty-four-hour baby hotels where children go—just like they're on holiday—and you never have to see them. Could I shove some freelance work your way?"

"Maybe," I say, picking up Ben and supporting him on my hip. Immediately the right side of my cardigan is soaked with warm wee.

"Are you panting?" asks Chase. "You sound knackered."

"Can I call you back?"

"Are you ill? What's that terrible cat noise?"

"Just the baby."

"Poor you," he says. "Are you sure you don't want to come back to work?"

Ben's mood has failed to improve by the time Jonathan shows up with Constance. She perches on the sofa while he shimmies skate wings around in an outsize frying pan. His bleeper goes off twice during the short cooking time. Jonathan has been put in charge of developing a crucial computer system involving billing those who are foolish enough to subscribe to his company's private healthcare scheme for a minimum fee of £7.95 a month ("which," Jonathan told me, "won't get you a splinter removed"). He has been given a generous pay rise and a team of five to manage. His boss says he needs to improve his management skills and is planning to send him, with a group of similarly lacking employees, on a training course in Bath.

Jonathan slaps skate wings onto plates and tips a bag of ready-washed lettuce into a dish. Until recently the salad would have included tempting accessories: blanched sugarsnap peas or toasted pine kernels. "If you don't check the data," he informs a colleague, "the whole bloody thing will fall over."

He places his bleeper on the table so it can stare at us. Constance prods her salad and says, "What's this in the lettuce?"

"It's not lettuce," I tell her. "It's radicchio."

"Actually," Jonathan snaps, "it's a kind of chicory."

Constance shoots him a look as if he's stamped on her toe and shunts the *chicory* leaves to the side of her plate.

Bleeper action continues throughout the night. By the time daylight seeps into the bedroom Jonathan has already left for work. Ben has spent a third of the night thrashing angrily, but now sleeps like a model baby advertising a mattress with sleep-inducing properties. Rather than wake him and battle with his ill humor, I am tempted to sneak back into bed, pretending I have forgotten about my appointment at Little Lovelies.

The taxi pulls up outside the premises a little after ten. The brisk poshness of Lovely's voice led me to expect glamorous offices with floor-to-ceiling windows and people employed to smile and lounge on velvet sofas. But Britain's Leading Child Model Agency appears to operate from a bow-fronted semi. Nothing distinguishes it from the other drooping properties in the road except a grubby blue-and-white sign bearing the words, in wedding-invitation script, "Little Lovelies."

"Yes?" parps a voice through the intercom.

"I'm here to see Lovely. I have an appointment."

The door opens and a squat woman stares at my chin. She has a bottle-tanned face and dimply cheeks. She looks like a tangerine. "Lovely's on a call," she says breezily. "Make yourself comfortable."

She leaves me in a hall the size of a dining table on a folding wooden chair. The room smells of paint. Hanging slightly askew is a clip-framed photo of a startled-looking baby in a woolly romper suit, possibly knitted by Constance. Ben squirms uneasily on my lap. A rich odor sneaks out from his bottom. Naturally I have come without nappies or wipes. I investigate the room marked Toilet and find only a dispenser of green paper towels.

"Hello, Nina." Lovely's head pops round the toilet door. Her apricot twinset lends her face a peachy cast. She's the color of waterproof plaster. "Glad you found us," she says. "Now, let me ask, do you know anything about modeling?"

"Very little," I say, tripping after her from the hall to the living room which appears to be the hub of the baby modeling world. Three women talk simultaneously on telephones. Enormous photos dominate the room: a little girl with a side ponytail, curtseying; a smug-looking boy biting fiendishly on a choc-ice.

"Did he?" says the tangerine woman. "It's not like

Nicholas to have an off day." She replaces the receiver. "Nicholas Horley in the Organica ad. Got hold of an open apple puree tin, sliced the end off his little finger. It'll never have a fingerprint, apparently."

Lovely squirms in mock-pain, causing her triple string of pearls to rattle softly.

"Well, they do say never work with children," I snigger.

"I hope they don't," says Lovely. "Our models are very professional."

"Unlike the parents," adds the tangerine woman.

"That's it," says Lovely, regarding me tersely as if about to grade my piano performance. "You see, what's going to make Ben a successful model—a star—is not just down to his visual appeal, but you."

"Me?" I croak. Ben starts to cry. I bounce my knees, gripping him tightly to my stomach.

"It's all in the parents' attitude," Lovely continues. "Ordinary mother turns up for a job with the child in a dirty babygro and runs out of nappies."

All telephone activity ceases as three pairs of eyes swivel toward me.

"But professional mother pays great attention to her child's appearance."

"Of course."

"And to her own."

I look at my shoes. They are not the footwear of a professional chaperone. They are park shoes. One toe has worn away, exposing something like cardboard.

Ben has grown tired of bouncing and reaches for the

tangle of telephone cords cluttering Lovely's desk. "I hope you're not expecting to make a fortune," she says. "There's not much money in this, unless you're one of the very lucky few."

"We're just doing it for fun," I insist.

She flares her nostrils, perhaps to inhale Ben's decaying nappy. "Modeling *should* be fun. Pictures only work if the child is happy in the studio environment. But please—" she rolls the pearls between her fingers "—never be late for a job. You can be fifteen minutes early, but never a second late."

As I step into the suburban street I realize that I have neither booked a taxi to take us home nor dealt with the foul condition of my son. I should be furious with myself or even crying but instead, I picture Ben in that Organica ad, opening his mouth on demand, doing nothing untoward with a discarded tin. *Organica*, the voiceover would say. *Doesn't your baby deserve the very best?*

I start walking, swinging Ben's car seat like a handbag. A black cab pulls up. "Been at that baby modeling place?" asks the driver as I clamber in. The back of his neck is wrinkled brown, like sausage skin.

"That's right. Little Lovelies."

"Thought so. Your baby, I'm sure I've seen him before. In that advert where the dad's cooking dinner and the baby unwinds a kitchen roll and tangles itself up? Something like that?"

I stare at bow-fronted semis. Bulbous, pregnant houses.

Family homes with clocks ticking and dust settling quietly. "He looks cute in that ad," says the driver.

"Thanks," I say. "He did pretty well. Everyone says he's a natural." We turn into the main street where semis give way to ramshackle greengrocers, their cabbages wilting in traffic fumes. Ben gawps at the cab's nonsmoking notice, shattered by the Lovely experience.

"You couldn't wish for more than a beautiful baby," the driver says. "Me and my wife tried for nearly ten years. Went through the embarrassing sample stuff."

On the pavement a woman in a vast Garfield T-shirt is walloping her son's behind. She chases him, hand flapping, into a dog grooming shop offering Clipping Flea Rinse Medicated Baths & Photography Of Your Pet By Qualified Professionals.

"We've settled for a Chihuahua," says the driver. "Like a baby really. Up in the night, gets into bed, follows my wife to the toilet."

On the radio a woman has just won a hundred thousand pounds and screams, saying she can't believe it. She tells the DJ it will change her life. "We'll move deeper into Essex," she says. The DJ laughs patronizingly.

"A very lucky woman," says the driver.

"I know I am," I say.

8

Your Postbaby Body

With no plans for the rest of the day I head home and play Jonathan's message: "Where are you? Thought you'd be in. I wonder where you are. The park, probably. Call me."

My voice comes out artificially bright. "I needed to get out of the flat," I tell him. Well, that bit's true. I'll add the missing pieces later, but not now, with the cogs of the working world clanking around him. "Anyway," I say, "did you want me?"

"Wondered if you'd mind if I went out with the work guys?" His voice swooshes up at the end, like a tick. "I'll be back by ten," he adds. "Just a couple of drinks."

"Of course I don't mind. Is somebody leaving?"

"No, I just feel the need. A breather from the whole thing."

From what whole thing? From me or the baby or the whole vegetable pureeing thing? Jonathan has never displayed symptoms of cabin fever. I thought he liked it.

"They'll be on the management course with me," he adds. "I should get to know them. Bond a bit. Maybe you could go out with Eliza another night."

"You don't have to ask. Just go."

The flat is so still and vacant that there's no question of remaining in it. I prowl the living room, wiping dust from the radiator knob with my thumb. Beth, self-appointed boss of the coffee morning circuit, is always involved in some petty household task when I call: tidying her pin cushion, polishing a light flex, marinating olives like those at the riverside restaurant. She details the task and I hear myself admitting that I am in the process of chipping limescale from the toilet bowl. I've started talking breathily, like she does. My old voice has gone. When Beth says she enjoys having her sleep disturbed ("How can I complain when it gives me extra time with Maudie?") I agree that the 3:00 a.m. blunder to the kitchen is a highlight for me, too. I must stop this, before a rabbit knapsack attaches itself to my back.

I've brought Ben to the swimming pool to escape from the radiator knobs. The changing room hums with sharp-elbowed girls talking nonchalantly about boys called Giles and Eddie. "He's so immature," groans a slender thing with bruised undereye shadows.

"Yeah, I mean grow *up*. Get it *together*. He's stressing you out," declares her virtually identical friend.

What do these girls have to stress about? They sit multichoice exams. Their tea is dished up in front of the telly by mums they despise. They can wear hot pants without anyone retching.

"What d'you think of Giles?" asks the bruised shadow one, applying mascara. She stretches her mouth like a fish.

"Gay," sighs her friend.

I'm staring with mouth lolling open and possibly drool seeping out. I turn away and place Ben facedown in the playpen. He pushes up on his arms, looking around with interest. The trouble with this pool is the fact that, during its upgrade, someone in authority decided to do away with segregated changing rooms and opted for the free and easy concept of a unisex Changing Village. Men roam about, toweling hair, scratching chests, buttoning up their trousers. There are wet buttocks and back hair and ruddy potbellies. Acres of dripping male skin. The challenge here is how to change into my swimsuit without exposing myself to the various men present, or leaving Ben unattended in the playpen.

The girl is covering her undereye shadows with concealer. It seeps from its golden tube onto a brush. A new cosmetic has been invented without my knowledge. "Excuse me," I say, frightening her, "would you keep an eye on my baby while I get changed?"

"Oh, what a sweetie," she gushes. "I love babies. Go on, he'll be fine."

I dart into the cubicle and strip off my cardigan and T-shirt in one, omitting to undo the cardi's top button which pings off and rolls under the gap. I kneel on the tiles, forgetting that I am wearing jeans, which are immediately sodden from the knees down. The button lies on the next cubicle floor, within reach. It shouldn't matter but my soft pink cardigan is the sole garment that has so far escaped baby-related splatterings. Magically its dusky pinkness makes me look a little less dead. This vision of softness gives the instant impression that its wearer is of sound mind and body, has enjoyed eight hours' uninterrupted sleep and certainly indulges in a wide repertoire of sexual delights, even on a weeknight.

Without that top button, it will never be the same again.

I slide a hand under the cubicle wall. The button has come to rest in a puddle. My fingers form a pincer shape, about to snatch it, when a hefty foot crunches heavily onto my palm.

"Hello?" the foot's owner says.

"I'm just trying to reach something."

A pause. "There's nothing here."

"There is. A button."

"I can't see anything."

"It's tiny. Mother of pearl. By your left big toe."

I peer under the cubicle wall as the foot—enormous with long, knobbly toes flecked with black hairs—is joined by a hand, which delicately extracts the button from the puddle.

Out in the Changing Village the girl with shadows now erased bobs Ben up and down before the mirror. He chirps with delight at each glimpse of his reflection.

A six-foot male in snug-fitting trunks emerges from a cubicle and observes my saggy swimsuit. My breasts droop thinly, like icing bags.

"Here's your button," says Ranald.

Does he recognize me? It's eighteen months since our camping expedition. "Thanks," I say. "You don't remember me, do you?"

"I know you from somewhere," he says carefully.

"Camping," I remind him. "Your uncle's place in Devon. We had a bit of a fall-out."

A tic appears beneath his left eye. "You look different," he says.

"Yes, I've had a baby."

His face collapses. A sturdy girl in a silver swimsuit with cutaway side panels strides from the showers. "Hi," she says to my breasts.

"Gabs," says Ranald, "this is someone I sort of used to know ages back."

Sharp nipples jut proudly from her costume. Ranald seems to be experiencing respiratory difficulties. "This is Gabrielle," he pants. "Gabs, this is...Nancy."

The shop assistant eyes the filthy buggy and accompanying clapped-out mother as we attempt to force entry. Eliza watches with interest as I ram the etched-glass door.

"Can you watch the door?" says the salesgirl. I wonder how it would be to work in such an establishment.

Naturally you would have to maintain a high standard of appearance, beginning your skincare routine at 5:30 a.m. But apart from looking stunning in a bored way—and sick around the gills when anyone weighing over seven stone tries to enter your shop—there doesn't seem to be much to it. "Can I help?" she asks, obviously concluding that I have thundered in by mistake and really want the Co-op.

"I'm just looking."

Eliza picks over sage-green garments hanging dismally from rails. The clothes are ugly, but smell expensive. "Hi, Cindy," she says.

"Oh, darling. I didn't see you. Looking for something special?"

"It's for my friend. She's a mother," Eliza explains unnecessarily, as the buggy dominates the shop like a forklift truck.

"That's nice," says Cindy queasily.

"She wants something to make herself feel better. Isn't that right, Nina?"

Cindy smiles bravely as if she's about to be given an injection. "Remember I've got my discount card," Eliza hisses. I check the tag on a cobwebby black sweater. "You don't want that," she scolds. "You never buy yourself anything decent and you're not starting with a dowdy black sweater."

Cindy pretends to straighten a gray silk dress on its hanger.

"You used to look great," Eliza adds. "There's no need for leggings just because you're a mum."

"I don't have any leggings," I say. But it's too late. Her briskness triggers my tear ducts into action. I examine a cream silk dress edged with antique-looking lace.

"And you don't want that," sniffs Eliza. "You'd want to be seriously thin to carry cream. Even I couldn't get away with it."

"Oh, you could," says Cindy. "You're looking great, really tanned. Been away?"

"Mauritius," says Eliza. She's filled me in on her latest trip: the insurmountable task of shooting nine bikinis over a three-day period left little time to sample the delights on offer at the beach resort, although she squeezed in a curious massage involving hot stones being placed on her naked bottom.

"Here, here and here," she says, snatching an assortment of garments in various shades of sludge.

"I don't like fawn."

"It's not fawn. It's putty. And you don't know you don't like it because you've never worn it." Instantly I see Eliza the Mother: "How can you say you don't like anchovies? You've never tried them."

"Can't I have something bright?"

"She's out of practice," Eliza informs Cindy. "Called me from a café all panicky, saying she wanted to go shopping but couldn't manage on her own. Said she couldn't make decisions. Upset over a button fallen off her chain store cardi."

Eliza has failed to notice a thin line of wetness spilling down one cheek. I squeeze my eyelids together, trying to suck it back in. She holds a long, narrow charcoal dress against herself. It looks like a funnel from a ship.

Ben opens his eyes and yawns at a rail of drain-water skirts. I make a gulping noise, like a frog. "Are you all right?" asks Eliza. Cindy swipes the cream dress as if she's trying to remove any skin cells I might have left on it.

"I don't know. I just feel so stupid." My lips are shuddering now, tears mingling with snot. I am liquefying in a shop where tights cost more than my pink cardi.

"Oh, sweetheart," she says, pulling me to her chest. Her sequined top scratches my face. Narrow arms wrap round me. "Can she sit down?" asks Eliza, like I'm an elderly lady having a turn.

"Oh, poor darling," says Cindy, registering my wet face. She leads me to a dimly lit back room. I am lowered into a brown leather armchair.

The two women peer at me. "Are you depressed?" asks Eliza.

"No, it's not that."

"Lots of women get it. They go mad and cry all the time. They throw their babies downstairs."

"I'm not about to do that." She's right, though: as a breed, mothers are particularly unhinged. In no way could my mother be described as normal. During parents' evenings at my secondary school, I would fidget at home, praying she wouldn't invite my French teacher's son round to play with me.

At *Promise* I interviewed a woman who, eight weeks after giving birth, had taken up with a schoolboy she'd found performing impressive 360-degree flips on his skateboard. He had peered into the pram and admired her baby. Three weeks later she was hanging about outside his school in lilac embroidered corduroys and a strapless satin top. She told me, "I don't care what people think. I love him, he loves me. The only problem is when his mates come round and polish off all our drink."

This woman isn't unusual. Mothers are primed to go off at any moment. They spend decades calmly encouraging small people to finish their fish fingers and say, "Please may I leave the table?" until one day: off they go, without leaving a note or even washing the frying pan.

"You're shaking," says Eliza.

"My brain doesn't work. I can't make decisions. Even little things, like do I go to the loo now or hold on for a bit? I don't know what to *do* with myself."

"Should you see someone?"

I think of Ashley and Mum's horse pills.

"What triggered this off?" Eliza asks. "I thought you were coping. Assumed you enjoyed your funny daytime world."

I tell her that, after being humiliated in the Changing Village, I'd attempted to calm myself with a hot drink. A new café had sprung up in the place of the friendly old one with its all-day five-item breakfasts. Dozens of unfamiliar coffee varieties were being dispensed in chrome-handled glasses and potty-size mugs, with or without white chocolate flakes or gingerbread crumbles or some kind of vanilla gloop. I'd stared at the blackboard, wondering whether the gingerbread crumbles would float on top or plummet to the bottom like overdunked biscuits. The menu milled with chalked words and wiggly drawings of steaming cups. "Coffee to go," I said meekly.

"What kind?" asked a girl with an airbrushed face.

"I don't know."

"Well, can you decide? We're busy."

I'd left the café without buying anything.

"You didn't call me because you couldn't choose coffee," says Eliza.

"No, I called because of Ranald. Remember Ranald, the camping man? He called me Nancy."

Cindy hands me a porcelain cup of unidentifiable herbal tea with the bag still in it, leaking redness.

"You need something special," said Eliza. "Something to remind yourself you're still a woman."

Cindy has Ben in her arms. He regards her with exaggerated blinks, wondering why his mother is never as well turned out as this. She plucks a narrow black dress from the rail. "Try this. The baby's fine with me."

I look at her: slender and ironed with contented infant. Magazine mother and child. She drifts back into the shop with Ben. I strip off my outer clothes and pull on the dress, expecting nothing: a stretchy black tube with miserly straps.

It drapes gracefully, creating the illusion that I have never seen the inside of a maternity ward.

"Shoes," commands Eliza.

Cindy reappears with sandals like tangles of licorice.

"Where would I wear these things?"

"Anywhere," Eliza says. "They'd do for when you go back to work. People wear anything to the office these days."

It seems so long since I entered a place of work that I cling to an image of sensible workaday shoes and enormous clanking computers. *Promise*'s offices were so dismally beige I was grateful for those triumph over tragedy interviews, and always willing to travel to the women's homes. Even Luton could be uplifting on a sunny day.

"We've got the old Nina back," gushes Eliza. I view my reflection and try to straighten my shoulders. Wet eyes and chunky bra straps aside, the effect is, although not quite goddesslike, a marked improvement on the woman who barged in through the etched-glass door.

And I have to admit, I rather like it.

By 10:30 p.m. Jonathan has neither returned from his after-work drink nor phoned to say when he'll be home. I resist the urge to call his mobile. Why shouldn't he stay out late? He needs a break. Everyone does. Even Beth goes out occasionally, with her coffee morning cronies, to bemoan the condition of East London's parks and slag off mothers who give their infants fizzy drinks. Jonathan and I could go out. I'd wear the dress—which I'm wearing right now—and he'd spend all evening staring at me in a funny way. But so far he's shown no desire to venture out after dark—until this evening, of course, when presumably he's rollicking from pub to pub with various female colleagues attached.

At eleven forty-five I rehearse my speech: "As you can

see I have bought something to make myself seem attractive to you. Though obviously I come way down in your list of priorities." By twelve-fifteen the speech has been rewritten to include: "You can fuck off." I wonder how he would react to a barrage of swearing. I have never heard Jonathan swear properly. Just the occasional "bugger it" when he's running late in the morning and can't get his cuffs done up. Even then he ruins a perfectly decent swearing moment by apologizing afterward.

At one twenty-six Ben wakes for a feed. It seems unimportant that I'm cradling him while wearing a dress that cost more than our new stereo, which we never use because Jonathan doesn't like music, not even classical. As Ben chugs his bottle, I make a mental note to inform Jonathan that I'm moving in with Eliza and would he mind driving round at some convenient moment with my things? Not that I own much. My belongings appeared instantly shabby in Jonathan's sleek surroundings. What use had I for my ratty paperbacks and the cookery books my mother donated when I left home, even though I couldn't remember her ever preparing a meal from scratch? One included a chapter on nightmare constructions requiring intricately carved fruit and piped cream. Jonathan frowned at it, suggested we rationalize my stuff, and dropped off the undesirables at a Sue Ryder shop. My black photo album—a present from Eliza, into which she'd stuck pictures of the two of us in Corfu— must have been packed into the box with the piped cream cookbook because I never saw it again.

I still have my clothes of course: prepregnancy outfits

now unfashionable enough to look faintly knackered, yet not so ancient that they'd create some kooky retro look. But I do have my new dress. It looks even better in the dim glow of the plug-in night-light. I fancy myself even if Jonathan doesn't. No point in pretending. It's over.

As the taxi growls outside the flat I roll words around my mouth: *We're finished. We've tried, made a decent stab at this, but it's not working. You can see Ben as much as you like. Take him to the park like weekend dads do. I'm sure it won't screw him up, if we separate when he's little. It needn't be messy. We're reasonable people, aren't we?*

A figure emerges from the cab and loiters at our gate. A burglar, sensing female alone with baby. Through the spyhole I watch the person rummaging in its pockets for something—crowbar? Knife?—then stagger against a galvanized pot of lavender.

I unlock the door.

"Hello," says Jonathan.

"Where have you been?"

He glides past me, self-consciously upright as if balancing books on his head. "You're wearing a dress," he says.

"Why didn't you phone?"

"It's very nice."

"You've had me demented."

"Can I have a closer look at that dress? I like the way it scoops down at the front."

I step back from him. "Don't think I'm mad because you had a good time. It's not that—"

"You're sexy," he says.

"Why did you make me so worried? You don't know what it's like, being here, waiting."

"I like *you*."

"Do you?"

"Can't we just go to bed?"

I'm about to tell him no, we can't, because we don't do that kind of thing—sure, we go to bed, but we don't *go to bed*—but he's already lurched for the bathroom, banging the door behind him. From in there comes a thud of something heavy meeting floor tiles. I try the door. It won't open.

"Jonathan, please let me in."

The something heavy shifts just enough to let me squeeze through the gap. Jonathan has crash-landed on the bathroom floor, tie strewn diagonally across his shirt. I crouch beside him, try to hold him, but he arches away like babies do when they don't want you.

"What's wrong?" I ask.

He fixes his gaze on the point where the blue tiles meet cream. Calming colors. His favorites.

"I drank too much," he tells the tiles.

"I'll get you some water."

"Nina," he calls after me, "it's not right, is it, any of this?"

I look back to see that his cheek is crumpled against the loo seat. When I'm closer I realize that he's crying without making a noise, not delicate teardrops but sheets of fluid, dripping from his mottled chin onto the perfectly pressed but grubbily fingerprinted collar of his shirt.

9

Making Baby Friends

Jonathan sleeps through the polite *peep-peep* of the travel alarm and refuses to respond to several reminders that the working world anxiously awaits his presence. I suspect that this is the first time in the history of Jonathan that he has failed to show up for work. "Shall I phone in for you?" I ask.

A timid growl comes out.

"What shall I tell them?"

He flips from his back onto his stomach, hair clinging to his scalp in moist swirls. "Sayamill," he groans.

"Just ill."

"Or sick."

"Right. I know," I say, reaching out to pat the wet head

and deciding to make the call instead, "I'll tell them you had bad seafood."

I dial and start, "It's Nina, Jonathan's..." I hate that. How you don't know what to call yourself if you're not married. Wife is plainly inaccurate, girlfriend too frisky considering we jointly own a food processor, and partner sounds so businesslike you'd never believe sex was involved (which it isn't, but still).

"I'm calling for Jonathan," I say. "He's been up all night with his stomach."

Jonathan's colleague chuckles and says, "Seafood?"

"That's right." I step into the bedroom to report that I have pulled off a fine act of deceit but Jonathan is unconscious. The room stinks of pub carpet. Old alcohol, fermenting in the gut. The sash window opens stiffly but crashes down again, snapping at my fingers. I wedge it with Jonathan's work shoe.

The doorbell rings. Beth marches in, skinny plaits tied with gingham ribbon, and Maud bound to her hip by a fragile-looking scarf. She pecks my cheek. Up close, she smells of baking. I'd forgotten that I'm hosting a coffee morning for Beth's new-mother gang. Therefore I have failed to prepare an impressive array of warm, home-baked goodies as is customary on these occasions.

I stumbled into the coffee morning circuit accidentally, introduced by Beth, who took me under her wing way back in those antenatal classes. "You need baby friends," she declared when we'd become proper mothers and it became apparent that she knew more than I did. A "support network," she called it. *Women who know what you're*

going through. My name was swiftly added to a list of
novice mothers who kicked off tentative friendships,
discussing sleeping patterns and the healing of Caesarean
scars. Tips would be swapped. Within weeks, fragile in-
timacies were formed. I hadn't been faced with so many
unfamiliar faces since starting school, aged four.

Phoebe arrives shortly after Beth, chomping some kind
of foodstuff, probably breakfast. She has a jaw like a brick
and an over fondness for blusher. Phoebe appears to feed
her older child entirely on breadsticks and crudités, but
thinks nothing of troughing fudge brownies all morning, which strikes me as unfair on the kid. No wonder
he has a disgruntled air about him, like something's missing, probably chocolate.

Beth met Phoebe at a painting workshop. The word
"workshop" implies light engineering, but this type involved placing babies and small children on a plastic sheet
and allowing them to express their creativity with stumpy
brushes and water-based paint. Beth mounted Maud's
creation in an outsize clipframe that hangs over their tra-
ditional fireplace. I feel obliged to say something intelligent about the colors—"the way that purple swirls about
with the red! The juxtaposition of lilac and green!"—
every time I go round there.

I rummage in the cupboard for some snack that might
pass as home-baked. A woman with blue-veined eyelids
and sun-blistered shoulders announces that her husband
wants to move to the country. "Why?" asks Beth. "The
country's all right to visit but—you know, what would
you do all day?"

"I've told him," she says. "Explained that I can't live outside a five-mile radius of a Hobbs."

I dump a plate of artfully arranged (but obviously shop-bought) oat cookies on the coffee table. "You can't get anything in the country," Beth continues. "Matthew and I are just back from Somerset. Everyone was friendly—happy and simple the way they are in the country—but you couldn't buy watercress or any kind of lettuce you'd want to eat and I'm stuck there, rustling up a salad with an iceberg."

"Coffee?" I enquire. Four additional women have arrived. They have bossy voices and mobile mouths. Their children are plonked on the rug where I have arranged a selection of what I hope are ecofriendly toys, produced from sustainable resources while encouraging hand-eye coordination. I'm learning fast. No palming off twenty-first-century baby with a gnarled Miffy book.

Ben observes his playmates fearfully. A new arrival removes her child from his front-loading carrier. I met her at Beth's but can't remember her name: so many new acquaintances to file correctly, plus the names of their babies. That's the hardest part. Unless a child possesses an outstanding feature—a dense rug of hair or vast, flapping ears—I can barely distinguish one from another. In a clump like this, it's virtually impossible. I often ask, "How's Jacob sleeping these days?" only to be met with, "*Joshua's* doing a full six hours, thank you."

This woman's name starts with *J* or maybe *K*, I know that much. She has a felt-making business requiring much rubbing of wool through an old net curtain and hanging the resulting sheets on her washing line. Her current project is an outsized slab to adorn the wall of a primary school canteen. Beth told me she lurks around skips, fishing out discarded objects—chest of drawer handles, scraps of moldering upholstery—to stitch onto the felt. "How's your felt thing going?" I ask.

"My what?" She reaches for biscuits, sees what's on offer and quickly withdraws her hand.

"That thing for the school," I say uneasily.

She rubs her powerful upper arms, making a rasping sound. "It's an installation."

"Is it nearly finished?"

Her child—an ill-tempered ball of a boy called Ernie or possibly Alfred—starts crying. She plonks him on her bosom while still standing. "It'll never be finished," she retorts. "It's a work in progress. That's the idea. The children keep adding to it, stitching on found objects for years and years—forever in fact—so it's constantly evolving."

"I'd like to see it when it's finished," I say. "I mean *not* finished."

The living room is stiflingly warm, perhaps due to the number of adults milling about it, or heat radiating from Jonathan's sweating corpse in the bedroom. Beth and Felt Lady are discussing their POOP campaign (Poo Off Our Pavements). Beth is to put pressure on the parks department to erect a dog lavatory, which I assume is a Portakabin with miniature toilet inside but turns out to be a designated fenced-off area.

Felt Lady offers to produce leaflets to thrust into the

palms of owners spotted with defecating dogs. She and Beth huddle over a notebook, debating the wording. "Your dog has been spotted soiling a public area," begins Beth. "Please pick up deposit and place in dog-mess bin."

"Not enough oomph," chips in Felt Lady. "Put: cut the crap. Dog owners must clear up after their pets or face a fine of—"

"We can't fine them," says Beth. "We're not the police."

Maud interrupts with a startling wail as if she's been bitten. Beth carries her to the kitchen, pointing at our storage jars of pasta. "Look," she soothes. "Tagliatelle. Penne. Spag-*yeti*."

Maud squawks angrily. Phoebe's kid—he's around two or three, I have yet to get to grips with bigger children's ages—investigates a drawer filled with treacherous cooking implements. "Haven't you child-proofed your drawers?" asks Beth.

"No need. He won't be crawling for months yet."

"Isn't he trying? I know he's only four months, but so is Maud, and she's desperate to get moving. The health visitor couldn't believe how advanced and determined she is. But, then, we do a lot with her."

I glance into the living room where Ben is sucking the ear of the black, featureless bear donated by Eliza.

"Perhaps he needs more stimulating toys," remarks Beth.

Phoebe's kid produces a miniature taxi from his dungaree pocket and raps it sharply on the door of our stainless steel oven. I'm unsure about the etiquette of telling off someone else's child. "Now then," I murmur. "Let's not do that."

Maud, unimpressed by our pasta range, writhes in Beth's overlong arms. "Do you have any rice cakes she could nibble on?" she asks. I locate an open packet of off-white tiles and hope Beth doesn't register their bendiness. Phoebe's kid opens the oven door and places his taxi on the wire shelf.

"That's an oven," I point out. "Very hot."

He twiddles the knobs, attempting to turn on all five rings and gas us. It's 10:27 a.m. Apart from Beth, who refuses to poison her insides with my freshly brewed offerings and accepts only plain hot water, we are all drinking coffee. This counts, then, as a coffee morning. Should Eliza burst in between skirt-choosing appointments, I have planned to say that these women descended on me without warning, forced their way in and started boiling the kettle. It's almost true. They're not friends exactly. We are linked by our lifestyles—wipers of bottoms, dispensers of milk—and a rabid desire for adult company.

"Can I ask you something, Nina?" says Beth. She looks especially greasy today. Her fringe and forehead form a buttery slick. She strokes the Peter Pan collar of her candy-pink blouse.

"Ask away."

"Is Jonathan romantic?"

"It depends what you mean. He's thoughtful," I say, then remember the previous night and add, "most of the time."

Beth breaks off a corner of flexible rice cake. "Matthew's not. He used to be. He'd buy me spontaneous presents in his lunch hour. Little things you'd never get for yourself—perfume, lacy underwear with the dangly bits for your stockings to hook on to—just to say he still thought of me as his lover, you know?"

"I know," I lie. Jonathan and I bypassed the cute present stage. His sole non-special-occasion gift to me was a crafty sperm that dive-bombed my egg. At least it was spontaneous.

"Do you ever feel they don't care?" asks Beth.

"Who's they?"

"Our menfolk. Our *other halves.*"

"It's different now," I say, like I know about relationships. "There's less time to—"

"Tell me about it," she sniffs.

"Is your gas supposed to be on?" asks Felt Lady. I turn off the rings. Phoebe's kid, who's yanked out a bottle from Jonathan's wine rack, receives a rap on the skull from his mother.

"You could damage his head doing that," reprimands Beth. "You're sending the message that it's okay to hit. You're normalizing physical violence."

Before Phoebe resorts to more serious violent tactics, I trap Beth by the nappy disposal machine. "I thought you and Matthew were fine," I say. "You're always out, aren't you? And you've just been away. Me and Jonathan never do that."

"What, Somerset?" she scoffs. "Some weekend that was. The cottage he's booked is disgusting. So we book into a hotel—baby friendly, all the facilities—and we arrive and everything's lovely."

"So what happened?"

"We settle Maud in the cot—a beautiful cot with a

Shaker-style quilt—and go down to dinner but the baby listener can't pick up a signal. I'm back up in the bedroom, going, 'Hello? Hello?' into the listener and of course Matthew can't hear me."

"Did you have dinner in bed?" I ask.

"No, in a nasty little conference room with a shiny board you could write on and wipe off—just me and him with the baby listener crackling. And you know what?" Her voice trembles. "We didn't speak a single word during that entire meal."

"That's good," remarks Felt Lady. "I'm always suspicious of those couples you see, talking ten to the dozen, trying to prove they still get along. Sitting quietly, just *being* together, sounds perfect."

"We weren't *being* together," snaps Beth. "We've nothing left to say. We've run out of words. There aren't any left, except, 'Did I tell you the extractor hood's not working?' and, 'Remember to put the bin out.'"

She's shouting now. I was wrong to dismiss coffee mornings as tedious get-togethers for the lonesome. All kinds of stuff goes on, if you look for it.

"How was the rest of the weekend?" I ask.

"We end up in a country pub. Horse brasses, sort of peasanty. Farm workers with big hands."

"Was that better?"

"Yes, until the TV comes on. Matthew never used to like TV. We didn't have one until this not-talking thing started. Now every night he's holding his hand up, silencing me, because he's glued to some dimwit quiz show. So finally, because he is not interested in any kind of adult discussion, I walk out and he's running after me and of course," she finishes, her voice thunderous, "you've got to face some stupid baby-sitter in your hotel room and her pile of teenage magazines."

"That's terrible," says Felt Lady.

"Maybe you need a break," I suggest.

"What, like Somerset?"

"Well, it sounds like it's getting too much for you. Perhaps you need extra help."

"I do. It's not like a job, this baby thing, is it? You're on call twenty-four hours a day. It's seamless. Even when they're asleep you're preparing the next meal and sterilizing toys and washing terry nappies."

"Oh, do you use terries?" asks Felt Lady. "I tried. Thought they'd be no bother at all—easier, in fact, than disposables—and you're not lying awake at night, worrying about landfill sites."

"I know," says Beth. "If all the dirty disposable nappies were laid end to end they'd stretch, er, right round the world, probably."

"Well, I'm sorry about that," says Felt Lady, "but do I have time to be boiling and hanging the damn things out on the line?"

"Like your felt," I suggest.

She blinks at me. "Felt isn't *boiled*. I binned the terries and I'm less hassled and a better mother for it. So really, in using disposables, I'm making the planet a friendlier place."

"At least you're recycling in your work," says Beth. "No one's perfect. You can't do it all. That's why we're getting an au pair."

Beth and Matthew's three-story town house gleams even more sweetly than our flat. In fact, I have noticed a deterioration in standards at our place. Worktops are smattered with crumbs. Jonathan has stopped loading the dishwasher immediately after each meal. "Do you need an au pair?" I ask Beth.

"I'm not talking about need. It's about having support. I can't do this single-handedly."

"What does Matthew say?"

"He doesn't say anything. I've had an agency send seven girls round—sweet foreign girls who are glad of the chance to live in a civilized country—and I just need to pick one."

"Where do they come from?"

"Some godforsaken eastern European country where it's freezing and they don't have any money."

"So you haven't told Matthew?"

"He wouldn't be interested. Anyway, it'll be done and dusted before he can put his oar in."

"You shouldn't keep secrets from your partner," scolds Felt Lady. "You'll lose your intimacy, your coupleness."

"That's right," I say.

"It's okay for you," says Beth crossly. "You wouldn't keep anything from Jonathan. Look at you. So neatly turned out in your lovely pink cardigan—has it lost a button by the way?—with this beautiful flat *and* you make all your own baby food."

"That's amazing," says Phoebe, restraining her kid from running his palm along our cheese grater. "Do you mash or use a mouli?"

I refill her mug, pleased that I have taken the trouble to grind Jonathan's good coffee beans. Above the hubbub the veiny-eyelidded woman shouts, "Nina, your phone, shall I pick it up?"

"Please."

"Someone called… I didn't quite catch it. Says it's lovely here. I said it's lovely here, too."

I snatch the phone and escape to the hall. "Gosh, it sounds busy at your place," says Lovely. "Are you having a party?"

"Just a few friends round."

"You mums. All that socializing." There's a soft rattle, like pearls. I imagine she's wearing peach. "Anyway, there's an audition for a commercial. Ben would be perfect. But it's short notice. Three-thirty this afternoon. Can you make it?"

Felt Lady looms anxiously before me, discomfort fuzzing her eye region. "I'm sorry, Nina," she interrupts, "but I really need to use your bathroom. Something's been in there for ages, making terrible growling noises. Do you have a pet?"

10

Crying and Comforting

When the last of the coffee morning mob have departed for various workshops I catch sight of myself in the bedroom mirror and remember Lovely's warning: the mother must be impeccably turned out. My underarms are wet beneath the pink cardi. Flecks of oat cookie are wedged between my teeth.

Jonathan is coagulating in the bath, lips hanging apart limply. "How are you feeling?" I ask.

"How do I look?"

It's been a long time since I saw him naked. He has delicate, faintly feminine shoulders and a light dusting of fair hair on his chest. Though he doesn't exercise, he is in reasonable shape. For one thing, he doesn't have an apron stomach.

"You don't look too bad," I say, feeling sorry for him. It's only through lack of drinking opportunities that I have avoided hangovers for more than a year. I used to rack up hideous morning afters until one ran into the next. It was pretty normal for me to feel empty-stomached and poisoned, craving eggs, my duvet and darkness.

I wonder whether to run out and buy Jonathan some milk thistle tincture, which Beth tells me is good for the liver. Hers doesn't need cleansing; she drinks only at Christmas, and then it's watered down wine. I suspect she just likes the wholesome sound of it.

Eliza's better on hangover remedies. On doddery mornings she scours the Internet and tries recommendations such as beef consommé soup with a splash of vodka and is hoping to track down a rare (and apparently highly effective) remedy made from dried bull's penis. I decide not to mention that one to Jonathan. "Are you well enough to watch Ben while I have a shower and get changed?" I ask.

"Put him in the car seat. He'll be fine."

"Then I'll take him out and you can have the rest of the day to yourself, recovering."

I expect him to thank me. All he says is, "Right."

By the time I meet Eliza I'm cutting it fine to make the casting by three-thirty. But I want this haircut. Eliza has arranged her crucial fashion PR appointments to fit in a spot of baby-minding while my head is sorted out.

Her idea. "You owe it to yourself," she said. "A haircut tells the world what's going on inside you. You want it to say, 'I feel positive. I'm in control. Life is *great.*'" Clearly, my hair is capable only of bleating, "Brush me."

Eliza is waiting outside the hairdressers. She wears a knee-length cream dress and fine silver hoop earrings. I fear for those earrings. Ben has taken to grabbing at dangling objects, forcing me to abandon wearing anything decorative. "What are you going to do with him?" I ask.

Her smile stiffens. "What do you mean, do with him?"

"You know. How you're going to spend the hour."

"An hour?" she splutters. "Is that how long it's going to take?"

"I'd say at least that. How long does your hair take?"

She regains her composure and says, "I could take him to the office, but I hoped he'd be asleep."

"He's already had two hours. He'll be awake for ages."

"Oh. I thought babies slept a lot. How about I take him to a gallery? He might find it relaxing."

"That sounds good." I glance inside the hairdressers. A woman is having her head massaged. Caramel aromas sneak out each time the door opens. "At least there'll be changing facilities," I add. "Here, you'll need this."

Eliza observes the changing bag, clearly wishing she was back at work, conversing with model agents. It is pillow-size with a repeat pattern of purple rocking horses. "Is he likely to… soil himself at this time of day?" she asks in a high voice.

"Probably not. But you never know your luck."

"I'm sure he won't," she says firmly.

★ ★ ★

The hairdresser is around nineteen years old and sports a retro sixties haircut that curls around his ears and neck. He is obviously appalled at having to attend to my head instead that of the tender, fair-maned creature sitting neatly beside me, and has therefore decided not to talk.

This is good. Since having a baby I have lost the ability to communicate with young people. Maybe it's a side effect of living with Jonathan. One evening he switched on *Top of the Pops* by mistake. A boy band perched on high stools, voices wobbling with hammed-up emotion. "Is this what they like?" he asked.

"Who's they?"

"Young people." I looked sideways at him. He was thirty-five and acted like he'd never been any younger. The boys who hung around our street made him edgy. One night, a vast adolescent rested his backside on the bonnet of our car. Jonathan spotted him, bouncing lightly, and asked the boy to remove himself from our vehicle. The boy laughed and spat in the road. The following morning we discovered cider bottles planted in the lavender pots.

Is this how Ben will turn out? Despising me, probably. You fritter away your thirties and forties worrying about what your offspring might be putting into their body, and at the end of it you are rewarded with a hormonal beast who regards you with the same blend of fascination/disgust they reserve for watching a fish being gutted.

"Been out lately?" asks the hairdresser.

"Oh, just the usual. I have a baby so it's difficult."

"I couldn't be doing with that. I don't want a baby until I'm at least thirty."

"Quite right," I tell the mirror. "I wouldn't have been ready at your age."

He smiles fakely, snipping with such speed that I suspect he wants me out of this chair as quickly as possible so he can do beautiful things to the tender girl. "What are you up to this afternoon?" he asks in a bored way.

"Taking my baby to a casting. For a commercial. He does a bit of modeling, you've probably seen him."

"Really?" The hairdresser brightens. "What's he been in?"

"Masses. Never stops working. It's hectic for me but at least I'm out of the house."

"You need that," says the hairdresser. "I model a bit. Just the odd job if I feel like it. I'm really an actor." He tweaks the ends of my hair and douses me with spray. "You like?" he asks. His first proper smile.

"I like," I say, blushing.

Ben, my dashing new haircut and I arrive at the four-story terrace at 3:37 p.m., seven minutes behind schedule. My mobile rings as I attempt to collapse the buggy while holding Ben. Our home number. I can't tell Jonathan where we are; not while his liver's creaking.

The audition suite is on the top floor. A squall of adults biff against each other. Babies busy themselves on a floor mat heaped with Duplo. I am handed a form by a tired-looking woman and fill in details of Ben's name, age, dimensions and agency. I leave the "special talents" space blank.

"Typical," says a woman in a heavy velvet shift dress and matching deflated beret (it reminds me never to attempt a soufflé). She dabs her daughter's fringe with a wet wipe. "Can you believe it?" she goes on. "She's perfect all week and today she falls over and smacks her forehead on the pavement."

"It doesn't look too bad," I reassure her.

"Yes it does. It's weeping. I'd pick the gravel out but I might make it look worse."

"You don't want it getting infected," says another mother. "It might fester and poison the blood."

The child with gravel in her forehead is wearing a high-necked dress in the same fabric as her mother's. I place Ben among the babies and open Eliza's magazine at the page with my son, Fern in the limp salmon dress, and the male model who isn't one really.

"Oh dear," says the woman, adjusting her soufflé. "That's bleak, isn't it? Raven does much more commercial work."

Raven fiddles with the ribbon at the neck of her dress. She doesn't look excited at the prospect of starring in a commercial. The ends of her hair are wet. She plucks a strand and sucks it.

"Don't do that, Raven," says her mother.

"Been waiting long?" I ask.

"Twenty minutes. Should be seen pretty soon. They're doing the older ones first, then toddlers, then babies. You might be here for hours."

I wonder if Jonathan is still stewing in the bath, and at what point he might start to worry.

"Would you like to see Raven's book?" the woman asks.

I don't like to say no. "Here," says the woman, handing me a fat portfolio stuffed with magazine cuttings. Each has been carefully mounted on white A4 paper with penciled dates and captions such as, "Required to tap" and "Raven performs somersault."

"Gosh," I say. "Raven gets lots of work."

"She's so in demand. It's a full-time job for me, of course, the chaperoning."

"Don't you mind?"

She shakes her head, causing the beret to wobble dangerously. "It's building up a trust fund for Raven. Are you saving your baby's earnings in an account until he's older?"

"Of course," I say quickly.

"Raven?" The tired-looking woman beckons the velvet duo. Raven is marched stiffly through the throng of parents and offspring to a door marked Auditions In Progress. Please Do Not Enter Until Called. One Chaperone Only Per Child.

By the end of the afternoon Ben has fallen out with the Duplo and I assume we've been forgotten. Should we hang about until the caretaker shows up and switches off the lights? I carry him to the baby changing room and remove the nappy that Eliza fitted too tightly. Red patches have sprung up at each hip. The nappy thuds into the disposal unit. Ben has grown heartily sick of the whole modeling deal and I consider slipping into the lift, heading home and telling Jonathan we've been shopping. Such a tiny lie won't count.

"Ben?" says the tired woman. "We've been calling for you, Mum. Could you take him in please?"

Ben responds to the darker room by burying his head in my cardi. "Hi, Ben," says a boy only slightly older than my hairdresser. "How are we doing today?"

Ben huddles deeper into my chest.

"Shy, is he?" asks the boy, glancing at his watch.

"It's his first audition," I explain, "but he's done a little job for a friend." I open Eliza's magazine.

"This is much more upbeat," says the boy. "We're casting for a gang of kids, all ages. They'll be messing about in a paddling pool, playing with the products."

"What products?"

"Little Squirts. Shampoos, body washes, conditioners."

"Conditioners? For babies?"

"A new niche. All the celebrities' kids use them. Makes the hair shiny, easier to comb. Could you pop Ben on the rug, sitting up?"

"He can't sit. He's only four months. All he can do is lie on his tummy and push up a bit."

"He's maybe a bit young for this job. All that water. But try him like that. He'd be splashing around, having a great time with the other babies."

I lower Ben to the floor. His face collapses onto the rug.

"Could you cheer him up a bit?" asks the boy. "We want a real sense of fun. It's what the Little Squirts range is all about."

Ben's forehead rises shakily. His red face appears briefly on a monitor before his arms crumple, sending him nose-diving into the rug. "Maybe he'd be happier if you were near him," suggests the boy.

I crouch beside him, hoping my backside doesn't appear on the monitor and fill the entire screen. "Ben?" I say softly. "It's okay. Can you smile for the man?"

What starts as a small, frightened cough revs up to a desperate splutter. I haul him over my shoulder. "God," says the boy, "is he choking?"

"Just emotional. Got a throatful of his own snot."

"Don't worry," he sighs. "Everyone has off days."

I clamp Ben firmly under one arm while I try to shake open the buggy and succeed only in bashing its wheels on the pavement. Ben's cheeks burn scarlet. He's plank rigid as I squash him into the seat. Two almost identically dressed females cross the road towards us. "How did it go?" asks the mother.

"Fine," I mutter, "though you never know what they're looking for, do you?"

She frowns at Ben's blotchy face. "He looks upset. You should get him straight home. I never make Raven do an audition if she's not in the mood."

"Was she in the mood today?"

"Oh, yes," the woman beams. "Charmed them. They didn't even mind about her forehead. But as you say, you never can tell. That's what makes it so exciting. Isn't it Raven?"

Raven sucks a vivid orange ice lolly. "Mummy," she whimpers, huddling into the deep velvet folds of her mother's skirt.

Jonathan appears to have made a full recovery. He crouches on the kitchen floor, squirting the oven's insides with an aerosol can bearing the warning: "Highly Toxic. Risk of Serious Damage to Eyes."

"You should be resting," I say.

"I feel better doing something useful. What have you been up to?"

"Walking. Just wanted to give you some peace."

"You've had a haircut."

"Oh, yes. Just had the urge," I tell him, stripping Ben to his vest.

"He looks cross."

"Got stroppy at the hairdressers," I say, heading to the bedroom for a clean vest, although he doesn't need one.

"Nina?" Jonathan calls after me.

I open drawers of socks and hats and babygros, but no vests. Jonathan follows me, still holding the can of oven cleaner. I wonder how he'd react if I told him. Whether he'd squirt me. "What are you looking for?" he asks.

"Where do we keep Ben's vests?"

He opens the wardrobe and plucks one from the vest shelf. "I have to tell you," he says.

I smile blandly at him.

"Great haircut."

"Thanks."

He looks at me curiously, as if he's about to draw me. "I like the way it flicks under and out a bit. Makes you look…cheeky."

"You don't think it's too young?"

"No. You look different, though."

"In what way different?"

"More like…before Ben." He takes a step closer. My instinct is to back away in case he spots something close up; my fibbing eyes which have flitted about an audition suite all afternoon. But my back meets the wardrobe. I'm trapped by a Swedish flatpack construction.

"We'd better check Ben," I say quickly.

"He's strapped in his seat. He can't go anywhere."

"What if he's crying?" I feel Jonathan's breath now, hot on my face. He tastes minty, and smells freshly bathed. He's still clutching the oven cleaner. My legs hook lazily around his. And nothing terrible happens. No clanking sounds come from my insides. I still work.

11

Choosing Child Care

Beth darts about her kitchen, chucking chopped dates into a mixing bowl, presumably to prevent the resulting cake from being too much fun. Three weeks have passed since her coffee morning outburst. She looks perkier. The forehead slick has been blotted away. Even her plaits look less dismal.

"Jonathan wants to get married," I tell her.

"Do you want to?" she asks.

"I can't see why not. We won't go for a big splashy do. And at least I'd know what to call him."

She smiles daintily. Beth thinks I met Jonathan through mutual friends at a dinner party. I didn't want her to assume I was sleazy or desperate or foolish enough to arrange a date with a stranger. Jonathan has been primed not to mention the ad, should we ever have another meal out with Beth and Matthew (unlikely, after the spewing incident).

I perch on a cottagey kitchen chair worn shiny by bottoms. Beth favors the country kitchen look: enameled jugs bearing delphiniums, fruit basket lined with a gingham square. In one of those drawers stenciled with yellow-beaked ducks, there's bound to be an apron. "When you're married," I say, "you know where you stand. It must feel more secure."

"I don't want to know where I stand," says Beth. "I want a night out, a surprise, planned and sorted without me having to do anything about it. 'Hey, Beth,'" she cries, mimicking Matthew. "'Don't bother cooking tonight. Put that spoon *down,* cupcake. Dig out your good shoes, the ones with the thin ankle straps. We're going somewhere special.'"

She places the cake in the oven. I wonder when I'll learn how to do that: click into Mother the Baker. Five years down the line, I'll be roped into the PTA and obliged to contribute walnut loaves and sugar-dusted sponge cakes in order to raise funds for crucial school equipment. By this time classes will be restricted to one workbook per seven kids. My son's academic career will rest solely on my ability to extract something from the oven that someone might actually pay 50p for.

"Why don't you ask him?" I suggest. "I'll baby-sit."

"We have a baby-sitter. We can go out whenever we like. And having to ask spoils the whole—"

"Who baby-sits?"

"The au pair, of course."

"So you found your eastern European?"

Beth laughs. "Not exactly. A lovely girl, Rosie, from Kent. Pretty little scrubbed-up thing. Went to one of those progressive schools where they only go to lessons when they feel like it."

"And what happens when they don't?"

She shrugs, wiping the kitchen table with an orange sponge shaped like a goldfish. "A lot of sitting under trees, it sounds like. Everyone had their own plot of garden. I've told her to make sure Maudie gets plenty of fresh air because, you know, me and the outside don't get on."

"Could she sort out your garden?" I ask.

"Well, I don't like to ask. It's not strictly in the job description. But I'm hoping she'll dig up that woody old flowering red currant. Matthew won't—he used to do the garden. Not now, with his telly. Look at the state of that lawn."

Beth's garden yawns from the kitchen window, bordered on all sides by a six-foot creosoted fence. She had the fence erected for privacy so she could practice her yoga on the lawn. The patio area has been decked, which Beth regretted instantly. Matthew's fault, she told me, for not sharing the burden; how thin she had grown from perpetual breast-feeding, fingers shrinking until skin hung limply at her knuckles (first place to show weight loss, apparently). And her ring slipped off, that serious diamond from Liberty, down a gap between the decking. The whole lot will have to come up. Not for sentimental reasons— though it was her engagement ring, purchased when he did still surprise her—but because she can't bear to think of another couple moving in, deciding that decking is very last century, and spying a glimmer of gold in the soil.

"Where's Maud?" I ask.

"Upstairs, playing with Rosie. You must establish rules, from day one. Rosie knows not to clatter about when I have friends round. And food—she can help herself from the everyday biscuit tin. But I don't want to open the cupboard and find my dark chocolate cookies all gone."

Sweet, youthful singing filters downstairs. Maud is laughing. I have never heard that child laugh before. Perhaps Rosie is playing a tape of anonymous babies giggling to stimulate Maud's sense of humor.

Beth sets two places for lunch on the kitchen table. With a flourish, she tugs the tea towel off an enormous salad dish. Nutty kernels nestle among glistening leaves and grilled peppers. "You must be feeling better," I say, "bothering to toast pine kernels and all that."

"Oh, Rosie knocked this up. You owe it to yourself to get one." She is about to pour sparkling grape juice but I've brought wine, and want some. "Just a sip," she says. I'm about to suggest pouring Rosie a glass but assume she'll eat later, picking at leftovers with Maud in the playroom.

The note Blu-tacked onto the maternity ward's toilet door went like this:

remember ladies
when you pee

clench to hold the flow of wee.
squeeze it tight
and hold it in
to keep the pelvic floor in trim.

It seemed a tragic waste of time, all that clenching and squeezing when there were ample visible areas to work on. But now I wish I'd put in the effort. I dribble wee constantly, like a mouse, and Beth's overreliance on stair-gates is enough to put you off going. I squirm on the kitchen chair and leave it so long it's threatening to spurt out before I've sat on the loo. But I make it in time and, awash with relief, find Rosie and Maud two floors up.

Rosie smiles gappily through a tumble of loose brown curls. This fresh, perky girl, with just the right amount of freckles, belongs on a TGV at the start of an Inter-rail trip, not flicking the wooden beads of an abacus in the upper reaches of Beth's town house.

"Thanks for lunch," I say.

"That's okay. Any time." She wears jeans, a white vest and no bra. Her skin is the type that adapts easily to the sun; none of your calamine lotion scenario. Maud bulges her cheeks blankly. Rarely have I seen a more un-attractive infant. Squeezed into a dainty madras-checked sundress, she looks like a transvestite. "Isn't she adorable?" says Rosie. "And so clever. I can't believe the stuff Maudie can do."

Maud jams a clenched fist into her mouth.

"Are you just out of school?" I ask, trying not to raise the pitch of my voice like you do when addressing a child.

"I've worked for a couple of years," Rosie says. "Waitressing, bit of modeling—you know, life drawing classes. Freezing, half the time. Some rotten adult education center. Two-hour sittings that felt like a week."

"That must have been awful."

"Last job, I was dancing. That was better."

"What kind of dancing?" I ask.

"Lapdancing. Great money but the hours—forget it. You can't do it, not for months on end. You're knackered. There's a cut-off point. So I thought I'd try this instead."

She presses the play button of Maud's cassette player:

> *Itsy bitsy spider*
> *Climbed up the water spout*
> *Down came the rain*
> *And washed poor Itsy out*

Who are they, these primpy singers? Three years at drama school and you wind up belting out nursery songs with such clarity that could ping your fillings out.

"Lapdancing?" I repeat.

"In a dirty old men's club?" barks Beth at my shoulder.

Rosie looks up, cheeks flushed prettily. "It's not just men. Women go, too. Lots of men take their girlfriends just for fun."

Beth breathes deeply, like a doctor's checking her chest.

"Maybe Matthew would be up for it," I tease. "There's your night out. You were moaning about him never surprising you."

"I don't think so." Beth's neck tendons jut out as if they might snap.

"It's not what you think," says Rosie. "The girl does her dance, that's the end of it. There's no touching."

"And what did you wear for this *dancing?*" enquires Beth.

Rosie plants Maud on her knee, landing a kiss upon scrubby hair. "Nothing. You have to wear knickers for pole dancing though. They're pretty strict about that."

Beth hoists Maud from Rosie's lap. The child howls in protest, straining towards her new best friend. "Where are we going?" I ask, following Beth as she clomps downstairs. Despite the lazy heat she bundles Maud into a chunky knitted jacket, striped like Neapolitan ice cream, plus a marshmallow sun hat, snapping the press-stud shut among Maud's many chin folds. "We're going for a walk," she announces.

"It's not like you," I say, "desperate to go out."

She stuffs Maud's left foot into a sheepskin bootie. "I feel cooped up. Actually, I'm nauseous."

"Maybe it's the wine," I suggest. "You're not used to it. Bad idea, drinking in the day. If I did it too often I'd be slugging all afternoon. I *love* wine."

I shouldn't have said that. That's the trouble with the coffee morning crew. Occasionally you forget that you don't know each other, not really, and that your friendship is built upon the terries-versus-disposables debate and a collective horror of dog muck.

Beth attempts to feed Maud's hand into a rainbow-striped mitten. "It's not the wine," she says, as Maud shakes it off. "How would you feel, knowing someone you'd hired—someone you trusted with your *most pre-*

cious thing—was willing to dance, stark naked, for men?" She squashes the now bellowing Maud into her buggy, aggressively strapping her in. "I'm not a prude, you know that. But she could have warned me, instead of landing it on me out of the blue."

"You didn't ask," I suggest.

"What would I have asked? Hello, darling, do sit down. Now tell me, is there anything I should know about your past?" Beth flashes a brief, manic smile.

"She seems lovely. Don't let it spoil things." Why am I taking the side of someone with whom I've conversed for less than five minutes?

"She's a prostitute," Beth hisses. "Tell me you really believe they just writhe on a pole. If they're prepared to do that, they'll do anything for money."

Rosie trips lightly downstairs. "You're not allowed to meet the guy privately," she says. "The club would lose its license if you did."

I steal a glance at her body, at the biscuity middle that dips in like a sand dune as she reaches for Maud's changing bag from the hook in the hall. On spotting her new primary carer, Maud relaxes and smiles.

"I'll bring the rug and some toys," says Rosie, "so Maud can play in the sunshine."

We buffet out of the house, with *Polly Put the Kettle On* chiming weakly from the playroom.

In the playing field Beth plants herself on a bench. Before I had Ben, I couldn't grasp the concept of urban parks. Those angular green shapes on the A-Z were in-

teresting only to rottweilers and their fat-necked owners. And those daytime people, shunting buggies.

Beth's park, in the green splodge pecking order, is
lower down the food chain than ours. "We were clever
to buy here," she confided once. She sounded like
Jonathan. No one bought flats where they wanted to live
anymore: they bought to be clever. "It's the next hot
spot," Beth insisted. "Look at the gift shops with their
wrought iron candlesticks and ethnic doo-dahs." Passing
through Beth's area, you might be conned by its rinky-
dinkiness: useless shops selling candles too expensive to
burn. But wherever you are, the park tells it like it really
is. Beth tries not to register the Bacardi Breezer bottles
slumped in the grass. When a man in a shimmering track-
suit allows his greyhound to defecate on the grass, she
doesn't have it in her to say anything or even thrust him
a POOP leaflet.

Rosie lies on the blanket with both babies. "Do you
mind if I strip her off a bit?" she asks. "She's roasting in
all these layers."

"Whatever you think's best," Beth manages.

It can't be easy, two adults doing essentially the same
job, stifled in politeness. I wondered how it would be to
have another female, especially one as eye-pleasing as
Rosie, emerging from the bathroom at 7:00 a.m., fragrant
and moist from her shower.

Beth hooks wiry hands into her hair. Her plaits have
come out. When she removes her fingers, clumps stick
out like birds' wings.

"We should have brought sunscreen," I say, to take her

mind off the dancing. She rubs papery fingers together. Beth has eczema. It bubbles up, she told me once, the instant she feels out of kilter inside. As if her skin is rejecting her body and wants to get away from it. "Nina," she says suddenly, "see that blanket?" Maud kicks happily on her back, batting the blanket with a rattle. "I made it," she tells me.

"You're clever. I wouldn't have the patience."

"Started it the minute we conceived. Well, as soon as the pregnancy was confirmed. We'd been trying for over two years. All the tests. By then it had become mechanical. Like putting oil in the car. At the wrong times, I wasn't interested. Seemed like a waste. And then, when it happened, I started working on that blanket, right until labor pains kicked in. Like a good luck thing, to make the baby seem real."

Beth has never before volunteered such personal information. I'm not sure what to do with it. "One hundred sixty-four buttercup squares," she continues. "Do you think that's why Matthew's gone off me?"

"It's a beautiful blanket," I say helplessly.

"And who'd bother, when you can buy one in John Lewis's baby department, probably better made? I had to bin half the squares, they were such pathetic, withered things. You know how your brain goes when you're pregnant? How you lose perspective? I was obsessed with that bloody blanket." She slides her wedding ring back and forth along a bubbly finger.

"Have you asked Matthew if there's anything wrong?"

"There's no chance to talk properly these days, not

with Rosie about, twenty-four hours a day, whizzing up Maud's juice."

"Shush," I say, "she'll hear you."

Beth stares ahead, hands now clasped tightly to her lap. Rosie stretches out slender brown legs. Beth smacks her hands to her mouth.

"What is it?" I ask.

"The cake. It's still in the oven."

Chase's flamboyant hair bushes upwards, its volume enhanced by some mousse-textured product. "My *girl,*" he says, bounding into reception. I'd forgotten my former editor's grand, cocky movements, which fill maximum space. "We've missed you," he announces. "There's a person-shaped hole where Nina should be." He takes a step back, appraising my appearance. I'm wearing a starchy gray jacket that wraps around me like cardboard. The buggy mars my professional aura. Ben sucks each finger in turn, hypnotized by the bright lights and Chase's beachball face.

From the moment we met, I liked Chase. On my first day at *Promise,* I'd slipped quietly to my desk to hide behind a PC. My colleagues gossiped about celebrities I'd never heard of and snazzy restaurants I hadn't eaten in. I felt too new, like shoes that hack holes in your ankles. Chase appeared at my desk, a hot air balloon of a man. "Let's have a chat in my office," he said, guiding me into his glass-partitioned cubicle. "Do you mind if I smoke? Trying to give up. I've been using this"—he waggled a white plastic fag substitute—"but you feel such a twerp. Might as well suck a biro."

The glass office quickly filled with creamy clouds. "You're doing an interview," he'd announced. "Pigeon woman of Bethnal Green. Loony. Feeds the birds, situation out of control. Neighbors, police, court orders. But she won't stop. Makes birdcakes from cornflakes stuck together with—I don't know. Some kind of grease. Now toddle along and don't forget to switch your tape recorder on."

Now I tail Chase to his office, feeling as much of a misfit as on that first day. The buggy clanks like unwieldy farm equipment. Will he light up a fag, even though I have Ben with me? What is it Beth says about passive smoking? Might as well offer your baby a cigarette. Cut out the middleman. Chase's words fling off in various directions: "I'd like you to take on the—I need you to come in and sort out the—" I hurry behind him, bashing the chair of an unfamiliar woman. Her nostrils flare at me.

"Bring the pram thing in," says Chase, barging into his office. His ashtray is shaped like a miniature Australia. Two butts rest in it, one eking smoke. With difficulty, I ease the buggy into the space beside floor-to-ceiling shelves bearing box files of rival magazines. The opposite wall displays the latest *Promise* covers. Each depicts a model showing her teeth (Chase's rules: big smile, bright lips, plain primary-colored top, though occasionally he'll allow pink), almost obscured by jangling coverlines and at least seventeen exclamation marks. To boost sales, some covers bear a taped-on free gift, like a sachet of hot chocolate or packet of pansy seeds. Just looking at them triggers a headache.

"I assume you want to come back," he says. "You can't dawdle about forever."

"Well, Jonathan keeps things going, money wise. I'm not in a hurry to start work." In fact, Jonathan and I never discuss my career options. The cashpoint always spouts the required number of tenners. I have nothing of my own, of course; less than nothing, having bought that ridiculous dress and sandals.

"You'll like what we're doing," continues Chase. "The whole triumph over tragedy thing's finished. Overkill. Every damn magazine chasing the same bloody woman who stashed her husband in a lock-up garage in Bradford. These people want paying, can you believe it? Not a sweetener, a few quid here and there. I'm talking *hundreds.*"

I'd forgotten how quickly he talked, how fast things were outside babyworld: staff darting from screen to screen, phones bleating for attention like hungry babies, and a willowy girl with stress on her forehead hammering a keyboard (*my* keyboard).

"The other weeklies," Chase rattles on, "they're so desperate they're making up stories. One woman who was supposed to have been married to a bigamist—picture of her at the front door with a suitcase—well, everyone knows it's their editorial assistant. The whole thing's set up, complete fiction. I interviewed her for a job once."

"So what's the new stuff you're doing?" I ask.

"Come and see for yourself."

I lift Ben from the buggy and check that he's in a photogenic condition. In just six months, *Promise*'s entire personnel appears to have changed. No one rushes forward, demanding to hold Ben. I feel like a work experience girl about to be shown how to operate a telephone. One lapel of my jacket is streaked by some kind of oily splash. I press a hand over it as if monitoring my heartbeat.

"We want warmth, a sense of caring," says Chase, indicating a double page spread on a screen. Two women are hugging in a nervous way. We Binned Our Cheating Love Rat reads the headline, And Now We're Best Mates.

"And we're bringing in a new regular page," Chase continues. "It's called My Secret, just a working title. An ordinary woman revealing something unexpected about her past."

"Sounds great," I enthuse in an abnormal voice.

"Could you take it on? One day a week. You can work here, you'll be glad to get out of the house. Or from home if you want—I'll get you a laptop."

"I have a PC."

"So what's the problem?"

"I don't have any child care," I mumble.

"You could bash this out in your sleep."

I want to say, "What sleep?" but hear my strained voice agreeing that I could fix something up, and leave the office promising to deliver the first My Secret in two weeks' time. Of course, I'll never find anyone. I've forgotten how to interview. I wonder what Chase will do with the blank page intended for my feature. What happened to star writer Nina? Can't find her computer's on button. Is this what childbirth does to the brain?

"I misjudged her," Chase will sigh. "Thought she could come up with the goods." And he'll ask Jess, my replacement, to slam in a giant crossword to fill the empty page.

With an hour to go before Jonathan is due home, I pore over the phone directory's Day Nursery section. Scamps, Tykes, Little Rascals. All imply that children are lovable, ruffly creatures rather than utter pains in the rear like Phoebe's kid with his mini black taxi and fascination with gas. I call Scamps to be informed that the waiting list stretches to almost a year, and that I should have put Ben's name down—accompanied by a sizable registration fee—when he was the size of an orange. At Tykes a panting girl wheezes, "Could you call back later? I'm manning the whole place myself."

I'm about to try Little Rascals when the phone rings. "Well done," says Lovely. "They want Ben."

"Who wants him?"

"Little Squirts, the bath products ad. Next Thursday."

"But he cried," I protest. "He was terrible."

"Maybe that's what they want. It's natural isn't it? Babies cry. They're not robots. Anyway, here are your details." She bangs out an address which I write on my hand and adds, "It's a classy job, Nina. Won't his daddy be proud?"

12

Making Bathtime Fun

Jonathan has cut himself shaving. He's applied a fragment of toilet paper to the nick which Ben tries to pick off during his goodbye kiss. "You're all bloody," I point out.

"I'm late," he snaps. "The alarm didn't go off. Did you tamper with it?"

"Of course I didn't. Don't blame me for your lateness."

He pulls on his murky blue jacket and trousers. An office suit, designed never to be worn for fun. "It's important, Nina, to be punctual," he says. "Especially today. You'll have to be up, rushing like I do, if you go back to work—*when* you go back to work." He laces up glossy black shoes, erasing a chalky smear with a licked finger.

"What do you mean, when?"

"Those nursery numbers by the phone. You're farming Ben out to strangers. We haven't even discussed it."

"I'm not farming him out. Chase wants me to do this little thing one day a week."

"You've always said Ben needs you at home."

Did I say that? I'm not sure I believe it. It's more logical, when you think about it, for your child to move into a nursery with competent adults who know how to prevent choking by sweeping small mouths with a finger, and who can construct vehicles with rotating wheels from milk cartons—people who've made babies their job.

"Look at Beth," Jonathan goes on. "She's happy. Maud's her priority. There's no question of her being put into care."

"Ben is my priority," I protest. "And Beth has an au pair. Most of the time she has *nothing to do.*"

Jonathan checks his watch. He's avoiding eye contact as if I'm a salesperson making him late by forcing my dusters on him. "I don't have time to discuss this," he says.

"You started it." I glimpse the scribbled address on my hand and hide it in the crook of my elbow.

"If you're unhappy, it might be a good idea to talk about it."

"I'm *happy,*" I shout, but he's already clattered out of the front door in a flurry of serious suit with a black zip-up bag containing casual clothes and his aloe vera skin conditioner. It's only then that I remember he's heading for Bath, to learn how to bond with his fellow men, and

I won't see him for three days. I want to run after him, say sorry and babble something about the Little Squirts ad. But he's gone.

I'm not worried about Ben's first, proper job. For all I care he can sit, Buddha-like, jabbing his belly button with a finger—because my child's debut advertising shoot will also be his last. The minute he's done his bit, sploshing in Little Squirts bubble bath (raspberry scented with skin-softening properties—as if babies are naturally lizardlike), I'll be on the phone to Lovely, telling her I'm not happy about Ben modeling at all.

I'm not sure I even like the woman. Surely, baby model agents should find children interesting and want to hear about their developmental milestones. Yet when I told her about Ben's new incisors stabbing right through our suede cushion cover, she said, "Really. So, if you have a pen ready, Nina, it's Unit B, Henrietta Wharf, ten-thirty start. Don't be late, or Marcus won't want to use him again."

It was that word: *use.* "Who's Marcus?" I asked.

"The director. You met at the audition?" she said with exaggerated surprise, as if I should be *au fait* with every big shot in the advertising world. And she rang off abruptly, leaving my questions—what should I take? How do I behave in front of these important adults?—unanswered.

Life without Jonathan is formless. I stay up too late, pacing the flat in the black dress and dangerous sandals imagining myself out, after dark, as a single person. I pout at myself in the bathroom mirror; even try to chat myself up. A stark, bitter face stares back. No one calls to check how I'm faring as a lone mother. I consider joining a support group. Jonathan's oldest friend Billy phones, but only to brag that he wound up at the end of the Northern Line and spent the night on a gravestone. "We're getting married," I tell him.

"Great! I'll start planning my speech."

I don't tell him that Jonathan is considering asking Matthew to be his best man, even though they only met through the antenatal classes. Matthew doesn't feel established enough to be a best anything. And Jonathan is concerned about inviting Billy at all.

The Little Squirts shoot looms constantly, clouding the space between my ears. I wake at odd times—at 5:56 a.m., worried that I'm a second late, my hand flapping for the alarm clock. It tumbles from the bedside table, knocking over Jonathan's carafe of water with the glass stopper to prevent germs from sneaking in. When Jonathan finally calls he says I sound distant, and why am I holding the phone away from my mouth? I'm not. I speak like there's a bubble in my throat. We ask each other questions like strangers ("How are you?" "Fine, how are you?"). He's not enjoying the course. The team has been instructed to build a pond at a young people's resource center. The idea is that they'll dig together and bond as a team, only Jonathan's been told not to bother with shovels and nip into Bath to buy cakes instead. "I'm not sure," he says, "that I'm really a team player."

Jonathan returns with a video of the pond work in progress. His colleagues grin at the camera, waving spades, and are splattered in mud. Jonathan stands a little away from them, looking clean. The night before the Little Squirts shoot, I'm aware of him guiding me back into bed. "You're sleepwalking," he says. "I found you at the wardrobe, rummaging through clothes, saying his blue fleecy jacket wouldn't do." I turn over my pillow and sink onto its cooler side. "Wouldn't do for what?" he asks.

"I don't know, just a dream."

"Maybe you've got a bug. Have you been eating properly while I've been away? There's hardly anything in the fridge. And your breathing doesn't sound right."

"I've got a lot on my mind."

He strokes my cheek. His finger feels like a spider. "Is it the wedding? It's no big thing, Nina. Promise you'll stop worrying."

"Promise," I say, hearing wind whistling through my nostrils.

Marcus's face pokes out from a crumpled shirt flapping over jeans baggy enough to house the seven babies and children present. He appears to be wearing the clothes of a larger, more robustly proportioned species. Despite being the director, and presumably in charge of proceedings, he doesn't talk to anyone. Certainly not the parents or children. I try to catch his eye, and give a little thank-you wave for casting Ben in the ad, but he stares crossly as if he's spotted me tampering with his car.

From the outside, the place appeared to be one vast, windowless slab. It took me fifteen minutes, circling the building miserably, to find a way in. Inside, though, the set gleams with food-coloring brilliance. Daffodils spring from fake grass, wafted by a wind machine. Toddlers slump on a faded sofa like their spines have been removed. On a TV with the sound down, Pingu pat-pats across pretend ice.

Across the building, two unkempt males stamp on AstroTurf, flattening bumps. A circular inflatable pool is being filled by a bony-bottomed woman with a gilt chain belt slung about her hips. In the area set aside for models and their parents—all mothers except one stiff-looking dad, who is flipping huffily through the *Daily Mirror*—everyone lolls about casually as if their children appear in commercials every day of the week. It's the done thing, I quickly figure out, to be utterly bored by such activities.

"We're only here because we know Marcus," boasts a golden-maned woman, windswept like she arrived by galloping horse. "He's Oscar's godfather. Oscar isn't even with an agency. Tots and Pepperpots want to sign him up but I'm not getting into that competitive nonsense."

"No, we don't have the time," says a West Indian woman, efficiently wiping her son's rear on a padded mat and folding the soiled nappy in on itself to form a dainty parcel. "If he's having fun, fine. But this friend of mine, her daughter did a picture for a magazine. Something about tantrums. The photographer kept them hanging about for hours in the rain, goading the little girl, even taking her favorite teddy away."

"Like he was trying to drum up a tantrum?" frowns the golden-haired woman.

"Exactly, though he didn't call it that. Said he needed a *defining moment.*"

Raven's mother is the last to arrive. She's sweating. Her hair is roughly bunched at the back of her head, like a shrub. "We'll discuss it later," she says, the child stumbling behind her, tugged along by a cuff. Lone father shuffles toward me to make sofa space for the latecomers. Raven's mother is wearing another velvet concoction, this time in a shade of dried blood.

The dad's toddler wants to sit with his face squashed against the telly and cries when he's told not to. I chuck the man a sympathetic look, as is my tendency when faced with lone father and child. Mothers go to pieces over men in charge of their children. I've done it myself, gushing, "How on earth do you manage?" to a dad pushing his child on a swing. A man has only to change a nappy—remembering to bring Pampers *and* wipes!—for women to burst into spontaneous applause and pin a Champion Dad medal on his snot-smeared T-shirt. A mother, on the other hand, can endure a supermarket shop, her furious offspring snatching at tins and opening cereal boxes to nab free CD-ROMs, and no passerby remarks, "You're doing a marvelous job." If they notice her at all, they merely eye her gnarled ankles and remind themselves to double up on contraception (coil plus industrial-strength condoms).

The skinny-hipped woman turns off the hose and pours pink gloop into the pool. "Hi, mums—and dad," she says, towering over us elegantly. "I'm Jackie. I'll be looking after you today." Lone father pays rapt attention to the strip of sunbed-fresh skin between her top and jeans. "Now, if you don't mind waiting, we're going to film with no children in the pool. The water's warm, but we don't want them in it for longer than they need to be."

"Wanna paddle," says Raven.

"There'll be time for that," Jackie says briskly. "Right, everyone happy?"

"Wanna go in the water," Raven thunders. Jackie shows her teeth and stalks back to the pool. She pulls several life-size dolls from a zip-up bag. They will float on their backs, surely, or facedown (hardly the fun image Little Squirts are aiming for). But, magically, the dolls bob the right way up; empty-eyed like the toys in a horror film that come alive as midnight strikes, wobbling eerily downstairs.

"I want that doll," says Raven.

"Look, darling, Pingu," her mother sighs.

"I want that doll with the big head."

"It'll be wet, darling. It'll soak your pretty dress." Raven's lips curl in on themselves. Her mother rummages in a secret velvet pocket and pulls out a tube of Rolos. Raven rips apart the gold foil, sending Rolos bouncing to the concrete floor. For a moment I feel sorry for the woman in her bleak velvet with nothing to do but drag her child from audition to audition and stitch outfits from Butterick patterns. Then I realize I'm not really so different except that, three decades back, her stab at making a cross-stitched sampler was undoubtedly better than mine.

Jackie places six pairs of padded pants on the table. "If you could pop one of these on," she says, "it'll save any little doo-doos in the pool."

"I don't think it'll fit me," I retort.

She grimaces politely and turns to Raven's mother. "We'll have Raven in the pool last, on her own, in this darling pink swimsuit. Would you do that for me, Raven?" Raven hunches before Pingu, posting Rolos between her lips. She doesn't appear to be chewing or swallowing. I wondered how many she'll manage to stuff in before they start falling out.

Ben wriggles excitedly as I feed his limbs into the padded pants. In the pool he bobs gently, supported by a duck-shaped inflatable seat. He flicks water experimentally. As the other babies join him, he busies himself by tweaking the duck's beak. Remarkably he is behaving as if this pool, crammed with unfamiliar babies, is our ordinary bath at home.

Each child appears on the monitor in turn, except Ben. He frowns intently, stroking yellow plastic, until a crucial part of his baby brain reminds him that he's not here to wallow in warm water, but to work. He looks up, wide-eyed and grinning, as if the unwieldy camera, sliding slowly toward him on a track, is a bulbous, milk-filled teat.

"Oh!" says the golden-maned woman. Ben's face fills the monitor in an advert not for Little Squirts gunk but parenthood itself: *look what you can make if you put your mind to it. Even if you don't. One little slip-up, and here's the result.*

Ben blinks at the camera. The lone father sets down his *Daily Mirror.* There's silence, then a ripple of applause. "Fantastic," says Jackie, scooping Ben out of the water and wrapping him in a yellow hooded towel. "You have a little star on your hands."

It's over so quickly, this happy scene that even Jonathan couldn't complain about. I'll tell him tonight. We'll have dinner and wine and afterward, I'll say something like, "Jonathan, I haven't been completely straight with you. Ben and I—we've been…" He'll look cross for an instant, and say it's the deceit he has trouble with, not the modeling. Couldn't I have told him? Did I really think he'd fly off the handle over something so trivial? But he'll understand that I'd only wanted a change, some respite from Beth and her floury kitchen. I'll hug him, relieved to have brought everything out into the open. We'll go to bed, and he'll climb on me and off again, the way he does these days, like it's a task to cross off the list:

Veg from market
Buggy tire
Wedding rings
Sex

And we'll get on with planning the wedding. Nothing flashy, bit of a wine bar buffet. We're married already, really. We have a married food processor and married sex. We might have been together for decades. As for the modeling, Jonathan will allow Ben to continue if it makes me happy. Next time—there's bound to be a next time—he might even come along too.

"You've done what?" rasps Eliza.

"Ben's done an ad," I repeat, my voice lurching as the cab jolts over speed bumps. "Marcus said he was a star. A natural. Soon he won't be getting out of his cot for less than ten thousand quid."

She laughs bitterly. "I didn't think you'd take it this far. Only used Ben in my shoot to get you out of the house."

I didn't expect this response. I assumed Eliza, scornful of stay-home-mothers, would be glad that I'd snatched a little glamour, even if only via my son's dazzling good looks.

"Greg, your photographer, recommended him to an agency," I start to explain.

"He's with an *agency?*" she splutters.

"It's just one little ad," I say huffily, "that'll probably be shown in Japan or something."

"What? On national Japanese TV?"

"I don't know. I forgot to ask."

Strapped into his seat, Ben sleeps in a haze of synthetic raspberry. I'm worried now. What if the modeling thing escalates out of control? If he starts demanding star treatment, batting away substandard food? He might get ideas above his station. Even demand a new mother. "What does Jonathan think?" Eliza asks.

"He doesn't know."

"There you are," she snorts triumphantly. "You know how he'll react. How much is Ben getting paid for this?"

"Not much," I say. In fact, I don't know how much. I haven't asked. It hardly seems important.

"You should have found out," she rattles on. "It might be child exploitation. Didn't you sign some sort of contract?"

I open the yellow box on my lap; it's adorned with pink squiggles and contains the entire Little Squirts range. Our thank-you present. Raven refused to get into the pool. She wore the swimsuit, but smeared melted Rolos all over the front. They didn't get a goody box.

"I'm not doing it for the money," I say lamely.

"Then why are you doing it?"

I fondle a tube of Little Squirts shampoo: a nourishing blend of kiwi and papaya, *because we care about your baby as much as you do.*

"Not for the money," I snap.

Jonathan shows up at around nine, whiffing of old wine. He's been out for a drink with Billy. Their nights out generally happen after three cancellations (by Jonathan) and leave him exhausted from the effort of trying to unfriend his oldest mate. It's the opposite to befriend. It happens when someone likes and needs you too much. "I don't know why he insists on this old drinking buddy thing," says Jonathan, draping his rain-speckled jacket on a chair. "I've never been anyone's drinking buddy. I'd rather be home with you."

He lands on the bed like a worn-out cushion. "Have you eaten?" I ask.

He shakes his head. "Could you rustle something up?" This throws me. I don't rustle; Jonathan does. I survive on snacks—plus whatever Jonathan cooks—and barely think about meals. "Perhaps," he says carefully, "you could start picking up a few bits during the day."

"What kind of bits?" I ask.

"Food," he says, giving me a sharp look. "You know— for meals. Seeing as you're home all day." He steps out of his trousers, aligning each leg's creases on the hanger. "All I mean is, maybe you could knock up the odd pasta sauce. If you have a spare moment. During the day."

He rubs his forehead as if trying to erase wrinkles. Since his promotion to team leader, Jonathan's clothes have become looser, his cheeks concave. He has started to bring home convenience meals, which he picks at. One evening, instead of presenting the usual fresh combo—a fig and Parma ham salad, say—he microwaved a ready-made thing called an ocean pie that leaked margarine as it heated.

"You're saying I have acres of time?" I blurt out. "Big, empty days, when I could be whipping up fancy sauces and freezing them?"

He unbuttons his white shirt slowly, casting it into the wicker linen basket. He shrugs on a mottled gray T-shirt that droops at his shoulders. "I know you're busy," he says quietly. "I've been calling you all day—your mobile's always switched off. I don't want to keep tabs on you, Nina, but it would be nice to know where you are."

"Why did you want me?" I ask cautiously.

"I wondered if you'd managed to sort out the venue. If the Fox can do the cold buffet with a poached salmon centerpiece. You know—for our *wedding*."

"I forgot. I'll do it tomorrow."

He gives me a quick look, strides into the living room and busies himself with Ben's tickly belly. "Time's running out," he reminds me.

"But it's three months away."

Ben is failing to respond to Jonathan's raspberry-blowing endeavors. Our son lolls, head flopped to one side, shattered after a hard day's modeling.

"Yes, and people spend years planning a wedding. There's a lot to think about."

I wish he'd give up, stop rasping on Ben's bare belly; I'm scared he'll detect a fruity whiff or a glimmer of glamour and stardom.

To Jonathan, of course, he's the same old Ben.

"I thought the wedding wasn't meant to be a big thing," I say to myself, chalking Call Fox with several underlines on the kitchen noticeboard.

Now officially in charge of food preparation for my entire family, I decide that it's unnecessary to cook from scratch every evening or even produce anything hot. Limoncello, the new deli that's appeared in place of the terrifying dentist's where you wouldn't want to open your mouth, let alone have anyone rummage about in it, is the answer to our culinary quandary. It's staffed by cheerful drama student types with affluent teeth and navy-and-white-striped aprons. I purchase ham, salami, ready-made salads and flour-dusted loaves weighing half a ton. Surely, if all the main food groups put in an appearance—protein, carbs, a scattering of leaves—nothing dreadful will happen to our bones or eyesight. And I won't have to cook *per se,* just assemble.

It works. Having meals put before him is such a novelty for Jonathan that I gain several thousand Brownie points. "Great salami," he says, tucking into my first offering. "Wonderful salad, Nina. Is this lamb's lettuce?" I nod, adding that we will eat from Limoncello from now on. We'll live simply, like the Italians or French with their enormous families and joke-telling grannies, clustering around vast kitchen tables. We might even have wine in the day.

"Funny you mention big families," he says. "There's no rush. It's not like your biological clock thing's going off just yet. But I was thinking…"

A scrap of salami sticks in my throat. Maybe I should have peeled off the stringy outer layer. What's it made of anyway? Pig gut or indigestible plastic? "Can't have Ben being an only child," he continues. "I'm one, you're one. Look how we turned out."

He looks up from his plate, smiling hopefully. I yank a strip of salami rind from between my front teeth. "We turned out okay," I say bravely.

After three weeks of deli cuisine, Jonathan suggests that we expand our repertoire. He eases the buggy through Saturday morning market crowds, apologizing each time he grazes a shin or ankle. Most of the stalls offer tie-dyed trousers and wraparound skirts made from sari material and other ethnic garments to suggest that your passport enjoys regular outings. Most of the shoppers have a hung-over air and are fit only for flicking through racks of scratched vinyl, and eating. Nearly everyone seems to be scoffing something. A bleary-eyed boy bites into pita bread, dolloping hummus onto Ben's soft leather bootee. We shove our way out to the quiet terraced streets, having managed to buy only a brown paper bag of organic radishes.

Too far from home, Ben starts bleating. "Let's stop and give him his bottle," I suggest.

Jonathan eyes a patch of grass bordered by haggard rose bushes and chipped black railings. "What, here?" he says. "It's not very—"

Ben roars his requirement for liquid refreshment. We park at a cast-iron bench graffitied with If You Want To Do It With Melissa Call… The number has been scribbled out in fat black marker pen. Jonathan's arm rests protectively around my shoulders. The small play area is entirely grassed, apart from a cracked concrete rectangle beneath the boat-shaped climbing frame, ensuring a serious head injury should your child tumble off. "Is there anywhere you'd like to go?" Jonathan asks.

I look up at the maisonettes clustered round the park, their balconies tumbling with lobelia. "We should head home. Ben's nappy smells serious and I forgot to bring a spare."

"No, for our honeymoon. We'd better book something soon. Any ideas?"

How strange that we've arrived at mum and dad-ness, yet have never actually been anywhere together. We haven't had time for holidays or even jaunts to the country like Beth and Matthew. They're away this weekend. Just the two of them. Shropshire. Couple time, Beth called it; vital for retaining one's intimacy. Reluctantly, she's weaned Maud off the breast. Bosoms like concrete for the first few days, and milk squeezed out in the shower to whirl down the plughole ("What a waste!" she lamented. "But it's worth it. I'm reclaiming my breasts. Actually, and it's probably no coincidence, Matthew's become interested in sex again, like he's remembered I'm a *woman*.").

With the bottle drained, Ben nods off on Jonathan's lap. "Where's hot in December?" I ask. *West Indies. Yes, the West Indies. White sand. Bikini. No, perhaps not bikini. A silvery one-piece with cutaway sides. I'll have to work on those sides. Forget pelvic floor squeezes. I'll do sit-ups. Crunches, they call them, which sounds dangerous. Start with ten a day and work up to twelve, maybe thirteen.*

It occurs to me that I have no idea of Jonathan's preferences in terms of countries. I can't imagine him in swimming trunks. It's me who takes Ben to the pool; we still brave it once a week, despite the Ranald humiliation. And the sun: Jonathan's skin wasn't designed for it. I wonder if he's ever taken a holiday. He's never shown me pictures or talked about places he's visited. "Where did you go," I ask, "when you were a kid?"

"Scotland," he says, "every year. A farm that did B&B. They got to know me and Mum over the years. They sent Christmas cards. If we went early enough they'd take me out to the fields and I'd feed the lambs with a bottle. Mum watched from the fence, scared I'd be bitten.

"They had a games cupboard," he continues. "Cluedo, Mousetrap, and that one with the spikes you pull out of holes and the marbles drop down." I imagine Jonathan and Constance agreeing that it didn't matter about the rain; there was always the games cupboard with everything just how they'd left it. No wonder she finds me difficult to be around. When there's only ever been two of you, a newcomer sticks out awkwardly with her big mouth and walloping backside. Maybe a family functions more simply and happily when there's hardly anyone in it.

"Did anyone else ever go," I ask, "on these holidays?" Jonathan dabs Ben's dribbling nose with the monogrammed cotton hankie he always keeps in a pocket, waking him instantly. Ben squirms crossly, backing away from the big, wiping hand.

"Who was there to go?" he asks.

"Well, your dad."

"All Mum has ever said is that there was someone. Obviously there was someone. But he wasn't available for her. That was her line. I never thought to ask any more." I want to ask more, to know everything. Why does he do this: offer only fragments of information? Maybe that's all there is to tell. "I wonder if they're still alive," he says. "That couple, the Brodies, at the B&B."

"You could look them up. Would your mum have their number?"

"We could go," he says. I wonder if this is a joke. I think about countering with Mexico. Eliza is in Mexico. The idea is to have the model diving in diaphanous dresses and shoot the whole thing underwater. "I'd like to show you," he adds, "and Ben would love it. Feeding the lambs."

"There won't be lambs in December," I say, feeling sick.

"Mum would be delighted," he adds. I am on the brink of vomiting. "What I mean is, Mum would love it if *we* went."

I'm so relieved I hear myself saying, "Then why don't we go?"

Jonathan kisses me with unexpected force. Ben yowls, alarmed at this public display of affection. "Kerplunk," says Jonathan. "That's the game with the sticks. Wonder if it's still in that cupboard?"

13

Involving Grandma

As a fashion stylist Eliza is concerned about my wedding attire and has thoughtfully stolen the last six issues of *Confetti* magazine. Its editorial offices are one floor up from hers, nabbing the best views. "Underworked ponces," she announces. "How hard can it be, bunging out four issues a year? 'And what shall we cover this time? Oh, I know. Wedding dresses. Honeymoons. Dainty shoes. And some sort of quiz: does he have husband potential or is he a lying, scheming ratbag?'"

I've left Ben at home with Jonathan. On my first night out since giving birth, I'm lying on my belly on Eliza's carpet, an autumnal swirl of rust and bile that you could be sick or even die on, and everything would blend in. Eliza's cat meanders in, eyeing me suspiciously.

Dear Natalie, Penny of Droitwich has written to *Confetti's* problem page. *Should I write the names of the individual people I am inviting on each invitation, or can I just put their names on the envelopes?*

Clearly Penny isn't getting out much. I wonder how long it might take for her prospective husband to discover he has made a hideous error of judgment and start going on too many overnight conferences.

Dear Natalie,
I plan to personalize the ribbon to tie my bouquet and have taken calligraphy classes. What sort of pen should I use?
Chloe, Saffron Walden

Dear Chloe,
I wouldn't advise writing on ribbon—it might come off and stain your hands, especially if they're sweaty with nerves on the day. Luckily several mail-order companies are happy to print ribbon with your own personal wording.

Natalie—help! My bridesmaids will hold pink rosebud posies but what should the page boys carry?
Sally, Dumfries

You're right to assume that boys won't want to carry flowers. How about satin ring cushions? They're light, easy to hold, and perfect for keeping little hands occupied.

What would little boys do with those hands, I wonder, without miniature cushions to clutch? I'll have to watch it, Beth warned, when Ben's old enough to investigate his private parts. "Boys are always delving down there," she shuddered. "Fumbling, can't leave the thing alone." As good reason as any, she said, to keep them bound up in nappies for as long as possible. Access denied.

"You don't want anything too fitted," says Eliza, joining me on the carpet. "You won't enjoy yourself, sucking in your stomach all day."

The sole source of light is an anglepoise lamp which dangles lazily, casting a creamy oval onto a speckled Formica table. Eliza's furniture appears to have been acquired from skips; precarious shelving, right angles not quite right, immense stacks of dusty magazines. There's a heady smell, pulpy and thick. Somewhere in the flat, bad things are happening in a fruit bowl.

"You don't want to *think* about your belly," Eliza continues, examining a picture of a frightful wedding gown that appears to have been constructed from doilies. "You want loose but not tenty—something you can put on and forget."

"You're right," I say. "I was thinking of a duffel coat."

She sighs, spreading out pages ripped from *Confetti*. Hot look for the modern bride: sleek and simple with ruffles at the neck and shoulders, lending a dandy edge. "How do you feel about bare arms?" she barks.

I'm not sure how I feel about anything. *Confetti*—with

its delicate veils, its lilac sugared almonds trapped in net pouches—makes me feel like some gigantic, snorting ox. The girl in the ruffled dress doesn't look as if she's about to get married. Too young, for one thing; let down the scooped-up hair with its lacquered crust and she'd pass as a schoolgirl like those in the changing village, all jutting collarbones and dangling arms, useful for batting off attention from boys.

No, you wouldn't look so poised, so serene, if your wedding was about to happen. You'd have a neck rash. I wonder whether dandy ruffles would avert attention from a blotchy décolleté.

Eliza's skinny knees crackle as she stands up. She heads for the kitchen in search of bread to make toast—the only food I've ever seen her eat, apart from sugar cubes. She seems disappointed. Maybe I'm not taking this seriously enough. The living room hums with decaying fruit, practically breathing all by itself. I feel like I'm inside a lung.

I flick through *Confetti.* So many crucial aspects I haven't considered: cars, seating plans, order of speeches. "No bread," calls Eliza from the kitchen. "Want a gin and tonic?" I have encountered Eliza's G&Ts: half pint of Gordons, token splash of warm tonic. No lemon or ice. She strides back with two tea glasses patterned with gold stripes and spriggy flowers. She used to collect them. She's collected plates shaped like lettuce leaves, intricate fans, asymmetrical hats that always looked a bit dented. But she always loses interest before there's enough to make a collection. Before it means anything.

"I've met someone," she announces, arranging herself cross-legged beside me. She gulps greedily from the tea glass.

"Why didn't you say? Who is it?"

She laughs, making light of it. "It's probably over already. And it's embarrassing. He's way younger. And I'm old enough to know better."

I have no idea of Eliza's real age. Several years ago, she celebrated her thirtieth birthday on a riverboat decked out in "louche chic," as she called it, with swathes of jeweled Indian fabric draped everywhere and some kind of twanging sitar music. The following year, a prissier affair in a small, blond-wood bar with waiters serving mini fish and chips in cone-shaped napkins was her real thirtieth, she claimed. She picks at a vexed-looking scab on her shin.

"He can't be that young," I suggest.

"Well, he's twenty-four, so it's ridiculous. Go on, slap me."

I laugh, testing the gin with my tongue. It feels wrong: too warm for its alcoholic strength.

"It's Dale," she says. "Remember Greg's assistant? You met at that shoot. I'm not expecting it to come to anything. It's just, you know, a physical thing."

"When did this happen?"

"Mexico trip. Disaster. Models deliberately burnt themselves. Hadn't heard of sunscreen, obviously. So we can't use them. Have to fly in someone else whose flight's stuck in Houston for seven hours and gets food poisoning from a chicken baguette she ate at the airport."

"I didn't think models ate," I say.

By some open-throated trick, Eliza tips the entire glassful of gin down her neck. "That's the thing. They pick out the fillings, leave the bread. And that's the dangerous bit. So we've nothing to do but get plastered until the poison works itself through. He's quite a laugh, you know."

When she's like this, grazed and tatty looking, I remember why I like Eliza so much. Her blue nail polish is chipped at the tips. Her shins are bristly. "Can I bring him to your wedding?" she asks suddenly. "Not as a boyfriend—he's an embryo, for God's sake—but just so I've got someone to, you know, just be with. Weddings make me feel so noticeable."

It hadn't occurred to me that my wedding, or any wedding, might make Eliza feel anything. I'd have thought she'd relish the opportunity to dress up. "Of course you can," I tell her. "So long as he doesn't bark."

Confetti lies open at the shoe page. Those pink, beaded objects aren't human's shoes. They belong in a museum or on a doll. I imagine the crystal-encrusted structures straining, eventually collapsing into sobs, if I managed to ram myself into them.

"Great shoes," says Eliza, "but not with your wide feet."

I am spending the night in Eliza's spare room on a blow-up bed that has defied her lung capacity and is therefore only partially inflated. When I lie on my side, my hipbone crunches into the floor. A flurry of tangled underwear bursts from a battered chest of drawers, possibly trying to escape Eliza's flat for an orderly home where it will be folded and treated respectfully.

Transparent dresses dangle on hangers at the windows, hazing the streetlight. Eliza has rented her flat for over a decade, having fallen heavily in lust with its cracked lilac bathroom suite. She didn't mind negotiating the abandoned fridge parked on the stairs. For several years she squeezed past it, bumping against the chrome handle. Then one day it was gone. A new family had moved in below, cramming their flat with ornately carved furniture, too many kids and possibly the fridge. The kids block the stairs with their intricate games involving witches' outfits and domestic mops which they ride recklessly. But Eliza won't move. Her flat has reached that comfortable point at which it cannot become any messier and may even begin to self-cleanse, like hair when you give up on washing it. It doesn't get dirtier. Or perhaps you just stop noticing.

I hear Eliza flicking off lights and clunking some bony part of her anatomy on something solid. From where I'm lying the fruit smell is worse. I investigate a glazed bowl on the chest of drawers. Bluish spheres, possibly once tangerines, fuzz uncertainly. My stomach growls, reminding me of the promised toast which never materialized. I can still taste the gin. I squirm on the bed, willing sleep to come, wondering if Eliza's bras might tumble from the open drawer and strangle me.

"Nina? Sorry to bother you on a Saturday morning." The cab rattles along the main thoroughfare which joins

Eliza's neighborhood to mine. "It's Lovely," says the chirpy voice. "Ben has another booking, but it's next week. I wanted you to know straight away. To check his availability."

I am barely awake and starving. Eliza was still semi-asleep when I left and muttered something about a crois-sant at the back of the fridge. I peered in there and found only a bottle of murky stuff, for detoxing.

"You didn't tell me," Lovely gushes, "how amazing Ben was on the Little Squirts shoot. Marcus—you know Marcus—says he's never seen such a natural. He comes alive, Marcus said, for the camera. You'd never think it, would you, when you see him in the flesh?" Her enthu-siasm bubbles out of the phone like lemonade. "So he wants him for another job. You don't even need to au-dition. It's on Friday—I take it that's okay? He'll be rid-ing in a supermarket trolley. Marcus just wants to check he can sit up."

"Just about," I say. "He's a bit wobbly, but if I—"

"And he's fine, isn't he, when you wheel him round the supermarket? He's used to that, is he?"

The cab pulls up outside the flat. Our bedroom cur-tains are closed. I feel grubby in yesterday's clothes and can detect the fruit smell, hanging about my hair. "Ben's never been to a supermarket," I confess. "We do all our shopping at a deli because it's easier with the—"

"So Friday's good?" she cuts in. "I'm so glad. I have a feeling—and I never say this to parents—that Ben's going to work and work. It'll take commitment, you know. You'll need your partner's full support."

The driver drums the steering wheel, wanting me out. I could have walked from Eliza's but felt too done in by a night on the blow-up bed. By the time I woke up, it had completely deflated.

The bedroom curtain flutters. Jonathan holds Ben at the window and waves. "Of course," I tell Lovely. "He couldn't be more supportive."

We arrive at Constance's just after two, although it could be any time of day or night. She keeps her curtains drawn, apparently to stop burglars peeping in. The room is bathed in brown shadow and smells biscuity. Jonathan likes to believe that we drop in on Constance every couple of weeks but in reality it's less often. I suspect that each time we leave he adds a mental tick to the brain compartment labeled Guilt About Mother. Certainly he is unusually buoyant after each visit.

Constance's living room is engulfed by a lumbering burgundy three-piece suite and glazed ornaments teetering on every horizontal surface. A cluster of shepherdesses and several porcelain birds of prey (life-size) gawk from the mantelpiece. The sofa arms are draped with peach crocheted covers, as if skin contact would damage them irreparably.

"No need to feed us," says Jonathan anxiously. "We've already eaten. A cup of tea will do fine." He says this each time we visit, presumably to avoid ingesting anything riskier than a finger Nice biscuit. He's scared of her food. Most of the edibles at Constance's are considerably older than our child. That jar of Schwartz All Spice bears a label of unfamiliar design; a box of sponge biscuits, intended for trifles, was possibly purchased during the poncho era. Odd ends of things lurk in the fridge: one halved peach in a dish, a leftover egg yolk, some kind of dense, gray fat, resting in a china teacup. When Constance goes to the bathroom, Jonathan springs to the kitchen and minesweeps the pantry, burying confiscated foodstuffs at the bottom of the beige plastic bin.

"I don't usually let strangers in," Constance is telling Jonathan. "But such a nice young couple. Smartly dressed. Clean and polite for young people."

"Who are these people?" Jonathan asks.

"Their church isn't my church," continues Constance, "but I'll listen. Such a well-mannered man."

"What church?" says Jonathan irritably.

Constance wanders to the kitchen. She steps onto a rickety stepladder to reach a carrier bag of potatoes from the shelf above the sink. "Get off that stool," says Jonathan. "Keep your food down low where you can reach it. What church?"

"Jehovah's Witness, I think. They didn't say. But they left me a color magazine and said they didn't want money, but you know me. Always pay my way. So I gave them five pounds."

"You what?" splutters Jonathan.

"They're coming back next week," she smiles. "It's nice to have the company."

Ben squirms on my lap, itching to acquaint himself with the shepherdesses. One has an extremely fragile-looking crook. I place him on the deep-pile hearth rug which he sucks experimentally. Constance squints at me like I'm a stain. "Well," she says, "I'd better check the meat."

"I told you, Mum, we don't want lunch," Jonathan calls after her.

While she's out of the room I want to hiss: why is she like this with me? Is she dreadfully disappointed in her son's choice of woman? But I don't know him well enough. I know him well enough to have a baby with but not to say anything even slightly controversial about his mother. Instead I stare at a porcelain falcon who eyes me suspiciously.

Constance reappears carrying plates loaded with dark meat, gravy and gray potatoes and sets them on an oval dining table. "Brown sauce?" she asks Jonathan.

"No thanks," he mutters, "this looks lovely as it is."

She hovers over us, watching us saw at the meat.

"Aren't you going to sit down?" Jonathan says.

She lowers her bottom onto a chair with a bobbly mustard seat. Perhaps Jonathan is wise to be cautious about her food. It's poisoned. Or at least mine is. She glowers at my plate, checking that I'm tucking into the right piece, the one with the strychnine.

"Mum, we have good news," announces Jonathan. He seems to be having difficulty with the meat. His jaws bounce, getting nowhere. "We've set a date," he says, swallowing with a gulp. Constance drags her gaze away from my plate and peers sadly at her own. Her hair fluffs limply at her cheeks. "For the wedding," he adds.

She dips her fork into the gravy and sucks it. "Those

people are coming back, did I tell you? Monday I think. They won't convert me, I've made that quite clear. But I like having visitors." She looks up at me, wondering why I haven't keeled over and cracked my skull on the hearth.

Unlike Constance, my mother was keen for me to meet someone. Anyone, in fact. She would invite young males round, embarrassing boys, like the sons of my teachers or the sick-looking lad who roamed our street with a radio jammed to his ear, talking to himself. She'd heat up food to get on their good sides, like Findus Crispy Pancakes. This was pre-Ashley when she'd never have dreamed of taping horse pills to her temples. She bought cheap yellow cakes and sprinkled sugar on everything, even Ski yogurt. It gritted my teeth. By secondary school I had eleven fillings. She wore too few clothes when these boys came round (or maybe she always did, but I only noticed when we had guests). You could see her thighs through her thin skirt, her graying bra under a faded nylon blouse. She reminded me of that boys' fantasy, the one where they're wearing X-ray specs, allowing them to see through women's clothes. "She's got good legs, your mum," said the radio boy, and he went a bit sweaty about the forehead.

These boys and I would mooch in separate rooms. The guest would fritter about in my bedroom, finding nothing of interest apart from a shoe box of dried up felt tips and a Spirograph set. I'd hang about in the spare room, huddled under abandoned ironing boards and chairs with tarnished chrome legs. Eventually Mum stopped bothering to ask anyone over. She called me unsociable. She was right; I didn't want anyone else in my house. I met a studious Glaswegian boy with an unstable complexion and a love of hefty literature but I didn't bring him home. He took me to the back of the tennis court where wet bracken grazed our legs. We kissed, then he pulled out his penis and waggled it furiously. His eyes glazed. I worried that he might burst a blood vessel. "Do you mind if I jerk off?" he asked, midwaggle.

I thought he said: "Do you mind if I Chekov?"

Jonathan is in his usual post-Constance mood (Visited Mother: tick!). "She has to get out," he says, glancing sideways from the driver's seat to check that I'm listening. "Those houses were new when she moved in. People cut their hedges. Talked to each other. Now look at them. No wonder she keeps the curtains shut."

"Aren't there lunch clubs and whist drives and stuff?" I suggest.

"She should move. She needs people around. We'll have to do something."

I picture Constance living with us, banging our pans and cooking her meat, and decide not to go there. "She didn't seem happy about our wedding," I say carefully.

He laughs. "I can't imagine Mum being happy about anyone I chose to marry."

Why do grown women wish to cling on to their offspring? Will I be that way with Ben, glaring at girlfriends, scaring them off with my cooking? Beth told me her mother cried for a week, constantly hurtling off into other rooms, splashing her face with cold water, when she announced her engagement to Matthew. Well, I can understand that. But I can't imagine feeling quite so cross, as if I've been burgled, when Ben leaves home.

My parents barely flinched when I moved out. They drove me south, becoming trapped on the M25, my mother flapping the map, saying, "It doesn't show individual streets. We'll be going round and round forever." Dad dived off at a random junction and we trundled around East London, passing the Museum of Childhood five times. A policeman glared suspiciously. On each occasion, Mum piped up, "That building looks jolly. What is it?" Finally Dad pulled up at a rickety house with a club called Jingles below it. I had landed a job as a reader of unsolicited stories sent to a women's magazine, most of which turned out to be written illegibly in blobby green biro. My new boss had told me about a vacant flat owned by her friend. One living room wall was painted gloss black and the whole place stank of drains. "This looks nice," remarked Mum. "You'll soon freshen it up."

Dad carried in grocery boxes stuffed with my rubble and looked like he might hug me, but didn't. "We'll be off," he announced. "We need to find something to eat before everywhere shuts."

Jonathan raps the horn as a cyclist zips in front of us. "We should get Mum and your parents together," he says. "I'm due holiday. Why don't I take Friday off, do a barbecue?"

Friday: Ben's maiden voyage in a supermarket trolley. "Friday's not good," I tell him.

He flicks his eyes at me, surprised that I might have a prior engagement. "The coffee morning crew," I babble. "Teddy bears' picnic in the park. As long as the weather's okay."

He pats my knee. "I'm glad you've made a life, Nina. I worried that you might not…adapt." I try to relax with his hand now plonked on my thigh, but I can't. My fib hums round the car. I wonder if he can hear it. "Some other time then," he says. "But it'll have to be soon. We can't have them sitting together at the registry office, not knowing each other from Adam."

I shudder to think how my mother will behave before Constance. In the presence of strangers, Mum regresses to girlhood, fiddling with her kirby grips, not hearing anything properly. She'll complain that she can't stomach Jonathan's barbecued food. When did eating become so problematic?

Jonathan stops at an amber light although he could have sneaked through. When the lights turn green, we can't move. A white Transit van has blocked the box junction. A horn blares. Ben wakes from his nap, disgusted to find himself confined to the car. "We've got to get out of this," says Jonathan. "This traffic, the violence—look at Mum's street."

"We don't live on your mum's street."

"We should move out. Why not? There's nothing to keep us here."

"There's Beth and Matthew," I said, desperately.

"We'd still see them, invite them over. They're good friends. They won't drop us because we live in the country."

This is moving too fast. One minute he's cross about traffic; next thing we're holed up in a low-ceilinged cottage with exposed beams, setting places for Beth and Matthew. "But I like where we are," I protest. And I mean it. I have surprised myself by settling into Jonathan's flat. The novelty of living in a reasonably clean, well-functioning environment has yet to wear off. I've even bought the odd small item—picture frame, candlestick, from those useless shops near Beth's—to mark my territory.

"Too small," he says. "Ben can't be in our room forever. We'll need another bedroom. Two, when we have another baby."

"We could use your study," I say uneasily.

"For a while, maybe, when they're little. But there's no point in us being here. We never go out. We don't want to. If we lived in the country we'd have everything: space, peace, bigger garden—*acres* to ourselves."

I feel woozy, though that could be Constance's gravy. It's still there, pooling inside me. A man in paint-daubed overalls stumbles out the van. Registering his unpopularity, he spins around, jutting his neck into the passenger window of a custard yellow Beetle. As if planted by Jonathan to demonstrate the awfulness of city life, a reedy man in a fluttering suit springs out of the Beetle and slaps the face that's raged at him.

"See?" says Jonathan. "This is no place to bring up our son."

Finally, the traffic eases forward. Ben's mouth wilts pathetically. Jonathan's is clamped shut. Maybe he's right: country life would be quieter, to the point of stillness. There'd be no road rage. We'd ease into middle age without noticing it. He'd wear cardigans with brown buttons and build a shed to hide in. I'd attend Women's Institute meetings, go to church, even though I can't remember any biblical stories apart from that one about the woman who turned into salt. I'd make marmalade. The kitchen would smell of oranges and sugar. Some people want that kind of life. Chase, my old boss, has a redbrick house in Surrey. Only he doesn't live there. He just goes at weekends. He just plays there.

"Imagine," says Jonathan, "having acres of land. Think what we could do with it."

Acres? I think. What the hell do I want with acres?

14

Your Mobile Baby

Beth looks like she might vomit when I tell her about Operation Wilderness. "You can't live in the country," she says, ramming her buggy over cobbles, causing Maud's plump cheeks to jiggle. "Trust me—I was trapped in a nasty little village until I was eighteen. Couldn't wait to leave. Next-door neighbors never took the plastic wrapping off their sofa. That's the kind of people you're dealing with."

We're shunting the babies around a city farm. What's the point of these places? They're not real farms. You're overshadowed by tower blocks and washing. Yes, there are animals, but those sheep know they're only here to be manhandled by clumsy eight-year-olds. They don't want to be poked or smacked. They're so fed up with these leering faces, sucking on Chupa-Chup lollies, that they can't even be bothered to have lambs. I have never seen a baby animal at a city farm. When we arrived, Beth spotted a smudgily-painted sign that read: Animal Nursery. Wash Hands Immediately After Stroking. She bounded into the slumped stone building, hoping to glimpse a baby bunny, but found only two hollow-cheeked girls, sharing a cigarette.

The city farm was Beth's idea. She felt guilty, she said, for doing so little with Maud since Rosie had come on the scene. If anything, Rosie is too efficient. Maud's rear is wiped the instant an unsavory whiff is detected, leaving Beth waving a nappy helplessly. No wonder she has taken to filling her time with unnecessary tasks: making her own strawberry ice cream and fancy loaves with sun-dried tomatoes nestling inside. You can hardly move in her kitchen for gleaming white gadgets and a tangle of flexes.

The cobbled yard is populated by several ratty hens pecking nervously at discarded sweet wrappers. "We're not moving," I tell Beth. "It's just a whim of Jonathan's. Probably tied up with getting married. He's agitated— keeps checking that I've booked everything. We've got the Fox doing the buffet. The registry office is sorted. Now he's worried about how we'll transport everyone from there to the Fox."

Beth doesn't respond. She often acts like this, hazing into a parallel universe, perhaps mulling over her next bread-making project. "Then there's his suit," I continue. "It came back from the tailor with one of the pockets sewn up."

Beth points Maud's buggy at a sheepdog curled up on the cobbles. The dog is licking a bleeding wound on its hind leg and rises unsteadily to its feet, causing Maud to squawk fearfully. "Don't be fooled," Beth warns. "The country looks great in the summer. Roses, clematis, honeysuckle, all growing round doors. You're tricked into thinking—I could live here. You imagine yourself manning the tombola at fetes. It's that tadpole thing, isn't it?"

I blink at her.

"Tadpoles in jars. Children growing up with scuffed knees, climbing trees. But you're trapped. Everyone's mad in the country and you can't get away from them. In our village, this crazy woman's corgi died. She put it in the airing cupboard to bring it back to life."

"Is it still there?" I ask, sensing a *Promise* story. Beth snorts and reties the knitted hat strings beneath Maud's chin.

We pause at a field where a cow is batting away flies with its miserable head. "It's just wedding nerves," I tell the cow.

Beth leans on a splintery fence. "You okay," she asks, "about getting married?"

The cow mooches away, displaying its moth-eaten backside. "I'm scared," I say.

"That's natural. But he's right for you, isn't he? Such a hands-on dad. You work so well together." I want to tell her: we do, everyone's clothed, no one goes hungry, we all have our shoes on the right feet. "You're a team," she says, giving me a wrong-feeling hug.

We have exhausted the farm's possibilities. The babies

flail miserably in their buggies even when shown a pond rich with frondy weeds and a solitary mallard duck. They would be happier at home, parked in front of the washing machine.

I want to leave now, to get away from this farmy stench, but Beth has brought a picnic. It's too chilly to eat outdoors. I'd hoped to pick up chips on the way home. We find a segment of bare ground where grass might once have been and spread out Beth's crocheted rug. "Isn't Ben crawling yet?" asks Beth, opening pots containing couscous and a herb-laden potato salad.

"He's not interested. I've tried holding a toy in front of him—that's what *Babycare* says. But it feels stupid, like dangling a carrot in front of a donkey. Anyway, Constance reckons Jonathan didn't really crawl at all. He sat on the carpet till after his first birthday, then developed this bum-shuffling thing where he'd shunt along the floor, propelled by one hand."

"Oh," she frowns, offering Maud a slab of pita bread. "Let's hope Ben doesn't turn out like that."

I must stop agreeing to these outings. Chase was right: I should get back to work. Hire a nanny. These women are trained for the job and therefore reasonably adept. The only training on offer for real mothers is witnessing photogenic children in movies who never regurgitate lunch or turn on gas rings. Even Felt Lady has a nanny now. She grew tired of taking her irritable child to the school where he'd growl his displeasure at the unfinished wall hanging. I'll tell Jonathan I've run out of steam with this full-time mothering lark and go back to my old job on *Promise*. If Chase will have me. The first My Secret is due in three days. I have no one lined up to interview. I could interview myself: *Little Ben's dad thinks his son spends the week doing ordinary baby things—playing on the swings, visiting friends. Only Ben's mum knows about their child's other life. "It started as a bit of fun," says Nina. "I knew Jonathan wouldn't approve. Trouble is, we're getting married in December. Maybe I'll tell him on honeymoon, when we're playing Kerplunk…"*

"This time next week I'll be off," Beth announces, nibbling her pita bread.

I gawp at her. Aren't she and Matthew getting along better now they have Rosie to shoulder the child-rearing burden? "Don't look so shocked," she giggles. "I'm going to Mum's in Oxfordshire. She's having this solid oak floor laid. Needs to pack everything away, every ornament, double-wrapped in tissue paper. She collects glass animals and makes settings for them. There's the woodland scene and a miniature zoo. She makes hedges out of lichen."

Now I see why Beth wears a rabbit knapsack. "Won't Maud go with you?" I ask.

Beth winces. "Can't have her inhaling all that dust. Rosie will take care of things. It's only for two or three days. And Matthew will be around in the evenings, of course. He's allergic to my mother. Convinced she's on a mission to put meat into him." I picture an elderly lady presenting the skinny-framed Matthew with a steaming boar's head. "It's a game," she continues. "Ways of putting meat into Matthew. Like her vegetable broth. He's eating it happily until he gets to the bottom and there's something gristly, like a knuckle. And Mum says, 'Gosh. Can't imagine how that got in there.'"

Ben removes a finger of pita from his mouth and places it delicately on the blanket. He parts his lips, allowing a dollop of cream-colored gloop to slip down his chin. In an attempt at recycling, he collects the mush in his fingers and happily reeats it.

Beth is clearly repulsed by my son's picnic manners. The city farm cattle moo mournfully. Beth glances at Maud to check that she's not picking up such dire habits. But Maud isn't there. The knitted hat lies crumpled on the blanket with no baby face in it. Beth springs to her feet, skinny plaits bouncing. "Maud?" she cries desperately.

I jump up, covering as much ground as I can while keeping Ben within sight. As a noncrawler heading for bum-shuffling territory, it's not as if he can go anywhere. At the peak of the developmental hierarchy, Maud could have tootled off to explore the labyrinth of walkways in the estate—or is heading for the tube to plummet head-first down the escalator. She might be on her way to Covent Garden for a shopping trip.

"The farmyard," I shout, running back to scoop up Ben. I head for the cobbled square. Beth clatters after me, sturdy lace-ups smacking against the stones. "My daughter," she cries, spilling into a sob. She flies into the baby animals building and emerges saying the smoking girls just stared blankly and didn't seem to know what a baby was. She gawps at the wounded dog, as if it might know something. It yawns, showing black gums. A young woman with roughly chopped hair and a barbed wire tattoo circling her upper arm sweeps the yard, pretending to be deaf. "I've lost my child," Beth shouts.

The woman leans on her brush. "What sort of age?" she says flatly.

"Seven months."

"Oh, a baby. Can't have gone far."

"She's a fast crawler," pleads Beth. "You should see her. Amazing, really, considering her—"

"Did you leave her unattended?" enquires the woman.

"Of course not. We were having a picnic. She was right there beside me."

"Have you thought of the pond?" says the woman.

"The pond? Oh, my…" Beth's eyes flood instantly. And then I see it: the duck, swimming in lazy zigzags, and Maud sitting waist-high in stagnant water, examining a handful of weed which hangs in slimy strands between her fingers, like the cat's cradle game. She looks up. Pond weed dangles from her mouth. "Silly girl!" cries Beth, teetering at the pond's edge. "Your dress. That horrible weed's in your hair. Get her out, Nina. You're wearing old clothes. No—get my phone. It's in my bag on the rug. Grab my phone and call home—tell Rosie to get down here with a fresh set of clothing and towels and some kind of strong disinfectant."

"Shouldn't we get her out of the pond? She'll be freezing."

But Maud seems to like it. She sniffs the weed in her hands and her tongue darts out to lick a deep green strand. The child looks past her mother, directly at me, and she laughs, her shoulders bobbing with the hilarity of it all. I can still hear her as I head for the rug, honking her fat little face off.

Within minutes of Rosie's arrival, every inch of Maud has been deep-cleansed and speedily clothed. "What are these?" asks Beth.

"Dungarees," says Rosie. "Matthew just brought them home. He says now she's crawling, she needs more hard-wearing trousers."

Beth frowns, looking sharply at Rosie. "He's home already? It's just gone three. Why isn't he at work?"

Rosie shrugs. She examines Maud's fingernails and delves into the bag she's brought, extracting pink-handled nail scissors. "Bomb scare. They evacuated the building. He would have come over and helped, but thought he might get in the way."

Beth stashes the picnic tubs in the bag and picks grass from her knees. "Bomb scare," she says under her breath.

Rosie and I walk together, briskly pushing buggies. Beth dawdles behind, barking into her mobile: "Yep. She did. So...? Right. Really. Good. No. I'm *fine.*" When I look back, she grins at me, her mouth stretched into a wide sausage shape to prove how one hundred percent fine she really is.

Matthew is in the back garden, halfheartedly raking up leaves. He has a should-be-at-work look about him, doesn't know where to put himself. Three women and two babies have burst in on him, wrecking his raking enterprise. "Wedding prep going okay?" he asks.

"Fine," I start, "though it's becoming a bit of a—"

He stalks into the house, tailed by Beth. Heads bob about in the kitchen, shouting. Rosie and I are left in charge of the children. She has them pushing toy trains along a track, shunting the vehicles intently. "You're so good at this," I tell her. "You always know what to do."

"Maud's pretty easy," she says, "but she needs a little playmate. There aren't many children I can invite round. Beth's, you know—" she glances toward the kitchen when Beth is slapping about in the sink "—quite particular about people. Except you. Maybe you'd like to drop Ben round sometime. I could have him for an afternoon."

This would be handy. The My Secret deadline is looming so close it's breathing down my neck. "Would you?" I say. "I could do this freelance job. I'm running out of time and haven't even found anyone to interview."

She sits cross-legged, piecing train track together. "What kind of person are you looking for?"

"Someone with a secret. Who's willing to share the juicy details and have their photo in *Promise*."

"How exciting," she says.

It's not, I want to tell her; though I enjoyed *Promise* world once. Found it easy. I'd trawl the local papers for quirky stories and track down that woman who'd been forced to move because her neighbors had objected to the saucy mural she'd painted on her house. It was art, she said; an expression of sensuality. The neighbors called her a tart and whitewashed over it the minute her removal van had rumbled down the street.

"What sort of secret?" asks Rosie.

"Anything," I say, desperately.

"Like being a lapdancer?"

From the kitchen window come snappy words and the banging of something; perhaps the breadmaker. I hope it's not broken. Can't have Maud eating bought bread.

"Would you really do it?" I say.

She nods. "I'm not ashamed of anything I've done."

I could kiss the lips right off that beautiful face.

As a mode of transport, the supermarket trolley wins Ben's approval. He takes to being shunted along the aisles as if he frequently accompanies his mother to buy baking ingredients. He is pushed by Norrie, an ageless model of the *Promise* cover girl type, but without a hot chocolate sachet stuck to her face. She has bland fair hair and a crisp, white smile that suggests she has never drunk coffee or smoked a cigarette.

The ad is shot in a real supermarket, with extras meandering along the aisles. But it's not real. There's no toddler, flat on the floor, howling because he's not allowed peelable cheese. The pretend checkout girl is unfeasibly cheerful. Marcus flashes pinched little teeth. It appears that I am the director's new best friend. He brings me a coffee and kisses my son on the forehead. "Ben's an absolute find," he enthuses. "Very responsive. You rarely meet a baby who's so relaxed in a shoot environment."

"He's not so bad," I say, already blasé like those parents on the Little Squirts shoot.

Marcus breathes sour coffee at me and says, "You're very professional, Nina. I can't thank you enough. I'm sure we'll meet again."

We come home to an urgent message to call Lovely. As a professional, I ring her straight back. "I'm putting Ben forward for a springwater commercial," she announces. "The idea is, a baby is cascaded with water like raindrops. He'll have to audition to see how he copes with the water but it's just a formality."

"Why?" I ask stupidly.

"The director's seen the Little Squirts ad. Ben's just what he wants. We should have lunch, Nina. Perhaps your partner could join us. I'd like to plan Ben's career, make sure he's in it for the long term."

"Let's do that," I say.

Rosie arrives next morning with Maud squawking excitedly from a front-loading carrier. "Sure you can manage both babies?" I ask.

"No problem."

"Do bring him straight back if anything—"

"Get on with your work," she says, laughing. I watch as they head for the park, then mooch around my PC, putting off the business of switching it on. Finally, I start to type:

Rosie Lyall looks like any other carefree twenty-year-old. When you see her at work, playing happily with the seven-month-old baby she looks after, you'd never guess that, until recently, she had a very different job indeed…

It doesn't feel right, sleazing her up. "Play on the secret aspect," Chase had urged. "The contrast between her respectable life with this poncy, middle-class family, and the dirty underworld of the lapdancing club…"

Rosie feels predatory eyes upon her lithe, young body. She is lost in a world of her own, feeling sexy and powerful…

I gaze at the screen. Words hover randomly. I delete a comma here, a full stop there. Fiddling. Putting it off. I switch off the PC, turn it on again and make little dotted squares with the cursor, then slope to the kitchen to make a salami sandwich which I eat on the back step, calculating that I have fifty-seven minutes until Rosie returns my son to me.

"We need a travel cot," says Jonathan, "to take on honeymoon."

"They have one," I tell him. "I've checked." It wasn't the Brodies at Netherall Farm in Kircubrightshire, Scotland. The woman who answered, Mrs. Jackson, had no recollection of a Mr. and Mrs. Brodie and seemed reluctant to let us book in for the week. She admitting eventually that she did do B&B but we'd have to vacate the room from nine-thirty till five every day. She sounded bossy and harassed. I decided not to ask if a games cupboard was included in the facilities.

"I'd rather he slept in his own cot," Jonathan says. "I

don't want him in some splintered old thing with a damp mattress." Somehow, this doesn't sound terribly honeymoonish.

We head for Oxford Street to purchase a travel cot on a gloomy Saturday morning. Or rather, we intend to head for Oxford Street but Jonathan points the car in the wrong direction. The air is heavy and moist. It feels like a storm might be brewing. We drive through an interminable clutter of terraces until we are on the motorway, then off it again, where there is nothing but fields and lazy cows and the occasional village nestling smugly around a village green.

I am determined not to ask where we're going. There's a slight possibility that Jonathan has located a purveyor of discounted baby equipment out here in Marmalade Land, but I doubt it. Jonathan hums to himself, like he's bought me a present and is bursting for me to open it.

"Is this a mystery trip?" I ask finally.

He gives me a quick, teasing look that says: you're going to love this. And I've guessed, even before he pulls in outside a pub called The Turkey and unbuckles Ben from his car seat. He cradles him in one arm as he hoists the buggy from the boot and shakes it open. "There's something I want to show you," he says, doing up Ben's straps and tying the laces of his pale denim padders.

"You couldn't commute this far," I suggest.

Jonathan strolls past immaculate redbrick cottages. "I've worked it out," he says. "It wouldn't take much more than an hour. I'd enjoy it. I could read on the train, even learn a new language."

"Why would you want to do that," I ask, "when you don't go abroad?"

We pass a church, its stained-glass windows watching us moodily. I'd have to go there on Sundays and I'm not even christened. "It's somewhere up here," muses Jonathan, checking a street name. Wisteria Lane. Hello marmalade.

The houses are now widely spaced, their boundaries marked by hefty stone walls. Somewhere a radio murmurs, and there's birdsong; you don't notice the absence of birds in a city. I could befriend birds, like that mad pigeon lady: tear bread into beak-size morsels and encourage my feathered friends to foul the village with their doings.

Jonathan stops abruptly at a handsome square house with four matching windows and a glossy red door, like a child's drawing. He swings in through the gate. Terracotta pots snuggle together on the white-painted step. Attached to a wooden stake, there by the birdhouse, is the sign: For Sale. Viewing by appointment only.

"Well," he says "what do you think?"

I think: it's perfect. I think: I don't want it.

"See?" he says. "You're lost for words. Gorgeous, isn't it? Better than it looked in the estate agent's blurb. The photo didn't do it justice."

"What estate agent?"

"Canning and Walker. They've been calling in details from their regional offices. I didn't want to raise your hopes—not till the right place came up." He grips my hand. "Let's just have a look," he says gently.

"We can't just barge in. You have to make an appointment."

He glances at his watch. "Gary should be here any minute. He'll show us around. The family is away. He says it's just what I'm—what *we're*—looking for."

He appears at the gate, the man who knows what other people want. He has a shiny tan and shakes my hand, jangling my arm right up to the shoulder. "Lovely baby," he says. Ben stares at him bitterly, as if chewing a lime.

I carry him into the wooden-floored hall where neatly-paired wellies, all facing the right direction, sit primly against the wall. The adults' are green, the children's silver, patterned with clouds. Three children of differing sizes. A big family. A big family house.

"You'll love the kitchen," Gary enthuses, assuming that this will be my domain; Jonathan will be out checking his cucumbers in the greenhouse.

The kitchen is floored with mottled slate and fitted with gleaming red units. Children's drawings are Blu-tacked onto cupboards. One depicts "Mummy"—a grinning lady with long black hair and spidery eyelashes. Another is entitled, "Daddy's new car," but it looks like a minibus.

And Jonathan is right: it is perfect. Neatly ordered, clean smelling, with just enough clutter to reassure us that a real family lives here. They function well. The Lego is stored in a trunk they picked up at an auction. The mum with the spidery lashes packs the kids' lunch boxes the night before school; it's good stuff they eat, fresh vegetables washed in that vast Belfast sink. What does the dad do? He's a solicitor. Eliza would like him. She wouldn't be so keen on the oven. I cannot imagine why it requires so many doors.

"Plenty of room to grow into," says Gary, directing us into the sitting room. "You want that, when you're starting a family." Good God: how many am I expected to produce? Am I to be permanently up the duff, patting my robust belly while manning the How Many Smarties in the Jar stall?

"Let me show you upstairs," Gary says. The adults have the biggest bedroom. Everything's white, even the floorboards. The embroidered bedspread is whiter than white. If they have sex at all, it's clean sex. "Peaceful, isn't it?" says Gary with a tight smile. "And the rooms are so light. Just the place you'd want to wake up on a Sunday morning."

"How old is it?" asks Jonathan.

"Late nineteenth century. It's rare to find one of this size. This is a popular village. The primary school's top of the table for the whole county."

Ben is on the white floorboards, trying to jam his forefinger into a gap. Jonathan keeps glancing at me, checking my face. "I've had a lot of interest," says Gary, leading the way to the children's rooms. Each door has a nameplate: Eddie's room, Sophie's room, Martha's room. Children who do well at school and sit at that homely kitchen table, tackling their homework to the cozy murmur of Radio 4. "I'll let you have a look by yourselves," Gary says. "Get a feel for the place."

Jonathan carries Ben to the sitting room and places him on a circular ethnic rug. "So," he says, expectantly.

"So," I say back.

"I think we should put in an offer."

"Let's think about this."

"Could you call him in the week? He gave you his card, didn't he?"

I rummage in my bag where Ben's bottle has leaked. Gary's card is sodden but still legible: not Gary but *Garie.* Creative spelling. I couldn't buy a toothbrush, let alone a house, from a Garie.

We say we'll be in touch; Garie takes Ben's hand and gurgles, "Bye-bye, little fellow."

Ben bursts into spontaneous tears. The sky has changed color, got a mood on. There's a thundery growl as rain starts to fall. We leave in a hurry, squeezing past an armchair in the hall; too big for its space, obviously intended for another room. It's plump and upholstered in burgundy corduroy, the kind you can never get comfortable in. And it's new. I know this because it still has its plastic wrapper on.

Eliza calls to say she has found the perfect wedding dress. "You've only just met him," I scoff. "He's too young for such a commitment."

"Not for me and Dale, stupid. For you. It's this blue, a delicate blue—I can't quite describe it."

"Larkspur?" I suggest.

"Like duck egg with gray in it. Nothing special on the hanger. But it's beautifully cut and won't emphasize your...you know."

"How much?" I ask.

"That's the thing. You can have it for nothing. It's a sample on loan from a publicist. I can keep her at bay for a few weeks, pretend we've lost it. And you're only wearing it for a day. Maybe just a few hours. She'll never know."

Getting married in a dress that's not mine? It's not right, although I'm not sure why. It's only a dress. Only a day. No big thing, Jonathan says, though he'd feel happier if I called the florist to sort out the table decorations.

"And I've got one for myself," Eliza says, more excited now. "It's plum, bias cut. The only problem is shoes."

"DMs?" I suggest. "Do they still do those oxblood ones?"

She ignores me and barks instructions that I am to go over to her place for a try on. "I'm quite looking forward to this wedding," she gushes, right out of the duck-egg blue.

I arrive at Beth's to let Rosie have a look at the *Promise* interview. I've trodden carefully, not wanting to offend her. The result is bland and, frankly, boring. Chase will chuck it back for a rewrite.

I hope, too, that Rosie might have a friend I can interview for the next My Secret. I'd forgotten how quickly a week speeds by: the minute one story's in, I should be hammering away at the next. Would Garie reveal something from his past if we bought that wretched house in Watton-by-the-Whatever-it-was? That's how desperate I am. In fact I'd pay someone to take the entire My Secret job off my hands. I'll be a waitress or a librarian. I'll take quiet lunch breaks and leave on time with no dead-line wheezing in my face.

I'm glad that Beth's still at her mother's. She won't ap-prove that I've interviewed her au pair. Beth thinks of Rosie as her property; another nonessential gadget, handy to have in the kitchen. I press the bell. Rosie is probably upstairs in the playroom with that song tape on. I hammer the door. Maybe she's in the garden. I try the door; it opens stiffly. "Rosie?" I call.

Music plays quietly in the living room. Something jazzy, meandering nowhere in particular. They don't usually play music in this house. Beth owns three token CDs: Phil Collins, Nina Simone, a love songs compila-tion with a silhouetted kissing couple on the cover.

"Rosie?" I shout upstairs. "It's Nina. I've brought the feature."

A cool gust drifts into the hall. The back door is open. I head for the garden, imagining her raking up the rest of those leaves with Maud asleep in the watery sun. But there's the baby, in the kitchen, lying diagonally across her playpen. She's snoring throatily. A wooden rattle rests on her open palm. Her broad chest rises and falls slowly. Her nappy bulges, full to capacity. She is wearing a vest, faintly stained, where tomato-based sauce might have splashed.

On the kitchen shelf, below Beth's cookery books, are Matthew's trophies: for golf and long-distance running. High achieving husband, good at everything. Happy to pick up the child care reins while his wife tissue-wraps glass animals in the country.

I check that Ben's still asleep in the hall, then peer

through the kitchen window. It's less sparkling than usual. The garden looks damp and neglected. In the olden days, Beth said, Matthew dug up the turf to create borders and planted perennials. Then he stopped bothering, unless Beth really nagged. He blamed it on Maud. As she grew, so did the weeds. The decking looks bleak. Back in August, Matthew made a cack-handed attempt at mowing the lawn, but gave up after one lap.

Down at the bottom, where the grass grows taller, no lawn mower ventured all year. There's Rosie, with her back to the house. She is moving up and down, her dress bunched about her waist. At first I can't make him out, with the grass being so long. Then I see him, flat on his back, his hands clutching her hips, just yards from the place where Beth's engagement ring came to rest, on a blanket made from 164 crocheted squares.

15

Couple Time

I'm turning the corner of Beth's street when I realize I no longer have the manila envelope containing Rosie's My Secret. It's not in the changing bag, swinging from the buggy handles. It's not rolled up, stuffed in my jeans pocket. It's been put somewhere. In Beth's kitchen, perhaps, beside the new fifties-style blender, perfect for smoothies and shakes so long as you screw the lid on properly, which she omitted to do first time around, splattering the Advanced One with pulverized strawberries.

Now I'm wondering if I even shut Beth's front door in my hurry to get the heck out. It'll be swinging idly, inviting burglars, while Matthew and Rosie finish things off in the garden.

I could go back and explain: *I came round to bring you the feature—look, here it is, silly me!—but you weren't in. Music was playing. Maybe you popped out and forgot to turn it off.* I won't mention Maud in the playpen. She was sleeping; I could easily have missed her. I'll say: I looked everywhere. Nothing. No one. *I didn't see a thing.*

They'll be finished by now. With Rosie on top of him, he won't be hanging about. He'll exhibit enthusiasm previously unseen in the garden. They'll ruffle the grass to erase the flat patch. Two flushed faces will check on Maud—still asleep? Good—and embark on ordinary dad/au pair activities. He might polish his trophies. She'll prepare Maud's midafternoon snack. When Beth calls, it'll be Rosie who picks up the phone. "Everything's fine," she'll say in her nice-girl-from-Kent voice. "Yes, of course she's missing you. We all are." And I think of Beth: trapped in the country, wrapping glass bunnies, counting the minutes until she's back where she belongs.

I won't tell her. We're not close enough; it's not in my job description. But she'll find out. They'll be careless. I hurry home, the buggy jerking over pavement cracks as I speed-walk, hoping the manila envelope will split into millions of particles and disperse in Beth's kitchen, like flour.

Jonathan shows up with simmering cheeks and two jam-packed carrier bags clutched before him like outsized testicles. "What's all this?" I ask as he unloads mixed leaves, prewashed and bagged in cellophane pillows. A polystyrene tray of twenty-four chicken thighs hits the worktop with a thump.

"This isn't all of it," he says, catching his breath. "I'll get the rest in the morning, start the marinades and light the barbecue around two. The forecast is good for tomorrow—I've checked."

It comes back to me now: the family gathering. My parents and Constance, getting to know each other just in time for our wedding. To give the impression that our families have mingled for decades. "Did you think about that house?" he says, lining up bottled oils ranging from beige to mossy-green.

I can't think. I'm still picturing Rosie's dark curls, springing about her shoulders. "We've got to make a decision," Jonathan says. "Garie called me. I told him we loved it. He warned me that three other couples are viewing this week."

Do we love it? There's nothing to dislike. You can't pretend that such a well-tended cottage is actually offensive.

"Of course he says that," I reason. "Have you ever known an estate agent to tell the truth? He wants to chivvy us along, grab his commission. There might be loads wrong with it—roof, damp, guttering…"

"Did it smell damp to you?" he asks, stuffing empty bags into the carrier bag holder (a white plastic receptacle with holes for easy bag removal, attached to the inside of the hall cupboard. A design classic, Jonathan says).

"Let's wait until after the wedding," I suggest.

"It won't be there after the wedding."

I picture a space where the house once stood. The welly boot family, bereft at the gate, staring at the vacant rectangle. "I went round to Beth and Matthew's today," I blurt out.

He exhales impatiently. "Tried to get Matthew at work. I suppose I should have some sort of stag night, or at least go out for a beer. But he'd nipped out to the cashpoint and hadn't come back. No one knew where he was."

I can't understand why Jonathan has picked Matthew for best man. He's not the best man. Billy is. At least he's interested in the wedding proceedings. He's suggested having the stag night at the dog track or an Elvis impersonators' club. At the ceremony he wants to play a little something he's written. Worryingly, he has bought an accordion.

With the shopping unpacked, Jonathan wipes his brow on his jacket sleeve. Why doesn't he take it off now he's home? I lift it from his shoulders. His shirt feels damp, as if blasted by steam. He kisses me tentatively, like I might bite. I hear Ben shuffling on the kitchen floor. Jonathan's hands are on my back and face and hair. Ben whimpers, fearing perhaps that his parents are about to adjourn to the bedroom and forget he exists. Babies won't tolerate adults showing affection. They won't have it, this lip-pressing thing that excludes them. Jonathan leads me into the hall. He kisses me less shyly now, against the cupboard, the one with the carrier bag holder inside.

"*Awaa,*" comes the cry from the kitchen. Ben's scared now, thinking: they're going to do it. Make a baby. A vile brother or sister who'll lie under the activity arch—*my* activity arch—and nab the best modeling jobs.

A louder wail. "He'll be all right," whispers Jonathan, "just for a minute." There are grunts as our son propels himself—definitely crawling, not bum shuffling—from the kitchen to the hall. His bottom lip juts out like a shelf.

"I have something to tell you," I say. There's an urgent tug at my ankle. Ben uses both hands in a futile attempt to pull up on my leg. "Matthew wasn't at work," I say carefully. "He was at home. In the garden. I went round to see—"

"About time. Have you seen the state of their lawn? They go to all that expense—the decking, those huge ceramic pots—and leave it to go rampant." When he uses that word—*rampant*—I have to escape to the kitchen and hide my face in the fridge.

Constance's unusually small feet are tucked into ochre lace-up shoes. She wears a dark brown cardigan done up to the neck and a pleated skirt that she picks at. She wants to help, and tries to break into the kitchen, but Jonathan guides her back outside. "Relax, Mum," he insists. "Chat to Nina."

Constance squints in the sharp October sunlight. She is trapped in the yard with her pretend daughter-in-law and Ben on her lap. He regards her as if she has stepped from a space rocket. Jonathan brings out two glasses of wine. Constance shakes her head at her glass and motions for him to place hers on the flagstones. She's in nonconversational mode. We stare at the brick wall bordering our backyard as if poised for the latest movie to be projected upon it.

My parents are late. Or perhaps they've forgotten. When I called to invite them, my mother appeared to have difficulty in remembering who I was. "We thought you should meet Constance," I said, "seeing as you'll be sitting together in the registry office."

"Constance?" came the distant voice, as if she were holding the receiver at arm's length.

"Jonathan's mother," I said, expecting her to say, "Jonathan? Who is this calling?" But just in time she said, "Oh! Of course we'll come. We'd love to see…the baby." Perhaps she had forgotten his name, too.

They arrive when the chicken should be sizzling nicely, filling the yard with tempting smells, but the embers aren't hot enough. Jonathan prods the coals with a long-handled fork; barbecue behavior, useful for enabling males to duck out of family situations. Constance rubs her shoes together and stares ahead. She holds Ben, but he could be a teapot for all the interaction that's going on.

Jonathan douses the coals with lighter fluid in an attempt to rev up the heat. Mum sniffs loudly. She wants to smoke, of course. It's allowed, as we're outside. And she's weighing it up: would anyone mind? Where should she sit so her smoke doesn't waft into Constance's face? She dips into her bag, pulls out a soft packet and lights up. Constance flicks her watery eyes at my mother, then looks back at the wall.

Dad hovers over Jonathan at the barbecue. "It never

cooks through to the middle, does it?" he says. "You think—it must be ready by now. And you bite it and it's bloody inside."

At the word bloody, Constance glares at my dad. "Don't say that, Jack," says my mother. "Jonathan's doing his best." She turns to Constance. "Isn't he good, doing the cooking? Nina says it's his area. All she does is grab a few bits from the deli and slap them on a plate." She finishes with a little laugh. Constance scowls, deciding—if further proof were needed—that I am not about to cut it as a superwife. "What sort of wedding food are you having, Nina?" asks my mother loudly.

"Just a buffet. Salmon, seafood, salady bits and pieces."

"We eat very simply in France, don't we, Jack? We have a place there," she tells Constance.

Now Constance views my parents as swanky folk, even minor aristocracy, with unnecessary homes dotted around Europe. Not that my mother looks grand—she's wearing a faded ivy-patterned dress, which looks like one more wash might finish it off—but she could just be slumming it.

"Looking forward to the wedding?" she asks, running out of steam with her Befriending Constance enterprise.

Constance stares at Mum's rumpled collar and says, "What?"

"The wedding. Are you—"

"I've never been to a wedding," Constance growls.

"Except your own," says my mother.

Constance's eyes, though insignificantly gray, beam

powerfully. "I have never been to a wedding. Jonathan's father and I were never married. Jonathan," she says, louder now, "will you take me home before it's too late? I don't like you driving in the dark."

"This is London, Mum," he says, examining a smoldering chicken thigh. "It's never properly dark."

"I'm sorry to hear that," my mother tells Constance.

Jonathan slaps chicken onto plates, forgets to pass round the salad which sits in a glass bowl in the kitchen, and tips wine into his throat, as if gargling.

Mum examines her plate. "This looks wonderful," she says, "but I might eat later at home. Ashley's concerned about the antibiotics in chicken."

"It's organic," says Jonathan.

"It's getting late," murmurs Constance. "Jonathan?"

Mon: springwater shoot. Bring white babygro & selection of toys.

Tue: My Secret due in. Who to interview????

Wed: Order wedding wine, order cake, check to Fox, chase up RSVPs. Transport from registry to Fox? Able Towing ad. 3:00 p.m. start? Eliza's to try on dress.

Thur: Xmas audition. 2:00 p.m.? Check with Lovely.

Fri: Jonathan's birthday. Beth baby-sit?

"They coped," says Beth, "but things are never done exactly how you'd do them yourself." She's back from the country, plumper and less greasy around the T-zone. "I missed him, you know," she adds. "Maybe that's what we needed. A little holiday from each other." She has brought back painted wooden letters spelling Maudie and two goldfish she won at a fete. They will go in the playroom. Rosie will clean out the tank because, according to Beth, fish count as playthings, and the cleansing of playthings is Rosie's domain.

"Take it you're not buying that country house?" says Beth, placing a miniature shipwreck in the tank.

"I'm fending him off, though it'll probably come up on Friday night. It's his birthday. Could you baby-sit?"

"No problem," she says, sounding nervous. Ben's a boy, after all, and he's already smashed the lid of her teddy biscuit barrel.

"Around seven?"

"Fine," she says, then adds giddily, "You know the best thing, when I got back? He'd cut that blasted grass."

The week passes in a flurry of scribbled reminders and the fear of being one second late. The springwater ad is shot against a stark-white background with droplets sprinkling from above. The director is a sorrowful man with a serious chin. He moves awkwardly, as if chipped out of stone. Ben sits squatly on the floor on mounds of what looks like bubble wrap. As the water starts falling, I expect him to storm off the set—or at least crawl like blazes toward me—but he laughs, batting sparkling droplets with his fingers. The other baby, the reserve baby, doesn't need to be used. "Never mind, it's just been a nice morning out," says his mother, her face flat with disappointment.

I spend the next morning scouring the papers for a My

Secret idea, but find nothing. I ask Eliza if she'd consider telling her story—"My Toy Boy Lover"—but she just honks down the phone. *Promise* isn't her sort of magazine. It's fit only to line her cat litter tray. I wonder what Chase thinks of the lapdancing story. There was no time to let Rosie read it first. She might have found it, plonked in the kitchen, but it hasn't been mentioned. I am keeping contact with Beth and Rosie to a minimum. I fear that my forehead, corrugated with worry, will blab: *I saw them, doing it. They left Maud in the playpen in a dirty vest, smelling off.*

Jess calls from *Promise* to ask if I could work in a little more detail this week? They'll run with the lapdancing piece as it is, no time for a rewrite. But they could have done with a twist. She talks squeakily, as if asking the school nurse for a sanitary towel. "Have you done the pictures?" I ask.

"Yesterday. Very natural, the photographer said. Lovely girl. You can't imagine her getting up to something so tawdry."

"She's a dark horse," I say.

"Will I have this week's piece from you today?" Jess wants to know.

"It's nearly finished," I mumble.

After Ben's lunch, I march him round the park until he drops off in the buggy. Back home, I bang out a fictitious My Secret, about a woman who knows her husband's having an affair, but lets it go on because at least he doesn't bother her for sex. By the time I've finished, coinciding with Ben's wake-up call, I almost believe it's a real story.

I e-mail it to Jess at *Promise,* explaining that the woman

refuses to have her photo taken. They can use a stock picture out of the drawer. Or take a picture of Jess. Like I care what they do.

The Able Towing ad is shot on the hard shoulder of the M1. All Ben has to do is simmer with photogenicness while being lifted from his car seat by an Irish actor well-practiced at the caring dad act. He's a Ranald type, looks like he could erect a tent in under a minute. The only time he smiles is when he hands Ben back to me.

Jonathan comes home from work complaining that his team aren't bonding, despite the three days spent digging a pond. "Everyone spins off, doing their own thing," he says. "I'm going to have a word." I wonder what kind of word that might be. Can't imagine Jonathan shouting, laying down the law. He says, "How did it go with the car people?" Was he spying, watching Ben being held by a surrogate dad? "You said you'd book a minibus," he says tersely. "To take everyone from the registry office to the Fox."

"Can't we use taxis?" I suggest. "There's only twelve people. They can—"

"I'll sort it out," he snaps. He plays an answerphone message from Eliza, reminding me to be round at hers at 8:00 p.m. sharp.

She looks like she's recently enjoyed too much sex for one person. Her flat has caved in on itself. It could be a jumble sale after the first surge has nabbed the best stuff. The dress droops at the window in Eliza's spare room, midway between blue and gray. A label hangs from the shoulder reading Sample: Must Be Returned. I try it on without removing the label. "Turn round," Eliza commands. My body feels saggy. I need some kind of support, like scaffolding.

"It looks all right from the back," she says.

The audition suite for the Christmas audition is decked out in clumsy green tinsel, presumably to get the babies in the festive spirit. The ad is for a catalog of toys and household goods: *straight from the page to your door.* How will I feel if Jonathan buys me a set of three glass-lidded saucepans? That's what happens. Beth was incensed last birthday when Matthew presented her with a dustbin. She was heavily pregnant, told me about it at the antenatal class. The bin was eye-pleasing as bins go—a sleek design in searing yellow—and contained three bottles of Moët. Well, she didn't want a bin. And, being *with child,* she couldn't drink champagne.

Jonathan and I haven't thought about Christmas. It's his birthday tomorrow; I've had enough trouble with that. Under our bed lurk two parcels: a briefcase with sharp corners and a hefty-looking combination lock (though his current one is perfectly good) and a three-step men's skincare kit in a charcoal corduroy pouch. The shop girl might have assumed they were gifts for my dad.

"Nervous?" pipes up a woman whose child refuses to be placated, even by the tinsel and frosted stars dangling from the ceiling.

"No, we've done this before."

She looks at Ben, then at me. "You're with Little Lovelies aren't you? And this is the famous Ben."

Famous Ben looks up at me with a fistful of stars and an expression that asks: do we have to audition? Don't they know who I am?

It's not Beth who shows up on Friday evening, but Rosie. "You don't mind, do you?" she asks, scooping up Ben in his zip-up sleepsuit. "Beth said she wanted some time alone with Matthew. I love your dress."

Apart from a couple of try-ons, the black dress has spent too long wrapped in tissue, in a dark place, like Beth's mother's glass animals. It smells musty and doesn't look as black as it should. The shoes are searingly un-comfortable. I'm not up to such brazen footwear.

Jonathan wears a light blue shirt and nondescript black trousers; it's as far as he is able to stray from the office look. He stares at my dress, wants to say something, but not in front of Rosie. We leave detailed instructions: what to do should Ben be reluctant to go down in his cot. *Babycare* recommends a trial run, having a baby-sit-ter round without going out, which seems pointless and embarrassing. What are the parents supposed to do? Hover in the kitchen, sipping wine, pretending it's a bar? Jonathan shows Rosie where nappies, wipes and Calpol are kept, although Ben's been changed and doesn't ap-pear to be running a fever. I've laid out his entire collec-tion of toys, except the rusting bike Mum brought for him, so he doesn't feel abandoned.

"Here's my pager and mobile and Nina's mobile and

the restaurant number," says Jonathan, handing her a note with everything written in capitals: BRAZIL UNTIL NINE THEN ODEON. FILM FINISHES 11:15 SHOULD BE HOME 11:45.

"That's our cab," I say, eager to escape before Ben clocks his mother's virtually nude feet and surmises that I'm off to a mysterious place where alcohol is served.

Jonathan climbs into the taxi, brushing invisible dust from his thighs. I turn back to remind Rosie that Ben tends to wallop back his evening bottle and demand a refill; she should take it slowly, give him breaks, make sure he's properly burped. She knows all this. She knows more about babies than I do.

"I liked the interview," she says, holding Ben in the doorway. "You wrote it just as I said it."

"Well, I tried."

"I just want to thank you," she says.

Jonathan doesn't like to eat out but Brazil is not a real restaurant: just a tapas bar, too hectic to pay much attention to what's on your plate. We stand near the door where it's less smoky, clutching glasses of wine. Jonathan smiles tensely each time someone buffets past him to reach the cigarette machine. A couple get up from one of the pavement tables, leaving an explosion of oily dishes, torn serviettes and an ashtray brimming with butts and beer bottle tops.

The table wobbles. Jonathan takes a business card from his wallet, folds it and wedges it under a silvery leg. But the table still teeters precariously when we lean on it. The waiter takes our order without looking at us. A gang of five, deeply tanned women at the next table applauds the arrival of an outsize jug of burgundy liquid, festooned with chopped fruit.

We're unused to being together without the distraction of Ben. I wonder if the tanned girls assume we're on a first date. We're still feeling our way. Our sentences start with "so." And of course the tanned girls don't notice us; why would they? One receives a text message and shows the others, who yelp like puppies. Jonathan takes my hand under the table and squeezes it.

And I will tell him, in a minute. I'll wait until the food's arrived; don't want a waiter delving about, arranging dishes, when I'm informing Jonathan that his son is soon to appear on national television, being wheeled about in a supermarket trolley with the voice of a forty-five-year-old man. You need a quiet moment to explain that the reason you're so wrecked is the springwater shoot and the Able Towing ad and the Christmas audition, not to mention the mounting pressure to concoct another My Secret.

I pick at baby squid and some kind of fish with a slimy tomato sauce and bones where you wouldn't expect them. I line up the bones on my plate. The tanned girls shout at a startlingly attractive blond boy with a portfolio tucked under his arm. He kisses each girl, smothered by cleavage.

Jonathan, I have something to tell you.

A fragment of squid, something like a tentacle, is wedged in my throat. It won't budge. It's jammed halfway down with the aid of its suckers. Jonathan looks at me, gripping his fork. The blond boy is playfully massaging the loudest girl's shoulders. Their jug is already empty. Three of them light cigarettes, taking quick, shallow puffs.

"I don't know how to start," I say.

Jonathan blinks rapidly, puts down his fork. "It's the house. You're not happy about it. You don't want to move."

The waiter appears at our table. "Finished?" he says, regarding the barely touched dishes.

"Yes, thank you," says Jonathan.

"Would you like anything else?" He watches the tanned girls while loading our plates onto a stainless-steel tray.

"No, thanks," I say. The loud girl beckons the waiter over, waving the empty jug.

"The house is sold anyway. At least they've accepted an offer. I called Garie to check. He's keeping an eye out for something closer to town."

How close exactly? You're either in town or you're not. I'd rather be stranded in Marmalade Land than in pretend country just off the North Circular. "It's not the house," I say, wondering if the tentacle will come back up or work its way down or have to be removed by that nine-year-old doctor at the hospital.

"You don't want another baby. That's okay. It's probably too soon. We have the wedding to think about."

He looks crushed. His neck is pink against the light blue shirt. There's a nick on his jaw from shaving. He twists the stem of his wineglass. There's a splash of meat-ball sauce on his wrist.

Someone heading into Brazil spots me and thunders toward us in an enormous, sapphire-colored dress. It hangs from her neck to her ankles with no discern-able seams or structure. Felt Lady's face is in mine, the voice booming, "Nina, sorry I haven't been in touch. He's had a chest infection. I'm worried it's the damp. I've started papermaking and there are buckets of pulp all over the flat." She looks expectantly at Jonathan.

"This is Jonathan, my fiancé," I croak. And I cannot remember her name. Does it begin with an *F* or an *H* or could that be her kid?

She extends a hand. Jonathan shakes it. "I'm Charlotte," she says, giving my dress a confused look before biffing her way into Brazil.

We pay and drink the rest of the wine. Jonathan holds my hand as we walk. I feel too old for hand-holding. We stop at the window of a home accessories shop selling globular lamps and delicate tables de-signed for baby-free homes. "Is it the wedding?" he says. "We don't have to do it, if you don't want to." Rosie flashes into my mind. She's curled up prettily on our leather sofa, channel hopping, every so often padding through to the bedroom to check that Ben is okay.

"It feels strange," I say, "being out like this. It's our first time, isn't it? Since we've had Ben?"

His hand touches the bare bit of my back. I pull my

thin jacket around myself. "As long as that's all it is," he says.

"I really want to marry you," I tell him.

As everyone else saw the film months ago, the cinema's only a third full. We've never seen a film together. I wonder if Jonathan sits through the credits until the lights come on, or bolts the instant it's over. I have him down for a credits man. Not a hot dog or popcorn or fizzy drink with straw poked through lid man.

. There are trailers for films I've never heard of, starring actors who must be massively famous considering the weight of importance given to their names. I should know about them, have the intricacies of their private lives stored in my brain. I'm a journalist, after all. But celebrities aren't my area. I interview ordinary people who do far weirder things than actors do. Failing that, I just make stuff up.

There are commercials. A model with limbs like a gazelle's, the kind of girl Eliza works with. She's on a jetty, drinking something made from peaches. It could be me on our honeymoon (although I've got bulkier legs), if Jonathan hadn't been so set on the B&B thing. I offer him my popcorn. He waves it away.

And there's a bath product ad. A flurry of infants splashing in an inflatable pool. Close-ups of features: wide eyes with wet lashes; a gurgling, toothless mouth. Now a whole baby: waist-high in water, supported by a duck-shaped floating seat. He splashes with a fist, brings a hand to his mouth, sucks a finger. The image freezes.

Little Squirts. Because we care about your baby as much as you do.

The film begins. Kevin Spacey in suburban America. Something awful's going to happen, we're told that at the start. A very sexy, very young girl rolls about in potpourri. There's a narky adolescent, the troublemaker. Somehow, my popcorn tastes both salty and sweet. The piece in my mouth shrinks to a hard kernel but won't melt away completely. For the second time tonight, I can't swallow. The kernel remains in my cheek, hard as a gem.

I can't follow the plot. Kevin Spacey is up to stuff with the potpourri girl but all I can see is a baby supported by a duck-shaped seat. Raspberry bath gel. Kiwi and papaya body and hair wash. Even conditioner. I steal a glance at Jonathan. His eyes are fixed on the screen, his lips pressed firmly together. Kevin Spacey's wife falls for a rival estate agent. He's flashier than Garie, with better suits. We leave, with someone babbling behind us: no wonder it won all those Oscars.

Outside it's drizzling. My dress appears to have shrunk. Its narrow straps dig into my shoulders. I undid the shoes in the cinema but have had to buckle them again. They too have shrunk. Jonathan flags down a black cab. I clamber in beside him, conscious of my knees and gusts of disapproval.

"What did you think?" I ask hopefully.

He stares out of the window. Pavements mill with good moods; for most people the night's just beginning.

"What do you think I think?" he says.

16

Tantrums

Rosie is stretched out on her belly on the tufted cream rug, as if sunbathing. She has been reading *InHouse;* it's lying open at a page about contemporary flower arranging (don't mix your blooms—just go for one variety, like hyacinths, displaying in a plain, rectangular vase).

Jonathan zooms straight to the bedroom. A dad's natural response. Checking on baby. Not because he is livid with bride-to-be. Not because anything has *happened*.

Rosie glances toward the bedroom, following his exit. "Enjoy the film?" she says, gathering herself up. She is wearing faded jeans and a snug-fitting black sweater. Her perfume smells of honey.

"Brilliant," comes my unconvincing voice.

"What was it again?"

All I can recall is the girl in potpourri. The title escapes me. I can remember an ad, with a baby. A grinning, finger-sucking baby, now sleeping soundly, having been given his evening bottle in the correct manner.

"Oh, weird stuff," I say. I just want her to go. She gets up, taking several decades to pull on a worn denim jacket. Each arm is fed, in slow motion, into a sleeve. She strokes her streamlined neck as if reassuring herself that it's not saggy and dumpy like mine.

"Thanks for tonight," I say, scrabbling in my purse for money. There's a fistful of scraps: deli receipts, directions to the springwater shoot, plus the number of a photographer Lovely recommended to take Ben's model card pictures. I must have the shots done within the next fortnight to make the deadline for the Spring/Summer Model Directory.

I have 27p. Jonathan is awash with cash but he hasn't emerged from the bedroom. Perhaps he's getting undressed. Is this how his birthday ends, with me creeping in to make amends, and finding him asleep? What about his presents? Rosie smiles and says, "It's a favor. We had fun. Buy me a coffee sometime."

Jonathan is running a bath. He has the taps on full-blast. I could pretend it wasn't Ben; don't all babies look alike, especially when naked? Would Jonathan apologize and mumble, "I thought...just for a moment...how stupid I was..."? But he knows. When you're fifty percent responsible for a child's genetic makeup, you are perfectly clear about who's eyeballing you from a twenty-five-foot screen.

He dries himself in the bathroom. I hear the soft flump of a bath towel hitting the floor. Normally he would slide it between the chrome bars of the heated towel rail. There are footsteps in the bedroom. The bedside light clicks off. I let my black dress drop to the living room floor. I kick off the brazen shoes. They leave pinched imprints on my feet as if I'm still wearing them, but in wrinkled pink. When I'm quite sure he's asleep, I slip in beside him.

He leaves for work before Ben wakes up. It's early; not quite seven. And he hasn't gone to work. He doesn't work on Saturdays. We go to the market for veg and prepare Ben's food for the week ahead on Saturdays. I assist by chopping herbs and cleaning the blender blades. I'm getting quite good at it. Heck, if he's going to react like this—over some insignificant bubble bath ad—I can get along without him. Who makes their own baby food? Beth does. Or rather, Rosie does. No one else has the time or the patience. What will happen when Ben eventually comes into contact with a factory-made dinner? He'll go berserk, like the kid who's never encountered anything sweeter than a digestive and chomps gobfuls of birthday cake before the candles have been lit.

I am tempted to test this theory. While Jonathan's huffing somewhere, I'll buy baby-food jars and drinks with maximum sugar content and loads of aspartame. See what he thinks about that.

Ben whimpers, pulling himself up on the cot bars. I lift him into bed. He propels himself into the space where Jonathan should be. His lips purse with disappointment. To distract him from Jonathan's absence—how do babies know it's Saturday, that Dad should be here?—I change and dress him briskly, singing to show how fine and normal and bloody *fantastic* everything is.

He's in his high chair, a new acquisition. Recently, Jonathan mentioned that this might be our last baby purchase; that the flat would soon return to normal. "When he's old enough to sit in a real chair, we can store this thing out of sight. Until next time," he added. I didn't mention that my mother had acquired a baby walker—an enormous plastic doughnut on wheels—at a car boot sale. Jonathan believes that such contraptions do untold damage to a child's developing limbs.

By midmorning, I've discovered that Jonathan's mobile is switched off and that he hasn't gone to talk best man business with Matthew. "Have you had a row?" asks Beth, the clink of crockery in the background.

"It's nothing. He probably said he was doing something. Maybe I didn't listen."

"Wedding nerves," she soothes. "He'll have gone for a walk. Probably working out his speech."

But Jonathan doesn't walk, not for fun. And we've decided we don't want speeches. Jonathan plans to thank our guests and the frosty couple who own the Fox and say a few words about Ben. Billy is still threatening to do something on his accordion. Eliza is delighted to have found appropriate headwear and called to check that I was okay with a tiara; that I won't feel upstaged by her sparkling headgear. Right now, she could show up with a chandelier on her head.

Jonathan's birthday presents still lie under the bed. I consider taking Ben swimming but can't face the rigmarole of the changing village. I could plonk him in the center of a circle of toys and try to rustle up someone for a genuine My Secret, but tap out Eliza's number instead. As her answerphone clicks on I remember that she's not due back from Nice until tonight. Eliza's trips are so commonplace that she rarely bothers to mention them. But she was revved up about this one. Dale was going. She had booked Greg for a shoot; Dale just *happened* to be his assistant. "I'd have booked Greg anyway," she insisted.

Lovely calls, apologizing for bothering me on a Saturday. "Something amazing's come up. Wednesday. Are you free? Zachary Marshall was booked but he's put his hand on the washing machine door, poor darling. Ninety degree wash. His mother was trying to get the gravy stains out of a dressing gown."

I try to sound sympathetic as if I know Zachary and care about his blistered paw. Ben raps his high chair table with a rubber spoon, exhibiting a newfound disapproval of Mother on the Telephone. "It's swollen up and bandaged," Lovely continues. "I biked over the Little Squirts and supermarket clips and they want Ben to take his place."

I point a loaded spoon at Ben's mouth, which jams shut: his mother is still on the phone and that isn't right.

"It's not that Ben's second choice," Lovely adds quickly. "I didn't put you up for the job because I'm worried about overusing him. But if you're available—"

"I'm available," I say, scribbling time and location in the small lined notebook I keep behind the formula milk in the cupboard. "What's the job?" It's almost an afterthought.

"The opening titles of a new breakfast show. His face will be superimposed on a boiled egg."

"I hope they don't bash him," I say, "with a teaspoon."

Splinters of laughter tinkle down the phone. "Don't worry. I'm sure it'll be tastefully done."

By lunchtime the flat has shrunk to a dingy box that's difficult to breathe in. How long does a Jonathan bad mood last? I'm not practiced at this. I try his mobile again, then Constance, but her face looms in my mind, assessing my wife-to-be credentials, pleased that we've had some kind of upset. I bang down the phone. Ben eyes me, crossly. "Isn't this fun?" I tell him. "Shall we play with your bricks? How about we have a roll on the rug?"

His eyes sidle to the front door.

I know what to do. I'll get ready for Jonathan, make things nice. I'll be wifely. Make dinner in advance. Jonathan's cookbooks are neatly lined up in the cupboard in ascending order of height. I select *Easy Suppers for Friends*. Supper once meant cornflakes or maybe toast and jam before bed; not a proper meal. Here, each chapter is headed with a single word: Cheese. Potatoes. Vegetables. Even the simplest recipes appear to require

ingredients I'd have to import from another continent or
at least obtain by mail order.

I remember something I ate with Eliza on holiday in
Corfu. Chicken in alcoholic sauce, with fruit bits.
Maybe rum was involved. And oranges. We have rum:
Havana Club, moved into Jonathan's flat with my ratty
paperbacks, somehow surviving his clear out of my
possessions. We have chicken, too, in the freezer, left
over from the barbecue. Jonathan overestimated our
parents' appetites. I set them to defrost. Ben cranes up
from his high chair, intrigued by the whirring of the
microwave.

Maybe I should cut up these chicken bits, like Jonathan
does. Allow the flavors to permeate. Gripping the breadknife, I saw a thigh. The flesh clings together, connected
by fatty strings. I slice harder, gripping the thigh, and the
knife slips, gouging a trough between my thumb and
forefinger.

I wash blood off the chicken and try to yank it apart,
but the effort squeezes more blood from the gash. There's
a bandage in the medical box, but nothing to secure it
with. Ben, who has so far regarded my cookery demon-
stration with rapt interest, bellows to be liberated from
the high chair.

I lift him out with blood trickling along my forearm,
inking his vest. He's crying, his face contorted. It's loud
enough to make a passing stranger glance at our flat
with pity, and hurry on. Finally his sobs subside into
hiccups. Scissors: that's what chefs use. Still cradling
Ben in one arm, I find some in the medical box.

Jonathan used them to neaten Ben's fringe. I was worried he'd make him look too prim for the supermarket shoot.

The bandage is secured with self-adhesive hedgehogs from a sticker book Beth gave to Ben. I thought he was too young for stickers but Beth said no, they'd help him develop fine motor skills. Maud can already remove a sticker from its backing. The chicken is snipped into misshapen strips, and doused with rum. I plonk Ben back in his high chair so he can watch my slick knife action as I chop a banana and an orange. As I open the oven door and slide in the dish, he waves delightedly. Yes: his mother can cook. This is the way things should be. If she'd grow a little less fond of the telephone, life would be pretty damn perfect.

My hand aches now, blood starbursting onto the bandage. Every half hour, I check the chicken dish. Nothing appears to be happening. I call Jonathan. When he spots me committing the phone crime again, Ben lurches for the hem of my jeans. Jonathan's voice mail clicks in. Ben roars, sabotaging any hope of leaving a message.

Later, the chicken appears to have heated through, although it still looks lank and uncooked. I wonder if the rum and fruit should have thickened and turned a more appetizing color. Banana slices float on top. I find candles under the sink and green glass holders to set them in. But I don't light them yet—can't have them flickering to nothing before he comes home.

I set two places at the table, checking wineglasses for smears. Ben greets his tea with morose acceptance. Even in the bath, he displays none of his usual enthusiasm. He places flat hands on the water's surface to see if they float.

I turn down the oven. Will a low heat cause bacteria to multiply at a terrifying rate? I don't want Jonathan poisoned on top of all this. I switch off the oven, figuring that when he shows up, I can blast my creation on the hob.

Ben lies across my knees, on the big bed, sucking his evening bottle. When it's finally dark I curl around him and drift, lulled by the steadiness of his breath.

I'm used to Eliza's grotty flat but I've never realized how potentially dangerous it is. It's Ben's first visit. I've brought my vulnerable son to a hazardous environment. Dotted red lines appear round the following dangers: a serrated knife lying across a breadboard on the sofa, evidence of a hurriedly prepared breakfast. A sturdy tripod, leaning against the fridge. The kettle, perched on a stool and on the verge of boiling point, which Eliza reaches by straddling an open suitcase heaped with bikini-type clothing. She greeted me and my bandaged hand with a hug that smelt of coconut.

She makes tea. The downstairs kids are practicing screaming in the hall. Ben investigates the flex of a chrome standard lamp. There are unguarded sockets everywhere, capable of shooting billions of volts through my son's fragile body. Eliza is wearing a scrap of black silk, possibly a robe, and the remains of tawny lipstick applied at least twelve hours earlier. "What do you think?" she asks, sipping fierce brown tea.

"His mother's, maybe. But he wouldn't. He doesn't *tell* her stuff."

She blows into her mug. "There must be someone he'd go to. Doesn't he have any friends?"

I shrug. "There's Matthew and Beth, but I've tried them. Maybe Billy, his old schoolmate."

"That's where he'll be. With someone who really knows him."

I can imagine Billy's response: "Oh, mate. What's it matter? Think how much cash the kid'll rake in. It's a laugh. Where's your sense of humor?" And he'd try to cheer up Jonathan with his latest alcohol-related incident, like the time he fell asleep while having a fag and was disturbed from his slumber by an ill-tempered firefighter, smashing down his front door.

No, he won't be at Billy's.

Eliza makes a feeble attempt to tidy a rumple of dresses on hangers which have been slung across an armchair. The electric fire glows sickly orange. Ben crawls behind the sofa, emerging with a brush, matted with hair, and licks it.

"He'll turn up," Eliza says. "Disappearing like this—it's an overreaction. An attention-seeking device."

"I should have told him at the start."

She pulls the robe thing around herself. "That's what he's mad about. Deceit. Not the actual modeling."

"Can I stay?" I ask suddenly.

Her eyes are on Ben, now gazing lovingly at the bars of the fire. During a long-ago sexual encounter, a lover of Eliza's had yelped on the floor as though in ecstasy.

Eliza had felt chuffed at his enthusiasm, until she discovered he'd jammed a toe between the bars of this fire. "It wouldn't be for long," I add. "He'll come back. He just needs to cool down."

Eliza's cat sneaks into the living room, making for a saucer in the hall. I'm not a cat lover; can't stand that claws-out dance they perform on your lap. It's behavior you wouldn't tolerate from a fellow human, let alone an animal with fish-breath. Enthralled, Ben follows the cat with a supercharged crawl.

Eliza's bedroom door opens. Dale steps out in gray striped pants; an overabundance of beige male flesh. "Hey!" he says. "I thought we had company." And he checks Ben's rear end, hoisted high and reeking even higher.

The cat stiffens. "I'll get dressed," says Eliza. "Make yourself a cuppa." And she heads for the bedroom with Dale, pants cling-filmed to his buttocks.

I feed Ben on the roof where there are no sockets or bubbling kettles; just a sheer drop to the pavement. He has mashed banana. How handy the banana is: neatly packaged, easily squashable. I wonder if babies really appreciate the fresh herbs that go into their meals. What do they get in the womb? A constant trickle of unidentifiable stuff, via a tube made of skin. Then they're born and it's papaya this, mango that. Talk about overegging the pudding.

I like being on the roof. It feels open and away from everything. Decades ago, someone tried to spruce things up with terra-cotta pots, now housing withered stumps, and wooden troughs, containing soil and bird droppings. There are no railings. The cat leaps up through the opening and prowls toward us, eyeing Ben's bottle greedily. It circles me, closing in. I delve into the bag of foodstuffs I've gleaned from Eliza's kitchen. "Help yourself to anything," she'd said grandly. I found a greasy-skinned apple and a hot cross bun, possibly left over from Easter. I break off a chunk and fling the rest over the edge of the roof. It hits the ground with a crack.

I tap in Jonathan's work number on my mobile. "He doesn't work weekends," says a middle-aged voice. "Who is this?"

"His wife," I blurt out.

In search of more food, I totter down the rickety stairs, clutching Ben tightly to my chest. And I hear them: muffled giggles from Eliza's room. An occasional thud, and a bed creaking painfully. The creaks quicken, and there's a grunt, like you make when you finally get the lid off a jar of gherkins. Then a whisper:

Do you think she heard?

No, she's up on the roof, feeding the baby.

Is she staying long?

Maybe. It'll be okay. She's my friend.

If I stay, I'll have to go back and collect the cot—we never got around to buying a travel cot—or have Ben with me on the blow-up bed in Eliza's spare room. *Babycare* warns that a child's sleep patterns are easily disrupted: *don't be too adventurous when holidaying during your child's*

*first year. Will your temporary surroundings offer the facilities
you need? Decamping to an unfamiliar environment can cause
unnecessary stress.*

I can't stay, even though we're all pretending this is an
ordinary Sunday morning, as if I've just popped in. I don't
pop in anywhere. My diary is scrawled with times and
places for castings and jobs, plus deadlines and must-re-
members. On the mum circuit people rarely pop in. I
have developed an aversion to popping. The one time
Felt Lady appeared at our door, blocking the light with
her hefty shoulders, I made her coffee with cold water
so she'd leave quickly.

Dale asks which paper I'd like and returns later with an
armful of newsprint, but not the one I asked for. He's
wearing greasy jeans and a hippie top with a tassel scenario
at the neckline. He distributes newspaper sections (him:
main paper; Eliza: color mag; me: travel, money and business and any other bits no one's interested in). Ben claws
the sport section. I read a feature about honeymoons: *Almond Beach Resort, Bermuda, offering its own private shoreland
and forty acres of landscaped gardens for a secluded break. Ideal
for unwinding after hectic wedding preparations. Couples only.*

Dale reads the foreign news pages, frowning and feigning grownup-ness. Eliza studies a feature on sweaters
constructed from knitted squares. No one seems concerned with eating, though Eliza crunches the occasional
Hula Hoop. She is still wearing the black silk robe. Dale
smells like the underside of a teenage boy's duvet. The
tea Eliza made me has brown scum on top. Ben sleeps on
my lap now, done in by the electric fire's dry heat.

The buzzer doesn't wake him. Eliza opens the door. Her robe thing is bunched up in its tie belt, showing her mottled thighs. Jonathan appears to have narrowed. Dale looks over his paper and nods amiably, as if another friend has popped in. So much popping. In an attempt to bring her robe thing to order, Eliza succeeds only in opening it at the front, showing high-waisted maroon knickers and a burning desire to be somewhere else.

Jonathan and I are on the roof because there's nowhere else to go. "What happened to your hand?" Jonathan asks.

The bandage is filthy and bloodstained and the hedgehog stickers are peeling off. "I cut it with a breadknife," I explain. For a moment he looks aghast, like he might topple off the roof. "Accidentally," I add. And I take my chance: "Can't we forget this? We're getting married in two weeks. We have stuff to sort out. Did you ever think it would be so complicated?"

He looks confused, as if a mad stranger has accused him of stashing his domestic waste in their bin and is threatening to call the police. "Like photos," I charge on. "We don't want a formal thing, not that soft-focus couple in a champagne glass thing, but shouldn't we put someone in charge, like Dale? Can he come, is that okay? He's not on the list, it's just started with them, but—"

He walks away from me. At least, with this being a roof, there's a limit to how far he can go. I follow him, glimpsing a jumble of rooftops and small, unkempt gardens and, far below, kids booting a football against the No Ball Games sign.

"The photographs," I remind him.

He turns to me. He looks tired and unemotional. "Nina," he says, "I can't marry you. I don't even know who you are."

17

Traveling With Your Baby

Is Ben sick? Has something happened? Do you realize how unprofessional this makes us look as an agency? You're duty bound to show up for jobs. It's for national TV. Extremely high profile for you, and for us. I don't know, Nina.

I ask what it is she doesn't know.

I don't know if we can represent Ben anymore.

At the edge of the ferry's soft play area, a woman with her hair gathered up into a wiry topknot shows me photographs of her children. They are creased passport photos. It's not necessary to show me as the real children are here: bounding from a PVC arch to a padded cylinder which they lie on and attempt to roll, with the smallest sibling squealing underneath.

"Stop that, Nathan," snaps the father from behind a creased paperback with barbed wire on the cover.

"On holiday with your little boy?" asks the woman.

"Just for a few days. My husband can't get time off."

She tweaks her topknot with burgundy fingernails. "Shame to be away from his dad. Beautiful little boy."

Ben rummages happily in the ball pool. Jonathan disapproves of this kind of play. He thinks bright colors overstimulate and worries about festering sandwiches and nappies in ball pools. He once said that such play facilities are for parents who can't think of anything more constructive to do with their kids.

"He might join us later," I tell her.

"Well, that's good." She studies Ben. "He doesn't look like you, does he? Is there more of your husband in him?"

I nod.

"Lucky you," she cackles, snapping a four-finger Kit Kat to distribute among her children. "We're off to Disneyland, Paris. Kids have been badgering me for years."

"They're not real, they're just cartoons," retorts a stringy girl in a faded vest, dangling from the PVC arch.

"Yes they are," says her brother. "You see them in the adverts, walking about."

"So how come you get Mickey in America and Disneyland, Paris, like two places at once?"

"It's like Father Christmas," says a younger girl with cherubic curls.

"Time difference," says the boy, tugging at his crotch as if he requires the loo. "Like, Florida's five hours behind us, stupid."

The older girl plummets from the arch in a jangle of scab-elbowed arms and thin hair. "They're dwarfs," she announces, jumping up. "Little people dressed up."

"I know," rages her brother. "Fuck off."

"Stop that, Nathan," says the father, jutting his nose farther into his book.

We have lunch together at one long table smattered with the previous customers' sauce sachets and soiled cutlery and a forgotten guidebook to Walks in Eastern France. Taking pity on me—though she has three times as many children—the woman says she'll order for me and returns with a Cumberland sausage, coiled like a glistening worm. Ben, already accustomed to a limited diet, makes do with mashed banana. The woman introduces herself as Linda and offers me her last finger of Kit Kat.

It's a calm crossing. Linda's family argues about how long the queues will be at Disneyland. The oldest daughter asks to hold Ben and plants noisy kisses on his forehead, leaving pink imprints. "That's not right," she snaps at her brother. He is slumped over a coloring book, tongue poked out in concentration. "Pluto's got down ears," she nags. "They don't stick up like that."

"He's running," huffs the boy.

While Linda explains that the ears are probably bouncing up, rather than permanently up, I marvel at her patience until my stomach takes over and saliva seeps into my mouth. There's no reason to feel sick. The sea is an endless flat puddle. Perhaps it's the smell of the fuel and the kitchens or the fragment of Eliza's hot cross bun that's only just forcing its way out of my stomach. But I'm on my feet, leaving Ben in the arms of an eleven-year-old, and running up scuffed metal stairs to the edge of the boat where the Cumberland sausage, a finger of Kit Kat and a rotten bellyful of guilt splatter down into the English Channel.

"Take the car," Jonathan had insisted, "if you're set on going to that awful place of your parents." He didn't say don't go. All he added was, "You have no idea how to get there. Are you seriously relying on this?" He clutched my father's map, drawn in marker pen on a paper serviette. The ink had blotched where he'd pressed too hard.

An open case lay on the bed. Jonathan played with Ben in the living room, singing and pretending to be happy. His voice sounded tight as elastic. He looked into the bedroom and stared at the case. "You'll be back in plenty of time, won't you?" he said.

"For what?" I asked lightly. I tucked socks into the corners of the case, not looking at him.

"The wedding."

"I thought it was off. You said—"

"I was just mad. The shock was bad enough. Then I started counting the lies. The times you'd dragged him round town and—"

"We're not getting married," I said, shutting the case.

He followed me into the living room. I wondered

whether to take toys. What Ben might need for entertainment. Maybe being away would be enough. Change of scenery. Wasn't that the whole point of holidays?

Jonathan perched on the suede cube, observing me. I lifted the case but he took it from me and carried it to the car. I had Dad's map in my purse and wondered if it bore any resemblance to the road system in Eastern France. Jonathan's smile was wide and brave. "Just a silly little ad," he said, trying for a laugh. He loaded my suitcase into the boot then felt in his pocket and handed me a small navy box. Inside was a watch.

"What's this for?" I asked. It looked like a man's watch. Silver face, without numbers. A serious watch.

"For telling the time," he said. "I planned to give it to you the night we went out, as a prewedding thing."

A prewedding thing for what? To thank me for marrying him? I put it on because I didn't know what else to do.

I wanted to ask him something. How many lies he'd counted.

"Have fun," he said, turning back to the flat.

Linda scoops up the soft toys, coloring books and windup plastic crocodiles with snapping mouths that litter the table but miraculously fit into her zebra-striped bag. The dad slaps his jeans pocket where the passports should be.

"In here," says Linda, patting the bag's outside pouch.

I check the zip compartment of my bag for ours: mine, the photo taken four years ago, before motherhood made me look craggier than my own parents. I'm grinning in a fresh, expectant way; I look like a toddler. And Ben's: a baby's smile, the mouth a black hole, with my hands holding him in the correct position in the booth. I'd applied for Ben's passport in good time for our honeymoon. That was before the B&B thing.

"Enjoy your holiday," says Linda, poised to shepherd her offspring down to the bowels of the ferry and into the car. She stops for a moment, gives me a look. "Will you be okay? You look a bit green."

"Sea sickness," I say. "I always get it."

"Poor thing. You'd have been better on Eurostar."

I can't tell her the truth; that some ridiculous part of me liked the idea of standing on the deck of a ship, watching my old world shrink to nothing.

"Mum," says Linda's cherubic daughter, "my arse is itching."

Linda laughs and ushers her away. "Funny," she says, turning back, "but I know I've seen Ben somewhere before. Are you sure we haven't met?"

I am so unused to driving on the other side of the road that I lumber around roundabouts as if I'm on my first lesson. I have no need to drive, not usually. My world is generally small enough to be covered on foot. I never drive to auditions; finding a parking space is too fraught. When it's a job, we're collected and deposited back home in cars with buttery leather upholstery and inaudible engines. In these cars I've worried about polluting the air-conditioned environment, just by exhaling.

I check Ben in the rearview mirror. His expression is

bright and expectant: he's looking forward to this impromptu holiday. It's like he knows this is France. The beginning of something.

The car smells as fresh and unsoiled as those posh account cabs, even though Jonathan has owned it for several years. He cleans it every Sunday morning, raking the seats with a minivacuum device. Ben is allowed only milk—no snacks—in the car.

After three hours on the road he is no longer prepared to tolerate the gaping cavern of his stomach. The whine starts up, becoming heartier as I fail to respond. He lashes his head from side to side, trying to bite at his car seat straps. I pop in the song tape from Beth's package. She called me on my mobile at Eliza's and insisted on coming over. I didn't want them to meet. You know when two departments of your life won't mix. They'll just curdle.

Beth and Eliza sized each other up in an instant, quickly concluding that they were of different species and not bothering to communicate. Beth hugged me with cranked-up grief and pressed the pink tissue-wrapped package into my hands. Apart from the tape, there was a sleepsuit for Ben. "It's fleecy inside, for warmth," Beth explained. "Look after him, won't you?" And she squeezed me again, saying, "It doesn't have to come to this."

The tape perks up Ben for almost a minute. Then the wailing kicks off again and no posh lady crooning *once I caught a fish alive* will convince him that life is worth living. I pull in at services and stopper his mouth with the milk he half drank on the ferry, and which is now fermenting beautifully. Could it have turned into cheese or even alcohol? At least it will soothe him. Didn't the lady with all those coats instruct me to add brandy to his nighttime bottle?

Ben's blanket, rolled into a fat sausage on his lap, props the bottle to the perfect height. I drive on, imagining Jonathan rapping at the passenger window and shouting, "Is this how you feed him? Is this what *Babycare* tells you to do?" *Never leave your baby unattended with a bottle. Dispose of heated milk after one hour. Be sure to sterilize your baby's bottles and teats until his first birthday. Never take your baby to a damp, decrepit hovel—Away From His Dad—unless you wish to encourage respiratory problems, in which case you have no right to be in sole charge of a vulnerable human being.*

I manage to negotiate Chatillon but from that point Dad's map lets me down. The village, Vanvey, is marked, and the house indicated by a think bubble splodgily drawn around it, but there is no line connecting it to Chatillon. It's raining now, and dark. I pull in at the roadside and study the serviette.

Ben makes sleepy murmurings in the back. The bottle has fallen from his mouth and lies empty on the blanket. I wonder why Dad missed out this crucial road. When he sent me the serviette, along with the key—a chunky lump of rusting metal—there were no instructions or even a good luck message. I have no idea how the village might be connected to the rest of Eastern France. All I have is a map (unfinished) and a serious five-inch key.

Ben mumbles dreamily, back in some cozy cot world where there's a freezer stuffed with organic delights. I nibble a torpedo roll I bought on the ferry. Maybe this is where we'll end up; mother and son in the car. People live in cars, even with children. Being trapped in his seat may hamper his gross motor development but it would do for now. Until I can think of something better.

A car passes, its outline smudged in the rain. It pulls up a few yards ahead. The driver's door opens. My back teeth set together. I keep perfectly still, like a child playing hide and seek, without hiding.

Someone bends at the window, head tilted sideways. I open it a fraction. Eyes peer in, the lids buttered with glittery stuff visible even in the dark. I wind the window down fully. "You're lost?" says the woman, shivering in a black evening dress with an embroidered cardigan on top.

I nod and poke Dad's serviette at her. "I'm looking for Vanvey. This house, at the edge of the village." Not the time for schoolgirl French: and what can I remember when I need it? *Je voudrais une tasse de café.* The woman peers at the map, running her tongue around her teeth. Her perfume wafts thickly into the car. "You don't know it," I say.

"I do," she says. "You can follow me, we're going that way."

"Do you know the house? It's old, and it doesn't have a number. I think it's kind of…ruined."

"I know this house," she says, casting Ben a sympathetic look. "It is bad, very bad. Can I show you the way to a nice hotel?"

In the dark, Vanvey amounts to a huddle of sturdy stone houses and a small shop with its shutters down: there is no indication of what it might sell. Soon we run out of village. Round a precarious bend, the woman toots her horn. I take it as my signal to pull into a track on the right and follow its curve to a cobbled area next to a low building. It's so dark, I can't make out whether I've arrived at the front, back, or some crumbling outhouse. Leaving Ben sleeping in the car, I prowl its walls in search of a door.

Dad's key fits stiffly into the lock. The door opens heavily, and I'm hit by the smell of wet dishcloth. The light switch is the old-fashioned kind with a knob at its tip and a firm click. I flick it on quickly, as if that will minimize risk of sparking or electric shock. I creep round the first room, which might be a kitchen. Uncarpeted stairs twist their way up to dank rooms in the eaves. Upstairs, no lights seem to work. Enough moonlight struggles through gunked-up windows to pick out the outline of a bed, unmade, and a stern-looking wardrobe with one door lolling open. I gather Ben from the car, feel my way upstairs and, without undressing either of us, pull him towards me beneath a rumple of moss-scented bedspread.

And I dream I'm wearing a red dress, so tight its seams threaten to split. "Get married in red, wish yourself dead," Constance warns. She laughs, showing big yellow teeth like peanuts. I follow her between flower beds, the sickly plants evenly spaced. Up the wide sandstone steps, through the chipped maroon door. First right into a lemon-painted room whiffing of Sunday school.

The registrar lady looks up, not at my face but at the too-tight dress, knowing my stomach hurts from being held in, that I'm faking my thinness. She suppresses a smile, as if she's in on a practical joke. Only then do I notice that guests have arrived: my mother, her hair partly obscuring wet eyes, and her hand at her mouth to stop giggles (or maybe she's crying). Beth holds Maud firmly, urging her to latch onto a fully inflated breast which hangs from her unbuttoned denim dress. Maud wears heavy black velvet, matching Raven who perches beside her, those petulant lips stained with blackcurrant ice lolly. Behind them is Matthew, his fingers interlaced like the child's game (here's the church, here's the steeple). Next to him, wearing a white cotton sundress, sits Rosie with hands on her lap, primly clasped.

Lovely hurries in late, hissing that I've missed the deadline for the spring/summer model directory and squeezes onto the end of the front pew, meant for important people. My parents and Constance shuffle along to make space for her. Later still are Ranald and his girlfriend, in swimwear, dripping onto the registry office's glazed parquet floor. "Are we ready?" says the registrar, glancing at the chrome alarm clock which dominates her leather-topped desk. *Let's get this over and done with. I don't have all day. There's another fifteen couples out there in the hall.*

She stands up to start proceedings when Eliza tumbles in, her lips glossy red, the wedding dress skimpily cut and edged with ruffles. "Sorry," she mouths as she reaches the spot before the desk where Jonathan stands, takes her hand and kisses her, in a way he's never kissed me.

I sit at the far end of the front row, close to the wall, half my backside hanging off the pew. Constance's papery hand wraps around mine, her fingernails spearing my palm. The registrar's alarm clock goes off with a deafening screech.

You know, before you're fully conscious, when you're in an unfamiliar bed. And you're already skimming through possibilities: your best friend's spare room with its molding tangerines? In a hotel that's falling drastically short of its brochure description? Or a misguided one-night stand: how could you? Who is he? What happened to your clothes?

The mattress is lumpen like porridge. Ben and I have sunk into the middle. His clammy head rests against my chest. Something rigid digs into my shoulder blade; a spring, trying to escape the vile mattress. Ben wriggles and shifts, moving perilously close to the edge. I slide both hands under him to pull him closer. He mustn't wake up, not yet, and start wanting things: milk, warmed to the correct temperature (how? Is there a kettle? Does the cooker work?), breakfast (not banana again?), and his dad (where is he? What happened to our family unit?).

Jonathan would never wind up in this mess. He'd have had the cool box packed with butter, yogurt, cheese and proper milk (not the ready-made formula in cartons I snatched in Dover). He'd be down there now, scouring the sink, making things work. I'd smell real coffee. The boiler would have been lit hours ago. By the time I made it downstairs, my parents' derelict shack would have been as gleaming and well-functioning as our flat.

I shiver, pulling up the candlewick bedspread to cover everything but our faces. Ben's is blissful (still sleeping and therefore knowing nothing about the domestic horrors that await him). Mine, I imagine, is a little tense and certainly unwashed, the frown lines etching permanently as I wonder what to do, now that I'm in charge.

Three voice mail messages:

Nina, Jess from Promise. *Is there a problem with your copy? Some misunderstanding? I've tried you at home and e-mailed you. We're having to fill the page with a puzzle this week. Call me. We're a bit desperate.*

Nina? Rosemary from the Fox. You said you'd call to finalize numbers. I'm assuming it's just wine and beer, no spirits, is that right?

It's me, just checking you arrived okay.

I wonder how long Jonathan will wait before calling the Fox to explain. How do you undo a wedding? Will he phone round personally or will Matthew, as redundant best man, do it for him?

Mum said, "I thought you were rushing things. You'd be better waiting until you've got your figure back." I told her there won't be a wedding, ever. "You can still have your present," Mum added. "It's a lovely lamp. Doesn't work, probably needs to be rewired, but it's pretty. You could hang things from it."

All Eliza said was, "It's better than getting divorced," thinking, perhaps, *thank God it's only a borrowed dress.*

Ben wakes hungry and irritable. His vest is damp around the nappy region. Gray light creeps in through the cracked window. The wallpaper, a faded pink and lime floral print, curls at the joints. On a pine chest of drawers at the window stands a blue-and-white-speckled jug, bearing flowers, now dried crisply. The room smells doughy, as if something is brewing, perhaps in the depths of the mattress.

A red wine bottle, an inch left undrunk, sits on the gray wicker bedside table. A pair of lilac knickers hangs on the washstand. As a child, I was unaware of my parents' lack of regard for domesticity: the twice yearly vacuuming session, so traumatic to the Hoover that it would clog instantly, to be jabbed by my mother with a straightened wire coat hanger. I'd thought this was normal until Imogen Priestley came round, stood in the doorway of my bedroom and said, "Why is everything dirty?" She perched nervously on the edge of my bed and asked my mother to call her dad so he could collect her early.

I carry Ben to the kitchen and fill his bottle one-handed. The rough kitchen walls look moldy. The kitchen cupboards have a homemade, out of synch look. A little cabinet with a wire door, presumably for cheese, sits on the scratched fridge. A mousetrap lies on the floor nearby, with a withered black mouse in it, the size of my thumb.

Ben settles on my lap, glugging his bottle, as if Jonathan

might emerge from a rickety cupboard and say, "So! Here we are. Shall I put some coffee on?"

But of course he doesn't. And I haven't brought coffee. I don't even know where the toilet is.

18

Cruising

*B*abycare doesn't warn you about the whopping developmental leap that occurs when an eight-month-old baby is left in sole charge of its mother. No one points out that infants are, in fact, wiser than their own parents in that they never embark on unsuitable relationships or willingly exchange a clean, warm bed, with its duvet from Heal's, for a dank mattress reeking of fungi.

Though still reliant on me for nutrition and toileting procedures, Ben matures at such breakneck speed that I expect to discover him mulling over the leaflet about Chatillon, left on the fireplace, which suggests an outing to the Musée Archeologique with its breathtaking artifacts including a bronze vase of Greek origin.

Instinctively, he knows what we should do. I huddle over the living room fireplace, recalling Ranald on our camping trip, barking instructions on the fashioning of newspaper firelighters ("What are you trying to make? A doughnut?"). When Ben witnesses his mother cursing over the grate, he crawls swiftly to the front door and batters it with a fist, demanding to be let out.

He's right: the fire can wait. We'll probably freeze and be discovered like mammoths, trapped in ice, but without firelighters nothing is likely to happen in the flickering flame department. What we need urgently (his hollow face tells me) is a supermarket shop. We can't live on bananas, aging torpedo rolls and cartons of milk forever.

As we drive to Chatillon I talk to him like the adult he has become. I ask him, "Should we get ourselves a proper map, instead of relying on Grandad's serviette?" Ben seems to think this is a good idea, and who else is there to ask? With a distinct lack of significant other/baby support group to hand, Ben is all I have.

In the supermarket he gazes thoughtfully from the trolley, accustomed now to this mode of transport. Chill cabinets whir lazily as I prowl the aisles in search of cleaning products. Once located, I am unsure whether to snatch anything with a lemon-fresh look about it (signifying an extended stay) or just washing up liquid and a spongy wipe.

The choice is too baffling and we leave with fresh milk, cheese, a bumper clear plastic packet of bald sponge cakes and baby food—salmon and vegetables which appear as alternate pink/buff-colored stripes in the jar, and contains both sugar and salt. Back at the house we eat quickly and messily, stoking up for warmth. Ben perches dumpily on my lap, nappy loaded with several gallons of wee, beaming all over his salmon-splattered face.

I imagine we're anonymous as we explore the village, or what village there is. Its inhabitants seem to have gone somewhere else—the West Indies, perhaps, or a cinema I have yet to locate. Occasionally there's a flurry of coat as someone slams a car door, or a smudge of face at a window. Only in the baker's—the shop turns out to be a baker's—do we witness a human being close up: a crispy-haired woman with firm lines from nose to mouth, regarding me as if I am planning to poke holes in her loaves.

So we fall into a pattern of driving to Chatillon every second day. That way we have some pattern to our lives, avoid the fierce bread lady and limit the chances of getting to know anyone. I'm not in the market for a new best friend or even a penpal. Days drift, with Ben snoozing off whatever striped delight he's devoured for lunch, and my voice becomes a strangled croak from underuse.

Nina, we're so worried…haven't heard…think about you… Then an adult male—presumably Matthew—butts in and Beth snaps, *I'm on the phone, for crying out loud. Leaving a message for Nina.*

Jonathan's voice is muffled as if coming from the inside of a dustbin. *Just seeing how you are. Let me know if you need anything. Right then, okay.* Knowing he'll be at work I call the flat, taking care not to sound so gloomy he'll assume something awful's happened, but not too party-spirited, either. "We're fine," I say. "Ben's trying to pull himself up. He's almost standing and—" My throat clogs with something creamy and I'm forced to ring off. Ben opens one eye, as if to check where the choking noise is coming from, and returns to the safe, mother-free zone of his nap.

The house becomes so familiar that I learn how to use its different rooms at various times of the day. Midafternoon, when Ben wakes up, I stroke him back to reality in the smaller bedroom. It's gloomy, and the sloping ceiling looms at you, but it's slightly less bracing than the rest of the house. "Most visitors come in spring and summer," points out Walking in Eastern France, which I filched from the ferry. "Winter can be picturesque, but is bitterly cold." So we huddle in the little room, every so often investigating the dark space off the kitchen where the boiler lurks. Spent matches litter the floor. I call Dad, hoping he'll shed light on the hot water situation. "We've never found it a problem," he says brightly. So I try again to follow his instructions and locate the red button which must be pressed for thirty seconds until the pilot light ignites, but there is no red button, and therefore no ignition of pilot light, and no hot water.

In the evenings I tuck Ben into my coat and button it up. We position ourselves as close as possible to the fire without clambering into the flames. The fire glows tentatively, lit with the aid of seven firelighters and a stack of paper doughnuts. Two spindly wooden chairs, laid on their sides, prevent Ben from investigating the flames. A kettle is boiled for the dual purpose of heating Ben's milk and washing the day's clothes to be draped on the chairs by the fire. We acquire a burnt smell. It's not quite *InHouse* magazine, although Eliza might say the place has a certain shabby chic charm.

Ben's scalp smells of dough. There's dirt under his fingernails which will never come out. I wonder what Lovely would say, were we to show up for an audition. *Professional mother pays great attention to her child's appearance. And to her own.*

At least, I remind myself, no one knows us.

But they do notice us. It starts with a nod, a quick smile of recognition, though everyone is too scarved up and hatted to speak. I have had to invest in a snowsuit for Ben. His ruddy face peeps crossly from a quilted hood.

One morning, I see two women chatting animatedly outside the bakers. One is dressed not in serious winter attire but a butter-colored suit printed with turquoise sea horses. She keeps patting her extravagantly sculpted auburn curls. Her companion wears a hairy brown sweater like a horse blanket. The sea horse woman waves. Up close I recognize her face: she directed me to my parents' place. "You found the house?" she says pleasantly.

"Yes, thanks."

She looks down at Ben and tickles the tiny cheek area accessible in the snowsuit. "The place," she says, "it's not so suitable for a baby?"

I wonder whether to agree—to detail its poor fixtures,

fittings and tantrummy boiler—but say only, "It's fine. We're having a fantastic time."

She speaks to the other woman; I smile dumbly. The sea horse woman pats my arm and says, "You're not staying long in that house?" *That* house. Instant disapproval. I can hear Constance now: "Well, I could have told you it wouldn't work out with *that* Nina."

"Not sure how long we'll stay," I tell the woman. "Our plans are sort of…open-ended." I wonder if she knows what open-ended means.

"No," she says, patting my arm with her leather-gloved hand, "no, my dear, listen, we have a hotel. Very quiet at this time of year. No one comes—not until spring." I wonder whether to sympathize over her ailing business. "And you're welcome," she says. "You and your baby— you can stay with us. It's warm and very comfortable. No charge." She smiles quickly and nods as if the matter is settled. "Here," she says, "call me, and we'll prepare a room." And she hands me a cream-colored card on which is printed Hotel Beauville, with a line drawing of a robust-looking building and the proprietor's name: Sylvie Laman.

"Sylvie," she says, patting her throat. "And this is my daughter, Nadine."

What Sylvie doesn't realize is that we have everything we need right here. The pilot light still refuses to introduce itself but I have found, in the bowels of the wardrobe, a snagged, green satin eiderdown and a mottled gray blanket embroidered with Girl Guide badges.

Despite the extra bedding I still sleep in my jeans, T-shirt, sweater and socks, and Ben wears the fleecy all-in-one with feet in, thoughtfully donated by Beth.

A parcel arrives, addressed to Ben. I shake the age twelve to eighteen month cable-knit sweater and checked woollen trousers, expecting to find a note. A few lines, perhaps, to indicate that Jonathan misses us madly and is falling to pieces and forgetting to put out the bin on a Tuesday night. There is nothing. I only know it's from Jonathan due to the forward-slanting writing on the brown paper wrapper.

But of course he wants us back, or Ben anyway. He's waiting, knowing we can't hold out for long. He has seen photos of the house. "Interesting," he said when my mother pressed snapshots into his palm. "It has potential. Quite an, uh, uh, project."

So he waits, continuing to prepare baby food, though now with a coarser texture so that Ben can learn to manage lumps. He won't ask us home for Christmas. Jonathan has never asked me for anything. He will spend Christmas with Constance and neither will mention the shimmering void where Nina and Ben should be.

I do my Christmas shopping in Chatillon. The department store is the obvious choice, but it's filled with shoppers thrashing their carrier bags with time to laugh and chat and kiss each other in that French way despite having so many people still to buy for.

These people make me sag inside. Sometimes Eliza does that to me. Back in London I'd be shaking antique crumbs out of the toaster and call her for some frivolous talk—maybe she'd tell me about a model who cried because the makeup artist couldn't provide her favorite eye cream with extract of squid—only to be told by a hoity assistant that Eliza had headed off for her Indian head massage and wouldn't have time to call until Fashion Week had finished.

Unable to face the department store, I creep into the pharmacy. It's quiet enough for me to enter with buggy and not gash anyone's shins. The shop is searingly clean with most products packaged in white boxes. For Eliza I choose a sparkly nail polish kit in a see-through plastic box. She'll understand, she knows things are tricky. For my mother I grab a purple leather pouch filled with finicky implements for manicures. For Dad I pick a black-and-white-striped sponge bag with wipeable lining, and consider buying a duplicate for Jonathan (what's the gift-buying etiquette for the man you've just left? Do you buy a little something to show you've remembered? Or a lavish gift—a digital camera, perhaps—to compensate for your guilt?).

No, a present from me would confuse and possibly even irritate. *After all she's done, she thinks she can make things right with a crappy zip-up bag. Like the one she bought me for my birthday in fact.* Instead I choose stackable plastic boats for Ben, optimistic that, come Christmas, the boiler will burst into life and we'll be awash with hot water and have bath after bath, for the sheer hell of it.

After a snooze in the car, Ben is revived and eager to demonstrate newfound skills. In the main bedroom he reaches up from a crawling position, hoisting himself higher by grabbing fistfuls of Girl Guide blanket. *Look,* says his bonkers grin.

He's standing up. He moves in unsteady sidesteps until bandy legs crumple and he tumbles backward, landing plumply on his nappied bottom. And he laughs: *You like that? Want me to show you again?*

December 4
Vanvey
Dear Jonathan,
Well, we're here and pretty settled. The house isn't as bad as it looked in Mum's photos. The roof leaks in around eighteen places but only when it rains, obviously. And it's less of a problem now I've figured out where water comes in and have found enough buckets and pots to catch the drips.

Great news! Ben is walking. Well, not walking exactly but standing up, almost cruising. Still a bit wobbly but you should see him! It really is amazing!

I crumple the letter, fling it into the impressive fire I've made and start again:

I don't know how to begin or even why I've come here. The house is terrible, far worse than Mum and Dad ever admitted. Ben's nose is permanently streaming. We can't wash properly—there's no hot water apart from what I boil in the kettle. I'm thinking of coming back and asking Eliza to put us up for a while, or even my parents. The house is just about bearable now but who knows how it'll be in January or February? Dad says there's often snow. If the pipes freeze there won't be any water at all. I never speak to anyone except Ben and I think I'm going crazy. Even Ben looks at me like I'm not all there.

I stop, check the date. Our wedding day. *Jonathan and Nina invite you to their wedding on December 4, at 11:00 a.m., at Hackney Town Hall and afterward at the Fox, Bishop Road, London N4.*

It's our wedding day and I'm spouting a weather forecast. In the little bedroom water drips from the light fitting into a chipped enamel jug. *Doop, doop, doop.*

Sylvie shows up in a quilted gold jacket patterned with raspberry-colored ferns. She smiles elegantly as if I should have been expecting her. Hefty gold earrings hide in her auburn hair. "I was passing," she says. "Look, I've brought you some things we won't use." I step back to let her glide into the kitchen. From her macramé shopping bag come tomatoes, an orangy pie topped with almonds and a paper bag of green beans. "I've been thinking about you," she says, pulling the jacket about her. "Are you warm enough? There's a heater I can bring from the hotel. Do you have enough firewood? My son will bring some around."

"We don't need anything," I say, backing away from her. "Thank you, but we're fine."

She looks around the kitchen. The worktop is dusted

with cake crumbs. Ben stands at a battered cupboard, clinging to its tarnished handle. His checked trousers are striped with chicken and broccoli with added sugar and salt. Is she expecting a coffee or what? I consider resorting to my old tactic—making it with cold water—to get her to leave. I don't want her here, noticing things.

"Are you staying for Christmas?" she asks.

"Probably."

"You're spending Christmas alone in this house?"

If only I had my coat on, I could pretend I was on my way out. *Sorry, Sylvie, but we're due to meet friends in a lovely warm restaurant. We know people here. See, we belong.*

"All alone with a baby," she says.

I swipe at Ben's unhygienic trousers with a rank-smelling cloth. "My husband was supposed to come," I explain. "For Christmas. But he's working, can't get away. We're just here a little while until—thanks for the food. It looks delicious."

She touches my arm and says, "Can I invite you for lunch? This Saturday? We'd enjoy having you." She trots out on clippy heels, wafting lavender like an underwear drawer.

Hotel Beauville lies at the end of a curved graveled driveway, a hunk of cheap yellow in the distance. Plaster animals cluster at each side of the path. A bird's house with a wooden man winding a handle juts from a dilapidated border. Ben struggles in his buggy, arching to making his escape. I feel conspicuously giftless. Ben and I perused the supermarket in Chatillon—and I hovered over prettily packaged olives, biscuits and cheeses—but what if these were everyday French brands, the equivalent of bringing Jacob's Crackers, or Branston Pickle?

Sylvie peeps though a flounce of white curtain and opens the door before we reach it. Ben is unleashed by her quick fingers and clasped in her arms. She guides me, a hand at my back, into a hall smelling of woodland glade room freshener.

"This way," she says, and we're in a mish-mash of a living room, its bookcase jammed not with books but soft toys: teddies with waistcoats and glasses and mice decked out in flamboyant evening wear. Each window is draped with ruched white satin, glimmering cheaply like highly flammable knickers. Damp wooden oars have been carelessly propped up against the pansy-printed wall.

Nadine makes sweet talk to Ben. She is still wearing the horse blanket sweater. Ben giggles, glancing from one animated face to the other. I realize how flat my face has become, like a paving slab. "Christophe!" calls Sylvie. There's a male mutter from somewhere higher than us and he appears, lolloping down three stairs at a time. He's a long-legged boy, a long-everythinged boy; too tall for his width, as if stretched. The nose is long too, the chin decorated with a beginner's attempt at a beard. *Don't kiss me,* I plead. *Don't do that double-kiss French thing.*

He does the double-kiss French thing and turns his attention to Ben, whose winter clothing is being peeled off. It's like shooting a commercial: everything taken out of my hands. Sylvie tells me to sit. Nadine dumps steaming mounds on my plate; green beans and dollops of mash and a meaty dish swimming in gloss. From his vintage high chair—clearly falling way short of safety standards—Ben is fed by Sylvie, his mouth stretching enthusiastically each time the spoon swoops toward him. My glass is sloshed with red wine, never allowed to be less than two-thirds full. There's a pudding of white stuff—cream and meringue, perhaps—flecked with berries.

I am aware, despite the perpetual chatter, of the sound of my eating; the slapping of my oversize tongue. Sylvie talks about extending the hotel with a conservatory at the back. Nadine regards me as if I'm about to do something amusing. Christophe watches my jaws moving. Sylvie licks a paper serviette and dabs Ben's face clean. I'm so full I can hardly breathe, let alone move. My parents' house is a continent away. Can I walk like a normal person, after so much food? It's the first cooked meal I've had since the sausage on the ferry, when my digestive system started to play up.

It's raining heavily. "You must stay," says Sylvie, "until it stops." She lifts a hefty green album from a bookshelf which I suspect contains photos. I tell her, "The meal was lovely, but we must get back. Ben needs to nap."

"He can sleep here," she trills, patting a rose-patterned sofa. Something rises in my throat; a fear, perhaps, of drowning in knicker curtains and meringue pudding. "Why such a hurry?" she asks. "On holiday, too."

"Sorry, we really have to leave."

While Nadine eases Ben into his snowsuit, Sylvie dollops the remains of the pudding into a green glass bowl which she wraps in a bag and slides into the basket beneath the buggy. "Christophe will see you home," she announces.

"I'm fine. It's just a short walk."

"But it's raining. Do you have an umbrella?"

"Of course not."

"Do you want to be wet, and the poor child ill for Christmas?"

"I have a rain hood for the buggy," I protest, remembering that although I do possess such an item, I thoughtfully left it back at the house. And I feel lousy for gobbling her food and kindness and doing a runner, but then, haven't I done a lot of that lately?

"Please, I don't need walking home."

"He wants to," she says. "Don't you, Christophe?"

19

Antisocial Behavior

Outside smells of wet soil. I am grateful for air; the hotel felt overheated and hard to breathe in, perhaps due to all those soft toys. Christophe holds the umbrella over me and the buggy as if we are VIPs treading the red carpet to a film premiere. Rarified creatures who must not be sploshed. Our feet crunch into wet gravel. The sole of my right shoe flaps as I walk. We turn into the road leading back to the village. There's no pavement, just a sodden grass verge, and we're too wide an ensemble to walk together.

Christophe touches my shoulder, making me jump. "Here," he says, "take the umbrella. I'll push." He pulls off his jacket and forms a waterproof cape around Ben, then walks ahead, pushing the buggy. His sweater is drenched. He looks back at me, laughing at the absurdity of the scene, and something not entirely unpleasant—like a glimmer of recklessness—flits through me.

We reach the village where the pavement enables us to walk side by side. Now he can ask me things. Curiosity is clearly a family trait. "So you're looking after your parents' house?" he says.

"Sort of."

"On your own, just before Christmas?"

I respond by batting back questions: *What do you do? Is this your life, helping your mother with the hotel? Why is your English so good?*

"I lived in London," Christophe says. "Worked there. Jobs here, jobs there."

He's at a lifestage where jobs-here-jobs-there is a viable way to exist. Not a Jonathan lifestyle. Not grown-up. We pass the bakery. The owner is using a pole to shake the canopy where water has collected. She nods at Christophe. Her eyes meet mine with startled disdain as if the flooded canopy were somehow my fault.

"What brought you back?" I ask.

"My mother. The hotel, she and my father bought it, worked together. And he left. We didn't know where he'd gone until the fax arrived, telling us he is living with a hairdresser."

So much information is gushing my way that I'm not sure how to respond. "His hairdresser? Did she cut his hair and—" I stop myself. I'm sensing a *Promise* story.

"No, my mother's," Christophe says.

"I assume she's not her hairdresser any longer."

He laughs, swerving the buggy down the track to the house, and says, "My mother still goes to her. She is very particular about who cuts her hair."

I let us in with the five-inch key which I leave under a lump of yellowish stone at the door. It's a game I play: hey, burglars! Come on in. See? Nothing to take, unless you're aware of a market for stale sponge cakes.

Christophe follows me in, shaking his hair like a wet dog. In one swift movement he yanks the sodden sweater over his head and, perhaps accidentally, the T-shirt with it. I wish I knew what to do with him. Linda from the ferry would have a warm drink pressed into his hands and something to occupy him whipped from the zebra-striped bag stuffed with coloring books (surely he's not young enough for a coloring book). "A towel please," he says.

I sniff the hand towel in the bathroom. It smells like it's been trapped in a bag with wet swimming trunks. When I come back, Ben has been decanted from his buggy, disrobed of snowsuit and placed in his car seat. He's nodding toward sleep.

Christophe towels himself dry. I busy myself with brushing cake crumbs from the work surface and cleaning Ben's bottles as best as I can with icy water. "Would you like a sweater?" I ask, keeping my back to him.

"Great," he says. He mooches out of the room, exploring. When I find him it's his back I see; narrow and shiny, the spine clearly defined. He lights the fire in my turquoise Gap sweater which finishes at his navel. Grinning, he holds up his blackened hands.

"No hot water," I say reluctantly. I don't want Christophe or any member of his family forming the opinion that I am managing anything less than brilliantly. And I want to ask him: why is your mother involving herself with me? And why are you here? I must have a look which announces: I need to be taken care of. But I don't. Look at me here, alone with my son. I take care of others, isn't that what mothers do? I'm one of those mums you see in the park; the real ones who know what they're doing, have clean babies and endless supplies of the right kind of snack, stashed in some kind of Tardis bag. I belong to that club.

I'm filling the kettle when it happens: that wave like on the ferry, only hotter this time, involving sweat and a too-close recollection of Sylvie's sauce swilling around my insides with the wine and meringue pudding. Your body does this when you're feeling unwell: conjures up images of intense, bile-making food—raw eggs, pilchards—just to taunt you.

It's having a laugh, this belly of mine; pulling a fast one when I have a young male—*two* young males—in the house. How much have I drunk? Wine: bad idea in the day. Shakily I make my way to the living room where Christophe is jabbing the fire with a poker I have never managed to locate.

I lower myself into the battered sofa, aware of its greasiness. Slow, deep breaths. Anything to take this thing away. As if sensing mother in distress, Ben wakes, depriving himself of his usual two-hour kip. He's instantly crotchety, kicking at his seat furiously. But I can't go to him. I am rooted to the sofa, panting into my hands.

"Is something wrong?" Christophe asks. "You look—"

It's a distant voice, well-meaning but unable to help. Ben's howls are more distant still. If only I could un-eat Sylvie's meal, get it out of me. It's there in my throat, splattering onto my park shoes, and he's at my side saying, "Poor Nina."

For a moment I believe it won't stop; I'll empty completely and sag like an ancient balloon. One arm hugs me, the other holds back my hair. Dignified. The sort of sophisticated look I always aim for when I'm with someone new. Fed up with wailing, Ben watches, transfixed, as his mother appears to be eating in reverse.

Christophe cleans up. He actually wipes up the vomit of a woman he has known for one brief afternoon, even finding disinfectant tucked behind the loo. To prevent Ben investigating the infected area, he constructs a kind of corral from three wooden chairs, placed on their sides around the sick zone. I am so ashamed I could cry.

Christophe says, "Feel better now?"

I shake my head and say, "A week ago, I was supposed to get married." He's still next to me in the striking combination of damp jeans and girl's turquoise sweater. "And I didn't get married," I tell him. "We had…a sort of row. About nothing, like most of them are. And I used it. As an excuse. I tricked him. It was a mistake—all too fast. We met though a lonely hearts ad, when you advertise yourself because you can't…do you have that here? Lonely hearts?"

He frowns, shaking his head.

"And we had Ben. Also too early. I wasn't ready. No one was ready."

He says, "It's better not to marry if you feel that way."

"I know that."

"Though you feel bad for hurting—"

"Jonathan," I say. The name comes out crookedly. I haven't said it aloud since I left him. I haven't even said "Dad." I wonder if Ben's forgotten he has one. How far back can babies remember? A month? Or mere seconds, like goldfish?

"And you came here because…"

"I don't love him," I say, wondering why it didn't occur to me to lie.

He stays into the evening, moving about the house as if he belongs. I feed Ben his nighttime bottle, drinking the coffee Christophe made, aware of clanking sounds from the dank space where the boiler lives. Something heavy and metallic is being moved. There's a scraping sound and a muffled yelp, as if he's hurt himself. I hope he knows what he's doing. Christophe may be unusually skilled in the efficient clearing up of vomit, but I suspect he might not have sat the complex exams required for fiddling about with gas.

But something happens. There's a rush of air like breath through a tube; then a faint *pwuff* as something ignites.

He stands before me and says, "You have hot water."

If I weren't double his age, and suspecting that I might still smell faintly of sick, I could hug him.

Christmas presents arrive. From Jonathan to Ben: a wooden construction with holes of varying shapes into which blocks are to be slotted to encourage manual dexterity. From Beth: a snowman card made with tiny scrunches of white tissue paper, glued into place, with perhaps a little help from Rosie, and blue rabbit slippers. The card reads: *Missing you. Have a very happy Christmas. Love, Beth, Matthew and Maud.* No Rosie. Perhaps she's considered too low in the hierarchy to merit a Christmas card mention.

From Constance to Ben: a custard cardigan with clumsy pearlized buttons. Nothing from Jonathan to me. Nothing from my parents to anyone. I reseal Ben's presents and place them high on the bookshelf.

I call my parents to remind them of their daughter and grandson's existence and brag about how well I'm managing. My mother says, "Are you finding the house comfortable?"

Slightly more so, I want to say, *now that I have hot water. Why didn't you warn me? What made you pack me off with a key and an illegible map and a baby?* But it's not her fault. No one made me do this. "It's perfect," I tell her.

"Oh, isn't it? Your dad and I are missing the place. We don't usually come in winter—absolutely freezing, isn't it? And so damp. But with you being there we thought, why not? So we'll be over for New Year.

Maybe you could make the place shipshape, get some food in."

"I'll do that," I say, warming to Sylvie's offer of an overheated hotel room, *sans* parents.

Presents come from Eliza: for Ben, a babysoft black crew-neck; for me, an aromatherapy bath kit (well timed considering the arrival of hot water). There's also a heavily discounted soul compilation CD—she's left the price sticker on—which, due to a lack of stereophonic equipment, I will be able to play only in the car. I rewrap the gifts so I'll have something exciting to open on Christmas day. There's an envelope in Eliza's jiffy bag which I assume is a card but it turns out to be a letter written in top-speed scrawl:

Dearest Nina,
Are you all right? Still at your parents' clapped out place? I've been terrible at keeping in touch. Sorry. Things have been complicated. But Jonathan called, wanting to know if I'd heard anything. Like what your plans are.
Conversation was a bit strained. Think he suspected I was holding stuff back—like I know more than I do. What could I tell him? He must be demented with worry. Is this some delayed postnatal thing? Why don't you come back and sort yourself out? You could get pills. Sarita at work is on some seratonin thing and it's worked a treat. She's sweaty at night and a bit spacey looking, but smiles more.

Nina, I have to admit I feel partly responsible for this mess, putting the baby modeling thing in your head. Please call.

Eliza xxx

P.S. Feel bad that I wasn't supportive when you were here. Swept up by the Dale thing. Well, that's over now. Says he wants someone just like me— funny, sexy, intelligent. But younger. My own stupid fault for getting involved with a younger man. At my age.

A tile clatters from the roof, causing Ben's feet to shoot up and kick the kitchen table. He's on my lap, breakfasting on fragments of strawberry tart. Someone is up on the roof—my roof—stealing the lead.

I hurry out, carrying Ben whose cheeks are stuffed with mashed tart, and look up. "Hi," says Christophe. "I saw you were busy. Didn't want to disturb you. But perhaps you'd better move your car."

"What are you doing?" I shout up.

"What do you think? Fixing the roof."

"It doesn't need fixing," I snap. Ben stares up, licking strawberry gloop from his thumb.

"But it leaks," says Christophe.

"Only when it's raining," I yell back.

If the roof episode isn't enough, he clatters in, hours later, and slams a grubby orange rucksack on the kitchen table. It's filled with winter woollies: my Gap one, now lavender-scented, plus three hefty sweaters in varying shades of gray, smelling of unfamiliar male.

"What are these?" I ask.

"They're for you. If you're here for the winter you'll need warmer clothes."

"I have warm clothes," I say irritably. What is it with this family and their urge to feed and clothe me?

"That's a jumper," he explains, as if I am incapable of remembering the names of basic garments. "Put on something warmer today. I'm taking you out in the boat."

Ben is pulling himself up with the kitchen cupboard handles. Christophe takes a hand in each of his. Ben stands unsteadily. Christophe moves backward; Ben follows with novice's steps. Boys of Christophe's age aren't supposed to know what to do with babies. He'll lose interest, let him fall back. Baby's skull meets stone kitchen floor. High-speed drive to Chatillon. Nurse asking: "What have you been doing with him? Where is this child's father?"

"Careful," I say. "He can't walk."

Ignoring me, he says, "So how about getting ready? I've brought food…"

"No," I tell him, "It's December. We'll freeze."

Ben's legs are bowing but his face is still tilted upward to meet Christophe's, seeking approval. And a latter chapter of *Babycare* pops into my brain: *Don't be afraid to let your child enjoy new experiences. Exploration is crucial to his learning and understanding of the world.*

"Where is this boat?" I ask.

The boathouse is close to Hotel Beauville where the river loops back on itself. Banks bush with rain-drenched weeds, dipping lazily into the water. There's a sodden wood smell in the boathouse. I park the buggy on the narrow walkway, making sure it's covered in case it rains.

Christophe fits a tiny life jacket around Ben, which fastens with Velcro and buckles. He steps onto the boat. It's just a rowing boat, toffee-colored and gleaming; a boat that trembles when you look at it.

He steps in and reaches to take Ben, supporting him in one arm. Then his woolly-gloved hand takes mine and he guides me in, as if assisting a pensioner. I'm not good with boats. Look at the ferry episode: heaving, on a glassy-sea day. With a little boat, the smallest movement— rearranging your legs, even blinking—causes it to lurch nervously. Christophe passes Ben to me; I grab my son, aware that my molars are clenched tightly together.

Ben sits upright and alert. What scares babies? Nothing much, it seems. He watches Christophe intently as he hooks in the oars and unties us, and we're off, with Ben eyeing his every stroke of the oar, thinking, perhaps, that his father has been replaced by a younger, more water-loving model with a beard.

We follow the river's lazy curves. Christophe doesn't speak. And Ben's right; there is nothing to be scared of as we drift, leaving the village behind. I spot the serious watch, eyeing me, and pull the sweater sleeve over my wrist.

We stop at a broad wooden post to moor the boat. Christophe steps off, taking Ben from me. We're in a small field bordered by unruly hedges. There's an ancient, stone-built hut, so ramshackle a sharp gust of wind might send it tumbling. Ben crawls through the field, his snow-suited rear waggling above the grass.

Christophe takes an armful of dry wood from inside the hut. A match flares. As the fire builds, we settle around it. Ben opens his mouth obediently as morsels of food, provided by Christophe, are posted in. His eyes widen in the firelight. *Take every opportunity to stimulate your child's senses. Let him discover how water feels as it runs through his fingers, and watch flames as they dance in a fire.*

So, *Babycare,* this is all right by you? That my son's nappy is so deeply encased in his snowsuit that it hasn't been changed for hours? That the food provided by this borrowed male role model—crimp-edged biscuits, mainly—is whittling away at the enamel of his newly formed incisors? How am I faring according to your new-mother rules?

Christophe says, "You don't notice it after a while."

"What?" I ask.

"The movement. On the boat. Next time you won't even think about it."

"I didn't think about it. You know, I even liked it."

"And you weren't sick," he says.

Ben is drowsy in my arms. We need to head home, though I don't want to. "I should go back," I say.

He says, "Back to England?"

The thought's in my head now. Back to what: to fix things with Jonathan? To do the right thing? We have a young family (such a big world—family—for two mis-matched adults and a baby too young to express opinions regarding his living arrangements). But Jonathan has called only twice, with brief messages. He hasn't seen his son standing on rubbery legs. The upright position: what a difference this makes. Ben is no longer a horizontal thing, batting the activity arch; he's a boy. And I no longer flinch when hungry whimpers start up. I can do this.

It's almost dark when we row back to the boathouse. Ben sleeps, splayed across my lap, not flinching even when placed in the buggy and wheeled home. I carry him to bed. His hair is flecked with grass and thick with wood smoke. When I come downstairs, Christophe is deconstructing the chair corral. The sick stink has gone. The room looks almost normal.

"You don't have to go back," he says. "Aren't you happy here? Doesn't Ben like it?"

"It's not that simple," I say.

Christophe says, "It could be. I'd help you. You could make this your home."

For one millisecond, it seems like a perfectly sensible idea.

20

Playthings

There are many reasons why I shouldn't sleep with Christophe. For one thing: his sheer nerve in assuming he's staying the night after risking everyone's health on his boat. As if I would. With someone who's even closer to childhood than Dale is (and look what happened there). Does he think I'm desperate? Or that I need him for various roof fixing and puke wiping duties and, therefore, some payment in kind is due?

We have nothing in common. Less than nothing to talk about. He hasn't done anything, been anywhere. Yes, there was London, but what did he get up to there? This job, that job, diddling about. My diddling days are so distant I wouldn't be able to remember how to diddle, even if I got the chance.

There are yet more reasons to avoid intimate physical contact with an arrogant, immature (though undeniably attractive) young pup:

I am a mother.

He lives with his mother.

He is a baby.

I have Jonathan (sort of).

I can remember Haircut 100.

His hormones are all over the shop.

He *smells* young.

He probably weighs less than one of my thighs.

And, most worrying of all:

What if he wants to talk about French pop music?

There's an impatient hammer at the door. It's so dark I can't see my own hand. I slip out of bed, bringing with me the satin eiderdown, and cape it around my shoulders. I feel my way downstairs, touching edges and flat surfaces.

Another hammering. I flick on the light and open the door a fraction but the postman pretends not to have noticed. He is in profile, his breath a white puff. Last night's rainfall has turned the ground to gloop. I open the door fully, feeling ridiculous in my satin cape. He hands me a parcel. To take it I'll have to poke a hand out of the eiderdown, but I need both to keep it bunched around me.

I nod at the ground. He sets down the parcel and tuts loudly. *Mad tourist. And not even dressed.*

Inside the parcel is a Christmas present wrapped in tasteful, Santa-free paper: silver stars on lilac with matching gift tag, which reads: *Nina, saw this and thought of you. Love, Beth.*

It's a book called *Start Talking, Start Loving*. On the cover is an illustrated couple, dotty like a Liechtenstein painting. His jaw is cartoon square. Her eyelashes curl lusciously. They are back to back with arms folded. He's late again, another dinner spoiled. Or maybe he's just witnessed his son in a cinema ad.

On the inside back cover there's a photo of the author: she wears a cream mohair sweater and a there-there smile. Chapter one kicks off with several questions:

Do you raise your voice to make yourself heard?

Does your partner shout to gain your attention?

Do you row in public?

Do you have the same old squabbles, over and over?

No, no, no, no.

Congratulations! gushes mohair lady. *You communicate without resorting to shouting or arguing. Yet we can all benefit from brushing up our talking and listening skills. With the exercises in this book, you'll grow even closer as a couple.*

Christophe appears before me, rubbing his upper arms where goose bumps have sprung. He is wearing the Girl Guide blanket sarong-style around his waist. Above it, ribs are visible.

I shut the front door and drop *Start Talking, Start Loving* into the wicker wastepaper basket.

"Come back to bed," he says.

★ ★ ★

Ben and I will spend Christmas Eve at Hotel Beauville, when Sylvie's family has their celebratory meal. There's no formal invitation; just an assumption that we'll be there. Sylvie is revving up for the big day, adding flourishes of ribbon to the scalloped drapes. A fir tree glints silver and white, heavily laden with glass baubles. The decrepit high chair has been embellished with glittery fir cones lashed on with what looks like gold dressing gown cord. Sylvie is breathless, tweaking and patting, delegating jobs to Nadine and Christophe but not letting me help. "You're our guest," she reminds me. "There is nothing for you to do. Nothing."

So I perch on the sofa accepting cordial drinks and soft, round confections, somewhere between biscuit and cake. Ben pulls himself up on sofas and armchairs, sucks soft toys and nibbles their swallowable accessories. I wonder if he prefers Hotel Beauville to my parents' house. There are no toys there, other than the presents reserved for Christmas. I haven't shown him a picture book in weeks. But how much stimulation does a child need? Ben can while away a morning by bashing a dented saucepan with a wooden spoon. In the olden days, no one fretted about stimulating children. From age three to eleven I spent most of my free time swinging on a gate. And look how well I turned out.

I have two homes now, like a posh person: one full of people and the clattering of crockery and one where I sleep. Christophe comes round most days with gifts of food, wine or his body. One morning he shows up with a toy truck made from a red and yellow cooking oil can. It has a certain rustic charm, though is desperately unsafe with ragged edges capable of shearing off a baby's arm (see, he knows nothing about children). I thank him and place it high on the bookshelf with the Christmas presents.

We drink just enough wine to fuzz things. I wonder if Christophe is using me as someone with whom to practice sex, so he's clued up for when he finds a proper girlfriend. Why else would he be here? I'm old. Done in. Distorted by childbirth. Still haven't managed to examine myself down there, scared of what I'll find.

Ben sleeps in the big bed, bordered on all sides by pillows. We slip into the little room and warm each other under green satin and mottled gray blanket. It doesn't feel like he's practicing. I don't know how it feels because I can't think. When I wake, half-covered by Girl Guide blanket, the Homemaker badge is staring me right in the eye.

My mother calls to apologize for not sending Ben's present in time for Christmas ("something we picked up at the car boot—though you'd think it was new, except there's something wrong with the horn"). She goes on to detail her dietary requirements for the New Year visit: "Dairy and gluten free, don't forget. Red meat's off and Ashley's not happy with chicken, so I'm better sticking to fish. Make sure it's fresh." According to Ashley, my mother's treatment has reached a crucial point. They are on the verge of clearing the blockage in her brain.

"Fish might be difficult," I tell her. "We're quite a hike from the coast, Mum."

She sniffs into the phone and says, "Your dad and I never have trouble finding fresh produce."

"Mum," I sigh, "are you sure about this trip? What if there's snow? You could be stuck here for days— weeks, even."

"Such a pessimist," she scolds. "So what if we're stuck? It's a wonderful place—you've said so yourself. I thought you'd be pleased. Stuck in the house with a baby. What do you do all day?"

Each morning, Christophe wakes before me. A warm hand on my stomach, or a breast, or a thigh. We're quiet as mice, a soft rumple of bodies, with the sloping ceiling looming over us.

Ben sleeps after lunch. Babies' naps are important. *At nine months your child will probably sleep for two hours or more during the day. Make use of this time. It's your opportunity to nap, too, and feel well-rested when your baby wakes.*

We learn new tricks. With a substantial lunch, high on carbohydrates, plus a full bottle of warm milk, Ben will conk out until four. We sneak up to the little room where I take off the serious watch and shut it away in the drawer, not caring that I'm destined for Hell.

Christmas Eve. Sylvie's table heaves under a jumble of scented candles and steaming dishes and a towering centerpiece of dried flowers, jabbed into a spongy silver dome. She is wearing a silky black dress shot through with narrow copper leaves. Nadine wears her usual lumpen sweater. The women are overheated from eating, talking and frequent flurries to the kitchen. Christophe eats calmly, as if it's an everyday meal.

Plates are cleared to make way for gifts. Sylvie is presented with a sandwich toaster made for giants. "For cooking meat at the table," explains Nadine. I nod, as if I have one just like it at home. Sylvie hands me a small parcel: perfume of an unfamiliar brand in a ridged glass bottle with a gilt stopper. I kiss her, grazing my face on her lacquered curls. I have brought a volcano-shaped cake erupting nuts and glacé fruit. Her gratitude is over the top, considering the quality of the gift.

I have yet to source anything remotely appropriate for Christophe. Lately, being so busy in that little room, I've had few opportunities to nip into Chatillon. I have yet to visit the Musée Archéologique.

I'm full from the meal but still hungry. This is happening a lot. All my jeans appear to have shrunk. Sylvie cuts me a slab of volcano cake, then brings her hands together in light, rapid claps. She raises her glass. "Nina," she announces, "welcome to our family."

I seem to have found myself a new mother. And a new something else.

Jonathan doesn't call. Perhaps he's staying with Constance, dutifully tipping down Meals with Mince. On December 26 I ring Beth, pretending to wish her happy Christmas. "Nina!" she says with fake jollity. "Did you get the book? Hope you weren't offended. I just thought, being stuck out in the back of beyond…"

"You're right, there's no bookshop," I say.

"How much longer are you carrying on with this? I thought about you yesterday, stuck in that miserable hovel. On your own, with no—"

"I have Ben," I butt in. There are rustling sounds as if she's wrapping something in foil. "Have you seen Jonathan?" I ask brightly.

"Um, let me think—a week ago was it, Matthew, when Jonathan came round for supper? Busy since then. My parents are here, wanted us at theirs for Christmas. Terrible sulks. But who'd want to be stuck out in the country? What if it snowed? We'd be trapped."

"How did Jonathan seem?"

"Seem?" she squeaks. "He's fine, considering what he's coping with."

"Only I haven't heard…" What do I expect to hear?

"Oh, Jana, watch Maud with that apple juice," Beth scolds.

"Jana?"

"New au pair. Czech girl. Terrible experience with her last family, thinks our place is a palace."

"What happened to Rosie?" I ask.

There's a bang, like an oven door slamming. "Didn't work out. It's like that with au pairs. Go through a heap till you find the right one."

"What's Jana like?"

"A worker. Never stops. Not the best-looking girl on the planet but Maudie doesn't seem to mind."

I drive Ben and Christophe to Chatillon. We will buy every item on the list dictated by my mother. For the duration of their stay, the fridge will bulge with fresh produce. She doesn't want any food intolerances ruining her holiday.

A vast dish of fruit will sit on the kitchen table. Apples will gleam. I shall wear lipstick at all times and keep my nails clean. Ben will sport a retro, minimal look comprising the black crew-neck and checked trousers. How can they fail to be impressed?

Christophe is amused by my lists, frequently amended and littered with question marks, asterisks and drawings of girls with tense faces. "Are your parents…difficult?" he asks.

I look sideways at him. He could be my son, blagging a lift to his girlfriend's. A softly formed girl in a white 32A bra with no porky bits under her arms. "You never grow out of trying to impress your parents," I say.

There are no creases even when he laughs. He's unlined, uneverythinged. A baby face. His mother washes his clothes, cooks his meals. He can't even drive.

He picks up the CD from the dashboard. It's the one from Eliza, the soul compilation. The cover depicts a close-up of a black girl's glossy lips. He slips in the CD, presses play.

Now that you're gone
All that's left is a band of gold

I skip forward a track: The Temptations. "Ball of Confusion." Christophe touches my thigh. I grip the steering wheel and stare into the rain that's starting to pepper the windscreen. Next track: The Jackson Five. "I Want You Back."

I click off the CD. "Hey, Nina, what's wrong?" Christophe asks, removing his hand from my leg.

"Don't feel like music," I say.

December 30. Snow, perfectly timed for my parents' arrival. The front door opens stiffly, sweeping an arc through a layer of white. Ben totters out, one hand in mine, the other in Christophe's. There is a suggestion of car shape, shrouded in snow duvet. "Do they clear the Chatillon road?" I ask.

"Eventually, perhaps by tonight. But if more snow falls—"

"They'll never make it."

"We should dig," he says. "If they manage to get here, they'll have to get the car off the road."

We spend the morning carving a lane from the house to the road, watched by Ben, who sits squarely on his rump. He licks flakes from outsize navy mittens. Fresh snow clings to his hair like miniature feathers. Inside, we huddle at the fire, wrapped in blankets; three faces, the way I'd imagined the scene after Ben's roadside delivery.

Although one of the faces should belong to the baby's father. What I'm doing is wrong. If she knew, that mohair lady would leap from her self-help book and slap me.

We have lunch and make the house parent-friendly. I comb each room for Christophe objects; on an armchair, his thick, hairy socks. In the bathroom, his menthol toothpaste. On the shelf by the little bed, condoms.

Ben falls asleep with the teat in his mouth. I carry him upstairs for his afternoon nap and tuck him into bed. When I look out, I can no longer see the track we made.

Christophe undresses. I pull off my jeans, sweater and underwear. He lifts the bedspread over us. His feet are icy, though his lips are warm, and the fingers warmer still. Much later, Ben's small cry comes. "I'll get him," says Christophe. But when he moves, it's only to hold me tighter.

"They said teatime," I tell him. "They should be here by now. Something's happened."

He has fixed the outside light and now digs snow in its yellowy glow. Somehow, insects have snuck into the sealed plastic cover encasing the bulb, and died there.

"They must have stopped," Christophe says. "Look, it's still snowing. They'll come tomorrow."

I wish he'd stop digging; it's fruitless. His forehead is slicked with sweat, despite the cold. "You should go," I tell him, "in case they show up."

"Why? It's a problem, me being here?"

He doesn't understand and why should he? He's never had to deal with someone else's parents. That comes later: the accumulation of in-laws. A mother who's not your own, just comes as part of the package.

"Who will I say you are?" I ask.

"You could say I'm a friend."

It's 11:30 and still no headlamps looming toward the house. I set my mobile on the cracked wooden shelf beside the single bed and fold my arms around his back.

It rings, some time later. "Where are you?" I say quickly.

There's breathing. Finally the voice says, "Nina. It's me." I can't place it. It's a man's voice, one I should know. "She's dead," says the voice.

I sit up. Christophe shuffles his limbs, aware that I'm no longer wrapped around him. "They think it happened yesterday," the voice says. It sounds tight, in difficulty.

"Who?" I say. *Who's dead? Who is this?*

"They found her in her chair. TV blaring. Those religious types. Jehovah's Witnesses. She'd left the door unlocked. Like she always does—and what am I always telling her?"

Christophe's arm emerges from the covers, feeling the space I've left.

"I'll come home."

Christophe moves, propping himself up.

"There's no need," Jonathan says. "I just thought you should know."

Christophe grips my hand. I shake it off. "How do you feel?" I ask. No, I've turned into mohair lady.

"I just wanted to let you know," he repeats.

"Jonathan, I'm coming home. There's the funeral. I need to—"

"It's not important," he says. "There'll just be me, Beth and Matthew of course, and Billy—though I'll try to keep him away, don't want him causing a—"

"I have to be there," I protest. My voice wobbles. Christophe stands up, picks through a bundle of clothes.

"Why?" says Jonathan. "Why do you have to be there?"

"Because I'm your—"

"My what?"

I watch Christophe turn his jeans the right way out. He pulls them on, zips up. "Is someone there?" Jonathan asks.

"Of course," I say, "Ben's here."

21

The Settled Baby's Routine

Christophe says I can't go. Not in the snow. I have a baby to think about. It's dark.

"I have headlamps," I remind him.

He says, "Come back to bed. We'll talk tomorrow." He paces the kitchen. He looks less fresh-faced than usual, like he's been glossed over with weak ochre paint. I wish he'd be still. There are things to pack: just essentials, enough for a short trip. We don't need much. Clothes, bottles, milk, nappies, wipes, food in jars. How easy it is to pack for a baby; second nature by now. I don't need the *Babycare* list. But I'm distracted by Christophe's barefoot pacing. I've bunged our passports into the zip-up bag and they seem to have melted away in an invisible compartment. Christophe has them. He opens mine at my photo. He's thinking: what happened? "I feel old," I say suddenly.

"You're just you," he says, slipping the passports into an outside pouch so they're easy to find.

I head upstairs to lift Ben from the big bed. He's startled by the sudden temperature switch, gulping sharp air as he's strapped into the car. Christophe watches from the open door. I'm wearing one of his sweaters. It scratches my neck and reaches my knees and yarn has come loose at the elbows. I feel like a bird's nest, slowly unraveling.

The engine growls irritably, as if disturbed from hibernation. "What about your parents?" he says, shivering now. "What do you want me to tell them?"

"Just say you're a friend."

Christophe turns back to the house. But he shouts something else, something that sounds like, "I thought it was over with him."

Like anything is ever that simple.

And he's wrong. Night driving is perfectly designed for mother and infant. *Babycare* would recommend it for those challenging long journeys. No stops for feeding or nappy changes; no Incy Wincey Spider on a loop. Ben sleeps with the Girl Guide blanket bunched round his neck. Should he wake, startled by service station lights, the engine's hum will send him back to warm oblivion. I stop for coffee, leaving Ben in the car, and stare wildly out of the window as the girl serves me. She has a round glassy face like a marble and can't find a lid for the cup.

I drink my coffee in the car and drive fast, recklessly.

I play the dare-you game. Dare you to swerve: what would happen? I used to play it with Tube trains. Stand on the platform, toes over the edge. Here comes the train. Dare you.

Snow faintly covers drab fields. Ben's lips open and close around an invisible teat; a milk dream. I envy him sometimes. He doesn't upset people or have to make difficult decisions. He is provided with food, warm clothing and a driver, and I want to be him.

We board the first ferry. The lounge feels like a party nearly everyone's left. A woman with black crash-helmet hair draws sausage shapes on a word search puzzle. The end of her biro is gnawed to bits. A bald man sleeps, his chin occasionally dropping to his chest and bouncing up again. The woman at the till is wearing a tinsel tiara. She taps in ham salad—the plainest thing on offer—and yawns noisily, showing gray fillings.

I feed Ben orange sludge from a jar. He pushes it out with his tongue. He refuses a warm *fromage frais*. I consider trying him with plain bread but realize they're pretend rolls, heavily varnished. *A break in routine can upset your child's eating patterns. Normal mealtimes should be adhered to. The wise traveler packs her baby's favorite foodstuffs in an insulated bag.*

I change him on the foldout table in the parents' room. A meaty stench floods out of the nappy bin. Ben is so squirmy I'm forced to hand him my serious watch to coat with saliva while I pin him down to secure the clean nappy. He squawks helplessly, attempting to propel himself onto the wet floor.

On the wall is a photo of a family on a ferry. The parents are healthy and toothpasty looking. They have a toddler and a baby in arms and are looking out to sea, pointing at something. I wonder if they're from Little Lovelies. As well as individual babies and children, Lovely rents out entire families. Obviously each family member should gleam with health and vitality. The woman mustn't have Spaniel-ear breasts. The man shouldn't sag around the eye zone. I examine my face; it's ashen, with spectacular pores. One eye is smaller than the other. But say I looked different—more delicately put together—and wore a peach crew-neck sweater tied loosely around my shoulders. Say Jonathan was more your mail-order catalog man, a Ranald type, with a robust jaw and the ability to look natural with one hand in a pocket. I wonder how he would react to the suggestion that we sign up with Little Lovelies as a job lot.

When I return to the lounge the helmet hair woman stares eagerly. "Do you like puzzles?" she asks. "There's another book in my bag."

"No, thanks. I don't have the patience."

"Or you can have this one. If you prefer word searches to crosswords."

"No, you keep it."

She grins like a wolf. There's a sinister hole where one of her canine teeth should be. "I'm going to write my resolutions," she says, producing a black mock-leather notebook from her jacket pocket. "Do it every year. Drink more water. Be better with money. Use the stairs, not the lift. And deeper things."

Her eyes are on me like dentists' drills. "I'm spiritual," she declares. "And you are, I can tell. You believe in karma. What goes around comes around. Made any resolutions yourself?"

"Just the usual," I say. "Must try harder."

Ben greets his homeland by reintroducing a wave of curdled orange. It smells like stomach lining and batters Christophe's sweater. Ben's schedule is to pot. He's grizzling for milk now but isn't due a bottle until after lunch. I give in, hoping he doesn't bring it up in the car, which is fouled up with polystyrene coffee cartons and cellophane wrappers containing crumbs and margarine smears. It smells of bin. I wonder what Jonathan will make of it, whether he'll charge me for valeting.

His mother is dead. Of course he won't care about the car.

I press the buzzer again, longer this time. Finally, a dull fumble of key. Eliza's skin is stretched taut across her cheekbones. "Can I stay?" I ask.

Her arms are around me, flimsy as bendy straws. "Happy New Year," she says into my neck.

I semisleep the afternoon away. Eliza is kind enough to let me have the real bed, not the blow-up one. She brings me a mug of brown tea. Occasionally the door creaks open and I'm aware of her, checking on me. But I keep my eyes shut. I can smell that cream, the stuff she uses on her neck.

And she does her best with Ben, considering she handles babies as if they might rip. "Don't touch," I hear her saying. "Careful, Ben. Let's leave that corkscrew alone." There's a flump, like a stack of magazines tumbling from a shelf. Eliza groans, and the door squeaks as she checks on me again.

I have no idea of the time as there's a gap on my wrist where the serious watch should be. If I left it on the ferry, would anyone find it? Could the tiara girl have it on her wrist so it eyeballs her each time she taps in an order? It was expensive, that prewedding gift. I could tell that from the box.

When I emerge from Eliza's bedroom nothing terrible seems to have happened. Ben does not appear to be suffering from malnutrition and is dressed in a clean babygro, though she's obviously had trouble with the fastenings. I don't feel like launching into a summary of the past month, so instead I ask, "What really happened with Dale?"

She shrugs. "Expected me to look after him. Cook meals and all that. Hands me the dirty plate. I say, 'What am I, your mother?' And he gives me a funny look."

She flings a pair of flip-flops into an open box. The living room looks like she's just moved in, or is preparing to leave in a hurry. Cardboard boxes huddle in corners, partially filled with dented lampshades and unidentifiable garments. One contains the unfinished collections of lettuce leaf plates and asymmetrical hats. "What's all this?" I ask.

"For charity. I'm space clearing, sick of the clutter. Have anything you like."

Is this how she spent New Year's Eve? Putting things in boxes? Her hair is pulled up clumsily, her neck longer and thinner than I remember. She looks exhausted. She sits nervously on the sofa as if it's upholstered with glass chippings. I say, "Were you out last night? Did anyone have a party?"

She blinks at me. "That's an interesting sweater."

I look down at it. One sleeve is flecked with regurgitated orange. "It's not mine. It belongs to a—"

"I've seen Jonathan," she says. It's unclear whether she means she saw him, as in *saw* him, or spied him briefly in the street. "He's been calling me," she continues. "It was weird, the first time. He's always been—"

"He doesn't know what to make of you."

"And it became sort of regular, and he'd ask about you and Ben and stuff, though I never had much to tell him." I wonder what to give Ben for lunch, whether any hot cross buns are still hanging around. "He needed a friend," she says.

"Of course he did."

"And he wants me to go to the funeral."

"Brilliant!" I say, ridiculously.

"I'm sorry, Nina, but he doesn't want you there."

"Yes, I know that. He made it quite clear." There's a tumble of unopened post, presumably Christmas cards, on the scratched coffee table. I busy myself by stacking them in a neat pile with edges aligned.

Eliza says, "So why did you come?"

"I thought he might need me," I say.

Constance is buried in a sprawling cemetery with gray gravel paths between rows of gravestones. I can make out Beth, who keeps one hand on her navy straw hat to stop it blowing away. She has swapped the rabbit knapsack for an old lady's black handbag. Matthew wears a business suit and stares at the gravel. Billy's black suit is set off by a flash of banana shirt. He is smoking and looking around at the graves as if sightseeing.

From where I'm standing, in a stone-built hut strewn with wet fish and chip wrappers, I can watch Eliza in her narrow black skirt and jacket edged with fur, or possibly feathers. She has bare legs and awkward high shoes that make her wobble like she's blowing over. Jonathan clasps his hands together, as if he's praying, but probably to warm himself. As the coffin is lowered, Eliza puts an arm around him, like any friend would.

Jonathan's flat looks like a hotel suite, minus the notice pinned to the door, detailing fire escape procedures. He is paying rapt attention to his cuticles.

I showed up without phoning first. Jonathan gathered up Ben in his arms but didn't look at me. "So," he says now, "how are we going to arrange things?" I wonder what the options are. "If you're stuck," he continues, "you can stay here. Until we decide how to map every-thing out. I'll go to Billy's."

"You don't have to do that," I protest. "We'll be all right at Eliza's."

He flings me a look like a dart. Ben is clinging to the sofa, and takes tentative sidesteps. I am horribly aware of my breathing. In less than an hour, my presence has rum-pled the cushions and brought in a rich stench of dog muck. I look like I've been mining.

Jonathan grabs Ben's hand, coaxing him to walk. He yowls in disgust, reaching out for me. The brief outburst causes him to topple back, smacking his head on the floorboards.

Jonathan holds him, wipes away tears with the flat of his hand, but Ben only stops crying when he's back in my arms.

Eliza is shopping at the sales, leaving me to put away hazardous objects and create a reasonably baby-friendly environment. Christophe calls my mobile to report that my parents are safe and well, despite the minor accident caused by Mum dreaming that they were driving the wrong way up a one-way street and shrieking so loudly that my father careened into a wooden shed full of chickens.

I'm glad Eliza's not home. I don't feel like explaining the Christophe thing. "What did she say about us com-ing back to London?" I ask him.

"Said you're always taking off. Complained that you'd taken her favorite blanket. Is she very forgetful? She can't remember my name. Calls me the handyman. Says, 'The handyman will do it.' She's told me to clean the chimney, says I must bring a very long brush—"

"Don't listen to her," I say.

"And wants me to find something in Chatillon, some kind of big pill for the forehead "

"That's her brain blockage."

"Drain?" he says.

"It's blocked," I tell him.

I clear Eliza's bath of clammy flannels and a nailbrush embedded with gray mush. It takes ages to fill, giving me time to snoop in the bathroom cabinet. It's jammed with mangled tubes and jars without lids. Despite being supplied with an endless stream of lotions and assorted gloop, she sticks loyally to the Dead Sea cream. I spot the unopened glittery nail polish set from Chatillon and loose tampons, like I used to use.

Used to.

I unzip my sponge bag and find the perfume from Sylvie. It's amber-colored, in cut glass. The bathwater isn't warm enough. It never is at Eliza's. The only way to have a proper hot bath is to pour only three inches so the water laps pathetically at your thighs.

I gaze at the tampons. When Mum told me about periods, she kept her back to me and said, "You'll find STs at the bottom of my wardrobe." I didn't know what STs were. They sounded like a disease. "How long do periods last?" I asked.

"Until your forties or fifties. Then the menopause

happens and everything shrivels up." I pictured decades of blood flow with no letup.

I hear Eliza come in, and a flump of shopping bags hitting the floor. "Okay in there?" she calls, angling her head round the door. She spies the open bathroom cabinet. "Help yourself to anything," she says, returning later with a cup of tea that tastes of sink. She looks at me, at the mum stomach that looks like most of the air's been let out. "Something wrong?" she asks.

The tampons lean precariously against a conditioner designed to nourish from the inside out. I wonder how it does that, how it gets right to the middle of your hair. "You know, don't you?" comes her voice.

My body could be having me on. What goes around comes around, the ferry woman said. I've been out of my normal routine. It's just a little scare, like when you saunter out of the deli with your brown paper bag of posh, nutty bread and realize your baby's still parked by the salami selection.

Eliza pushes her hair back from her face. She can't look at me. "He needed someone," she says.

The water's way too cold now, although there's a pocket of warmth where the hot tap drips. I climb out and wrap myself in a towel that smells of fungi.

She says, "It only happened once."

Christophe calls with the fantastic news that he has located a source of free firewood. His father has broken off with the hairdresser, triggering her to tear up the fence he made and attack it with an ax. The wood has been sawn and chopped and piled in the living room of my parents' house, to dry out. My mother drapes her washing on it. She's had Christophe clearing the snow and driving to Chatillon for the linseeds Ashley recommended she incorporate into her diet. "There's enough firewood to last until spring," he says. "When are you coming back?"

Beth is making miniature cakes, each iced individually with fancy pink swirls. Jana made the sponge part and is now scouring a splat of mixture from the floor. She grunts with the effort. Beth says that's the trick with au pairs; not to be embarrassed about making them tackle grittier jobs. Jana washes windows, cleans tiling grout and even fixed the ball cock in the cistern. Beth gets to do fun stuff, like playing with food coloring.

"I assume you're only at Eliza's as a stop gap," she says. "It's not right, is it? You're Ben's parents. You belong together. God knows what kind of message you're sending."

Ben is strapped into Maud's high chair, jabbing fingers into an eggcup of icing. As far as I can tell, he's unaware of any negative messages. His teeth are tinted pink. Maud is not allowed to join in; all that sugar. Think of the enamel. Beth has already had to point out a few basic facts to Jana; like please don't buy jelly snakes again. You can practically smell the additives.

Beth's thumb and forefinger are stained cranberry as if she's been smoking a scarlet cigarette. "You'll be stronger as a couple after all this," she says. "Look at it as a learning experience. That's what me and Matthew did. We've had our difficulties."

Jana looks at her with moon eyes and gravitates to the ironing mountain. Matthew's jaunty boxer shorts sit on top of the pile, expecting to be pressed. "It's nothing you can't solve," Beth adds tersely. "Did you read that book I sent you? It's about communication. That's what we focused on. Talking, expressing needs. We're even trying for another baby. Seriously now, considering how long it took last time. I'm plotting my fertile days. We're following a one day on, one day off program so he can—you know—replenish."

Jana is now slumped over Matthew's penguin-patterned boxers. "We're looking into sex," Beth adds. I feel bilious. Maybe it's all this pink icing. My teeth feel sticky, like they need to be shot blasted. "Naturally we want another girl, a sister for Maud," she continues. "Don't think I could cope with a boy." She glances at Ben, whose tongue is a cochineal dart. "Sorry," she says.

I do a test which winks predictably blue and see Dr. McKenzie who uses a flat plastic wheel covered in numbers and says I am due at the end of July. Dr. McKenzie has wide, flat cheeks and comforting freckles. I sit on a red hessian chair, not wanting to leave. The room smells of wet plaster. Ben delves into a box of battered plastic toys, forcing his arm through the window of a double-decker bus. "So it's definite," I say.

"Of course. You're nearly fourteen weeks. Haven't you noticed any symptoms?"

"I've been away. I thought maybe my cycle was messed up." Dr. McKenzie has a stack of patients waiting to show her their mysterious lumps and fungal toenails but not the heart to sling me out. "The nausea should subside," she adds. "You'll feel better soon. You'll glow."

"That's great," I say, rooted to the hessian scat.

Eliza is preparing for a trip. She's off to Crete where a boat will be hired and decorated with models who'll pretend to handle the tiller and sails. She's on the phone a lot, arguing with the photographer. Hector is a rising star with an attitude that spills out of the phone and onto the carpet, like lava.

"I don't want to take Mimi," Eliza snaps. "Too blond, kind of cheap. I'm fixed on Jade. She's not really modeling any more—she's an artist. We're lucky to get her."

Hector's voice rattles like coins in a tin. All this effort and angst to fill seven pages of a magazine that will be bunged under wonky bed legs. I can't see the point of it. Maybe Eliza can't either. She has tired-looking lips and gray fingerprints under her eyes. "He can't go changing his mind on a whim," she complains. I suspect she's relieved for a little drama to talk about. It stops anything else being mentioned.

The evening before her trip, Eliza hides in her room with the door shut. When she does emerge, to fetch the Dead Sea cream from the bathroom, she smiles anxiously like a shoplifter. I find her cross-legged on her bed, examining a model card: Mimi, a light and airy girl, like froth on beer. "Maybe Hector's right," she says. "We could fly her out halfway through the week, give her a try. She's dollyish, but we could make it kind of ironic."

I curl up on her bed and we flick through model cards together, just like old times, each of us pretending that Jonathan simply doesn't exist.

I am back at Dr. McKenzie's but this time for Ben who is wheezing and oozing snot. I wonder if Eliza's flat has anything to do with it. The space clearing enterprise has gained momentum. Boxes of unwanted items are stacked in my room, blocking the lower two-thirds of the window. Eliza returned from Greece with lightly grilled skin and a fierce determination to put everything to rights. She tackled the scary innards of her bathroom cupboard, flinging dried-up tubes into a bin bag. She tossed me an opaque blue perfume bottle, saying it wasn't her thing. It turned out to be a display bottle filled with water.

Dr. McKenzie fixes her green eyes on me while I tell her about Ben's breathing. She says, "I don't think he's asthmatic. He's had a virus, that's all, and his tubes are clogged with mucus." I picture wormy colored wires, like those in the fuse box in Vanvey. "Bring him back," she says, "any time you're worried. And I hope you're looking after yourself."

"Of course I am," I say, grinning ferociously. "Never felt better."

I leave the surgery and stop at the chemist where Ben's cough ricochets off a display cabinet of cruelty-free lipsticks. I leave with a clear syrup and instructions from an elderly lady buying fierce red blusher to set a bowl of hot water in his bedroom. I don't mention that he doesn't have a bedroom, or that his sleeping quarters are over-shadowed by a teetering heap of *Confetti* magazines.

When I reach Eliza's I fill the plastic medicine spoon to the halfway mark. Seeing it, Ben's mouth slams shut. I prize his lips apart with one hand while keeping the spoon steady and clamping the bottle between my knees. Ben tumbles back, booting the spoon, which shoots syrup onto Christophe's sweater. Ben screams, traumatized by a mother trying to do something horrible to his face. I have dropped the bottle. The syrup makes a sticky pool which shivers on the carpet, not sinking in.

I lean against an empty cardboard box, wondering what Eliza plans to put in it. The box is open, waiting for decisions to be made. That's the thing with old stuff. What to throw out, what to keep hanging around in case you need it one day. That's the hard bit.

22

Emerging Independence

Garie Bartholomew has been transferred to the London office. A small sadness hangs about him, like his pet has died. He is on the phone, saying, "Sorry, but they'll laugh at that offer. They've had a lot of interest. You're talking the best state secondary in the borough."

He looks at me, rubbing a sunburnt nose. His eyes are ringed with skiing goggle ovals. "Mrs.——" he says, digging for a name.

"Nina," I say. "You showed me—*us*—around a place in——"

"Cedar Cottage, right? Gone weeks ago I'm afraid. But we have plenty more, and if you hang on a tick——" He opens a drawer, flicking papers. His suit shines as if it has been lightly oiled. "Here," he says, handing me details of a modern house pretending to be old with Greek pillars straddling a white-and-gold front door. "Newly built," he says. "I know you and your—you were looking for a period property, right? Well, you'd never know this was new. It's faced in real stone—see how solid it looks?"

"It's solid," I agree.

"And you're not dealing with someone else's botched DIY. You're not talking a complete renovation job. What I'll do is, I'll give you Tanya's number. She'll set up a viewing."

"Thanks, but I'm looking for somewhere around here." He peels a sliver of skin from his nose. "Do you have any places to rent?" I ask. "Two bedrooms or even just one?"

Garie says there's nothing, at least nothing that we'd consider taking.

"I'll look at anything," I say, "anything you have."

Christophe calls to report that the roof is entirely leak-free and as soon as the weather improves he'll dig out the bank at the back of the house. That should sort out the damp problem. My parents have headed south, sick of the cold, and left Christophe with a long list of tasks. "Thanks," I say, "for the roof."

"So it's ready for you," he says.

The flat is on the middle floor of a maisonette block that skirts a market selling fruit, veg and cheap household goods in plastic baskets. Garie unlocks the door but seems reluctant to come in. He strokes his trousers and examines the palms of his hands. Every room is the color of artificial limb, except the bathroom, which is custard. "It's not ready to be let," explains Garie from the open front door. "The owner had to leave in a hurry. Some kind of emotional problem." The kitchen is long and skinny with cracked orange units and the smell of old gravy. "He wants it decorated before he puts a tenant in," Garie adds.

"So when will it be available?"

"April?" he shrugs. "Leave me your number. I'll let you know when it's in better shape."

At one end of the living room a door opens onto a balcony. An antique microwave is parked out there with a lame pigeon staggering upon it. "Could you open this door?" I ask.

Garie sighs and checks his watch. I step out and stare at a jumble of neglected roof terraces. When I come back in, I catch him looking at my belly. There's a suggestion of a shape there, impatient flutters inside. "I need a place right away," I explain. "I'll take it just the way it is."

He looks up from my stomach. "Of course," he blusters, "your partner will want to see it."

"There's no partner."

He looks irritated as if I've wasted enough of his time already. He could be showing nice couples serious houses with playrooms and utility rooms and purpose-built annexes for the au pair. "But I thought you wanted somewhere more rural," he says. His eyes light on the cheap red watch I bought from the market stall.

"No," I say, "I never wanted that kind of place."

★ ★ ★

Ben's wheeze dies away, leaving a souped-up baby exploring new territory with a speedy crawl and an obsessional love of the balcony. Jonathan calls, a little friendlier, to offer me Constance's old bed. "It's solid," he says, "properly made, though you'd need a new mattress. I'll hire a van and bring it over." I tell him it won't fit up the stairs, then buy a new one, self assembly, its slats designed to be lashed together with some kind of cord. The mattress is propped against the bedroom wall. The men delivering it had to feed it around the corners of the stairwell, ripping its plastic covering.

Jonathan told me to take anything I need from our household account, but instead I arranged a loan, bluffing that payments for my freelance work would soon be rolling in. I have also purchased a flat pack table with fold-out leaves, a portable TV, and a shelving unit for the stereo which I don't have yet. The pink living room carpet is strewn with paper diagrams. To escape, I head out for bananas but instead find Felt Lady, transporting her son in a backpack. She marches across the road to the fruit stall, stopping a car with her outstretched arm.

"So sorry to hear about you and Jonathan," she begins, snatching a plum from the stall.

"How's the felt?" I ask quickly.

"I've moved on from felt. Still doing paper. And I'm making a bottle tree. Dig them up at tips and saw off their bottoms and feed them onto the branches of trees." The fruit stall man moves a handwritten notice to a more prominent position. It says Please Don't Squeeze. "Can I count you in on the POOP protest?" barks Felt Lady.

"What will it involve?"

"Me, Beth and the others are meeting at six every Sunday morning. You'll need chalk. We're splitting into groups. Ringing every piece of dog crap we find. We'll write This Is Disgusting next to each deposit. We'll shame them, that's the idea."

"I don't think—" I begin.

"Come on. We need as many bodies as possible. Are you living round here?"

I point at the maisonette block which borders the market square like a staple.

"God," she says.

Six pregnant women arrange unwieldy legs on bean-bags in Jennifer's living room. She's an antenatal teacher and is burning lavender candles to create an aura of re-laxation. There are four men, all pretending to be com-fortable. A woman with a vast meringue of a bump says she's having twins. "My sister has twins," says Jennifer. "Teenagers now. They're actresses. There's a big demand for twins, you know. Directors like them because if one's tired or having an off day, they can bring the other one in. They're very marketable, twins."

The woman laughs and says, "I don't think that's our sort of thing." A glum-looking man hovers behind her like a cape.

She sits next to me during herbal tea break and asks, "Can't your partner come to classes?"

"We're not together," I say.

She clutches her belly and says sorry, anyway, hadn't we better get back to the living room for the pain relief talk? "It's fine," I call after her. "I've done this before."

Later, I notice that she has assumed a position as far as possible from me and, when I catch her eye, she twiddles her wedding ring as if embarrassed for having a husband.

I'm not the only woman without a man. The other has gappy teeth and a proud, watermelon bump. She assumes an all-fours position with her head dipping close to the floor and when she looks up she says, "Hi, Nina."

"Rosie," is all I can say.

Two messages:

Christophe reporting that some of the tiles have blown off the roof. Water pouring into the little bedroom. Bed soaked. No hope of drying it out. Disappointment seeps from the answerphone.

Beth's quivering voice saying would I believe it? She specified a nonsmoker. But she smelt something. You can detect it a mile off, can't you, when you've never had a cigarette in your life? And the top drawer of the chest? Meant for underwear? Stuffed with Jana's fag butts. No wonder she bought all those mouthwashes and mints. Maud has been passive smoking since November. God knows what it's done to her respiratory system. The agency is sending a Swiss girl called Beatrice who enjoys outdoor pursuits.

★ ★ ★

I buy emulsion paint in enormous tins and soon each room is a stark white box, except the bathroom where the custard shows through. Ben wakes up and squints. The white walls make the pink living room carpet appear instantly tawdry, so I scoop up Ben and rap at the downstairs flat's front door.

She is younger than I am and smells of sweet peas. Her hair is pulled back carelessly from her face. "I've just moved in upstairs," I explain, "and I will get a Hoover, only I haven't got round to—"

"Of course," she says, "I'll bring it up." Her name is Helen and she child-minds a clutter of infants of various shapes and sizes. Charlie, a boy of around five, tails her into my flat. He seems to belong to her. He's pretending to help carry the Hoover, but is banging the button that winds the flex back in.

"So are you…on your own?" she asks.

"Well, I've got Ben."

"And you're—"

"Yes, due at the end of July."

She smiles kindly. Charlie gazes at my stomach as if it might open up and reveal a twirling figure, like a musical box.

The Hoover has such an effect that the carpet changes from dusky to startling pink, like cheap lipstick. Someone hammers on the door as if their life depends on it. I assume it's Helen wanting her Hoover back, or someone from upstairs complaining about the frantic vacuuming noise. But it's Charlie and I don't know what he wants. He's small for his age with pale wrists, like leeks. I let him in, not sure what a child of his age likes to eat or drink. I wonder what he'd make of an activity arch. "Is this your flat?" he asks. His voice is unnecessarily loud, possibly from making himself heard among the other children.

"Sort of," I tell him. "It's where I live."

He stalks around the living room and peers at the microwave on the balcony. "Do you want that?" he asks.

"No, why, do you?"

"I could keep stuff in it. Can I go out?"

I let him onto the balcony, hoping he's not thinking of trying some treacherous stunt on the railings. "Are you revorced?" he shouts back.

"No, I'm not divorced."

"Does your baby have a dad?"

"He does," I say patiently. "He just doesn't live with us." I sound like a book intended to help children through challenging times: *I Don't See Daddy Much But That's Okay.*

Charlie's stopped listening. He's marched back in, turned on the TV and is laughing gutsily as a cartoon girl with ginger pigtails wallops a boy with her schoolbag.

Jonathan wants to formalize things. He looms over me while I bathe Ben, watching as I slosh chunky limbs with a fluorescent pink sponge. He is too polite to comment on my shoddy paint job.

Charlie is in the living room, making a potion by bashing Space Invader corn snacks into a blend of tomato sauce and milk. He eats startling mixtures, jumbling food groups. Sometimes he shows up saying he "needs" cold pea and ham soup with a swirl of mayonnaise. I've found him daubing raw carrots with Marmite. He's always chewing or crunching, sometimes simultaneously. His front teeth are graying where they meet the gums. He behaves like he's pregnant.

Jonathan and I are supposed to be discussing arrangements but he's staring at my wrist, wondering why I'm wearing a red, cheap-looking thing instead of the serious watch. It's difficult with Charlie here, making grinding noises with a metal spoon. "We need to set up some kind of system," whispers Jonathan.

"Why? You can see Ben whenever you like."

There's an irritable twitch about his lips. He says, "I'd like things to be more organized."

"How about you have him at weekends?" I don't want this, not really. Don't want my weekends empty and babyless.

"It might be difficult, having Ben overnight. Billy's staying with me. He's off the rails. Went for a haircut and a quick cider afterward and next thing he's having his stomach pumped."

I lift Ben from the bath and wrap him in a towel with a hood. I wonder if Jonathan really minds about Billy. Someone to cook for. Another body in the house.

While I dress Ben in pajamas Jonathan examines antique sockets, and the kitchen sink plug hole, as if expecting something vile to spurt out. He has brought my post. In fact one is addressed to Ben with Little Lovelies in navy script on the back of the envelope. Inside is a cheque for Ben's advertising jobs. I'm astounded by the amount. Jonathan plucks it from my fingers and says, "I'll put this in his savings account," as if I am considering squandering the lot on fancy moisturizers with gold particles in. "Will there be any more?" he asks.

"No. We've stopped all that. Anyway, the agency dropped us."

Charlie looks up, licking the spoon menacingly.

Jonathan teeters back. "You're in denial," he snarls at the door. "This pregnancy. You're carrying on as if all this is normal."

Spring arrives on April Fool's Day. One day I'm wearing Christophe's bird's nest sweater, the next I'm sweating in my pink cardigan in the office of a heavily lipsticked woman with a beaky nose and an Australian accent. Catherine is setting up a new magazine. Eliza gave her my name, possibly to make up for the Jonathan episode, but more likely because she has decided I need to be out of the house more often.

"We're not looking for the same old relationship shit," says Catherine viciously from behind her bare desk. "Our readers are highly intelligent. They don't care about pleasing men." I don't point out that she doesn't have any readers yet. She says there are two vacant positions in the features department. She has misunderstood me; I can't take a job. Not now. I breathe in, hoping she doesn't look south of my neck. "I'm looking for some freelance work," I explain.

"Fine, got any ideas?"

"I can think some up. I'll send them to you. You see, I've been out of the country for a while."

This seems to make me a little more interesting. She's thinking L.A., New York, not a pimple of a village in Eastern France. "I like your stuff," she announces. "Downmarket trash but funny and sharp. I'll call you."

Before heading home I venture into Hamleys in search of a stimulating toy for a one-year-old. It's Ben's birthday tomorrow. Maud has already had hers, being one step ahead in every sense. Beth had her old doll's house renovated, the seventies furnishings replaced with a more pared-down, Scandinavian look. Actually, Beatrice, the Swiss girl, did it. She's settled in well. Beth says she's very good with her hands.

The sale is on. Hamleys is heaving with sweating parents snatching cut-price Action Men with growling huskies. A woman with a rip in her tights is chasing her daughter up the escalator. A wizened boy with challenging eyes pokes a light saber up my skirt. I emerge giftless, reassuring myself that, at a year old, a child hasn't figured out the concept of birthdays. How long can I get away with this? No present from his mother and little contact with his dad. At what stage does a child start demanding his own Action Man with husky and an adult-size male about the place?

When I pick up Ben from Helen he is engrossed in a satisfying game of snapping Charlie's Lego towers. Charlie's dad is eating a curry with the naan bread draped over the arm of the sofa. He smiles at me over his fork. He's older and softer than Helen, and looks like he'd need a crane to hoist him from that sofa.

Charlie is chewing a pakora and decorating a square white cake with a red icing pen. "I'm drawing a tank," he says, but it looks like the imprint of a jam sandwich.

My flat is too hot. I open the balcony door and let Charlie out to play with the microwave. He has brought the cake, and streamers, which he drapes over the brass wall lamps, sprinkling their fluted glass underskirts with silvery strands.

Jonathan arrives at 2:00 p.m. sharp with a flat blue parcel and a worried Adam's apple. Helen and I carry food from the kitchen to the table: egg mayo sandwiches, animal biscuits with chocolate on their fronts, and Charlie's cake. I open the balcony door to let out the egg smell. Jonathan plays with Ben on the floor, showing him the wooden puzzle he's brought. It's a Noah's ark. Jonathan removes the animals and sits back, perhaps expecting Ben to replace them in the appropriate holes. Ben bites a wooden zebra. Jonathan snatches it from his mouth, causing Ben to bellow miserably. Jonathan blinks at the cake.

Beth arrives with Maud and Beatrice who wears her hair scraped to the side, secured by a schoolgirlish hair clip. "Would you like me to take charge of music and games?" Beatrice asks loudly. She is carrying a portable CD player. No one seems very keen on games. Charlie removes egg filling from a sandwich to smear on the chocolate animals. The other older kids—thoughtfully donated by Helen to make up the numbers—are demanding piggybacks from a girl of around Charlie's age, but who looks like she was constructed in a shipyard.

"We need music," says Beatrice, smiling like a head-mistress.

I only have one CD; the soul compilation from Eliza. My favorites are still at Jonathan's. She puts on "Sex Machine." James Brown. The shipyard girl giggles. "Maybe we won't have music," I say.

The party seems to last forever. I keep going to the toilet to check my cheap watch in secret. "Awful, isn't it?" sympathizes Beth, catching me creeping out of the bathroom.

"Is it? The children seem to be enjoying themselves." The older kids are rapping each other with balloons. The shipyard girl has drawn on hers, making it The Devil.

"I mean the toilet thing," says Beth. "The constantly going. That pressure on your bladder. How many weeks are you now?"

"Lost count," I tell her. "Two thirds through, I think."

She gives me a bizarre look and drifts away to separate Maud from the cake. The Genius of Bethnal Green has been walking for ages. She's probably the earliest walker in the world, ever. Ben has been standing for what feels like a century. He'd be up on his feet, running mini marathons, if I'd paid proper attention to his diet.

Everyone except Jonathan leaves in a surge on the dot of four, clattering out like the flat's on fire. Despite Beatrice's clearing up efforts, the room is devastated.

Jonathan stares at the pink carpet where the Noah's ark animals are scattered. "This place, how can you live here?" he says. "Someone's been sick on the stairs, have you seen it?"

"That's not sick. Charlie was making a mixture. It must have got kicked over when—"

"And that kid," he says. "Is he hyperactive or what?"

"He's just a boy."

"Doesn't his mother watch what he eats? He practically had all those biscuits, and took the sandwiches to bits—I watched him. Doesn't she care? Doesn't she *police* him?"

When he's gone the flat feels calm and unusually spacious, like an empty school hall.

I am swelling. Bigger and rounder than last time with a bump expanding like pizza dough, stretching right round my back. I wear black dungarees from an army surplus shop and enormous white knickers called Superpants. I eat five meals a day, all devoid of flavoring, and wake several times every night, needing a pee. The toilet makes a strange booming sound after each flush.

Ben approves of my bigness. He sprawls on me, grabbing fistfuls of breast, wiping the sweat off my face. It's blisteringly hot, with the kind of fierce sunlight Eliza travels to Antigua for. My parents write to explain that they are still in the Roussillon district and have fallen for a dear little grain mill which they hope to purchase when the sale of the Vanvey house goes through. The purchaser is a local woman, and they've given her an excellent deal, taking into account that her son has done much of the renovation work. The woman—Sylvia, my mother calls her—intends to turn it into a small hotel. *We could have done that,* my mother writes, *but who do we have to help us? Sylvia's son, the handyman, is such a keen young man. Not a drifter like you. He asked a lot about you, Nina. Wondered if you were coming back. When we told him you'd taken a flat in London he looked quite cross which is unusual, as he's usually ever so pleasant.*

Charlie likes shopping with me. He pushes the buggy with reedy arms, wobbling dangerously close to dusty curbs. The area is what Garie would call "improving." There are families with wealthy jaws and children called Hannah and Max. A vegan café and yoga center have opened. But there is still a smattering of pound shops and mysterious Turkish bars with blue lights and men who hover in doorways, smoking, and a frightening pub with a wet carpet where you might have your eyeballs removed for ordering a lemonade. One night, an angry man tumbled out of the pub, and ranted into the intercom that he knew I was there, "and you'll be sorry next time, Shirley."

Charlie carries my shopping upstairs, explaining that he'd like a boiled egg, and do I have any of that marmalade made out of limes? I let him in and pour him an orange juice. "Do you want another baby?" he shouts.

"Yes," I say, "what makes you ask that?"

"My mum," he says, "she's got a thing in her from

the doctor so she can't have any more children. She's not allowed. There's something wrong with her blood."

He falls back onto my new blue corduroy sofa. Jonathan insists I buy whatever I need, helping myself from our current account. He appears every few days to inspect the flat and play Noah's Ark puzzle with Ben and steal sly looks at my belly.

She arrives three weeks early at 2:27 a.m. My daughter is so keen to be born that she's here, in my arms, with only Helen to help us. The midwife arrives, and I am whisked off to hospital, apparently in shock. Helen has agreed to look after Ben. He'll wake up, knowing nothing about a new sister or what happened on the living room carpet where he plays with his toys. You can get up to all sorts while your baby sleeps.

Jonathan visits the ward to remind me that I'm in shock and brings Ben, who wears stiff-looking tartan dungarees and his fringe cut in a sharp line. Ben tries to break and enter the bedside cupboard, removing the chocolate digestives supplied by Helen and a book donated by Beth about managing postnatal depression without prescription drugs.

Jonathan holds the baby but gives her back to me when she cries. He perches on the edge of my bed as if testing its springiness. "How are you feeling?" he asks.

"Fine. I want to go home."

"No," he says, "you might feel fine, but you're not. It's

your hormones. They're boosting you temporarily. In a day or two you'll crash."

Ben cries when Jonathan carries him out of the ward. "I'm going home," I shout after them.

23

First Steps

I'm in Jonathan's flat and it's just the same except there's the baby, who mews daintily from a carrycot, and Billy, who doesn't. He has grown an extra layer, been fattened up by Jonathan. He looks less likely to wake up in Ongar and play with the frogs.

I sleep with the baby in Jonathan's bed. He remains politely at the furthest edge. He could be in another continent. When the baby wakes, Jonathan watches me feeding her. He arranges the pillows so I'm comfortable and fetches me water from the kitchen. *Although he may not have the equipment, there's lots a new father can do to support his breast-feeding partner.*

In the morning he whispers, "Don't worry. Billy will find himself a place, now you're back."

"Nina! I've just shot down an airplane." Charlie is playing in the stairwell, firing an invisible gun at cracks in the ceiling. He has broken up for the summer holidays and clearly intends to spend seven weeks alternating between his flat, with its hordes of children, and mine, with a more manageable two. He's glad I'm back. He missed playing with the microwave. He clatters in and grabs Ben's hand, intent on locating his walking button.

Catherine calls to report that prelaunch research indicates that potential readers are baffled by her proposal with its intelligent features and political analysis and would prefer the same old emotional shit. "Like to do a piece?" she says in a tired way. "We're thinking of—Can Your Relationship Survive an Affair? You know the drill. Get some psychologist biddy to harp on about communication, good stuff coming from bad, all that guff." She will pay me an astronomical fee which will convert neatly into a stereo. I might even buy another CD.

Charlie helps me bathe Ben by lobbing stackable plastic boats into the tub which bob among Little Squirts froth. When he's gone I feed the baby to sleep and bash out the affair feature without coming up for air.

My parents show up with startlingly brown faces and a construction kit consisting of rusting metal components intended for a child of around twelve. Mum shows me pictures of a clapped-out barn and says, "You must come next time we're at the mill. It needs work, admittedly, but there's huge potential to convert it into a, er, isn't there, Jack?"

Dad holds the baby as if she's a fragile fortune cookie with a scary message inside. Mum flicks her eyes around the electric fire's plastic coals. "You're just here temporarily," she says. "Until you've found your feet."

"No, it's where I live."

Charlie saunters in without knocking, stopping dead when he meets my father's corduroys. "When are they going?" he asks.

Mum stares at the closed front door long after he's gone. "I suppose," she sighs, "you can live with us."

I have started to like cleaning. There is so little of the flat, so few murky crevices, that it's ridiculously easy. I have stocked up on products with spray nozzles and even a Hoover with a special attachment for upholstery. I intend to use my cleaning time to think up feature ideas for Catherine but realize, when the job's finished and the bathroom smells pleasingly citrusy, that I haven't had one work-related thought.

When I do work, it's at night, when Ben and the baby are asleep. The occasional personality clash tumbles out of the wet-carpet pub. It's around 2:00 a.m. when Jonathan calls, his voice pulpy with alcohol. *It's all in the past.* "Pasht," he says.

"Has something happened?"

"I'm sorry," he says. A deeper male voice prompts him. There's a groan from an accordion.

"There's nothing to be sorry about," I say.

"Yes, there is. The modeling, what does it matter? Great idea!" He burps and apologizes.

"That's all over now."

"I'm sorry," he rants on, "about the country. You don't want to move. That's fine. Sorry."

"For what?" I ask.

"For getting you into all this—"

"Please," I say, "can't you come over tomorrow? We'll talk then. You're just upset. We don't have to—"

He's sorry for letting me go to France.

For not making me stay.

For criticizing my flat.

And being sexually predictable.

Sorry for not letting me come to his mother's funeral. And trying to bully me into staying at that B&B. Did I know it wasn't quite true, the way he described those holidays? His dad was there. He'd invent sales trips and leave his picturesque family behind. This man would spend a week in Scotland with Constance and a son who wasn't allowed to say Dad. The man was a family friend, that was all. Jonathan was told to call him Tony.

"I shouldn't have done it," he babbles, "that night with Eliza. It only happened once, do you know that? In fact, it didn't really happen. Not really. It was an accident." He says *ackshident*.

There's a hollow bellow of accordion. He's sorry for not understanding. For not listening. He'll change.

"Jonathan," I say, "I'm going to bed." He says something else, but it's drowned by a groan, like someone trapped under the accordion.

My daughter falls into an easy pattern of feeding, sleeping and gazing at jumbled wet rooftops through the balcony window. She stares levelly when Ben, a humongous toddler, towers over her. Her name is Jane. Short and simple, like the way she slipped out of me. Beth says she's small—even smaller than Ben was at this age—but anyone would seem miniature next to Maud, who clomps about my kitchen in terrifying boots.

Eliza says she looks like me. She has my sturdy nose, apparently, and dark, unremarkable hair. But I wonder if Eliza is seeing anything clearly. She has decided to leave her magazine to work exclusively for the photographer with an attitude. "Hector wants me to be his muse," she says, and when I asked what a muse actually does, she explains, "I'll stimulate him visually. We're going to create together."

I tell her to be careful, look at me and Jonathan and what happened when we got down to creating, but she goes dreamy and says she doesn't have it in her to work with one more model who's been flown to Morocco and bleats about missing her boyfriend.

Eliza says it's different with Hector, the sex thing. It's creative. Part of being a muse. He wants to photograph her. He is entranced by her neck, apparently, though he likes her to remove all her clothes for a photography session.

I've just sunk into the bath when Ben wakes. He's

babbling and rattling the bars of his cot. This is unusual; since we moved here he's slept through the night. I warm his bottle and hold him on my lap. He drinks steady with one brown eye on me, like a raisin. The milk fails to make him drowsy. He's fired up, kicking to get off my knee. I put him down, wrap myself in a dressing gown and open the balcony door.

There's karaoke in the pub and a gang of girls surging in, chirping like chickens. Ben sits in the darkened living room, rattling the clear plastic sack containing the metal construction kit. Beyond the balcony are forgotten roof gardens and a sky that never gets properly dark and someone singing: *I will always love yew-hew.*

When I look back at Ben, he's up on his feet. There's no hand to hold, no solid object to grip. He totters toward me, toward the houses and the terrible singer now sounding like her molars are being removed with no anesthetic. He's tottering on the cheap pink carpet, towards the balcony door. Here, his steps falter and he clangs his head against the door frame.

I'm expecting tears or even blood and a frantic trip to hospital but his mouth forms a smile, like you see in the ads, and nothing terrible has happened, nothing terrible at all.

"You're walking," I say. "You're actually walking."

He looks at me like this is the first sensible thing that's ever come out of my mouth.

HARLEQUIN® flipside™

It's all about me!

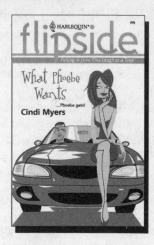

Coming in July 2004,

Harlequin Flipside heroines tell you exactly what they think...in their own words!

WHEN SIZE MATTERS
by Carly Laine
Harlequin Flipside #19

WHAT PHOEBE WANTS
by Cindi Myers
Harlequin Flipside #20

I promise these first-person tales will speak to you!

Look for Harlequin Flipside
at your favorite retail outlet.

The Solomon Sisters Wise Up

by Melissa Senate

Meet the Solomon sisters:

Sarah—six weeks pregnant by a
guy she's dated for two months.

Ally—recently discovered her
"perfect" husband cheating on her.

Zoe—a dating critic who needs to
listen to her own advice.

Suddenly finding themselves sharing a bedroom in Daddy's
Park Avenue Penthouse, the Solomon sisters are about to wise
up, and find allies in each other, in this heartwarming and
hilarious novel by Melissa Senate, author of *See Jane Date*.

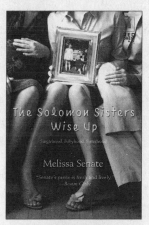